I0550470

Smith's
MONTHLY

Every Month Original
Novels, Stories, and Articles

USA Today Bestselling Writer
Dean Wesley Smith

TABLE OF CONTENTS

SMITH'S MONTHLY ISSUE #1

Thanks for Supporting This Project!

Dean Wesley Smith

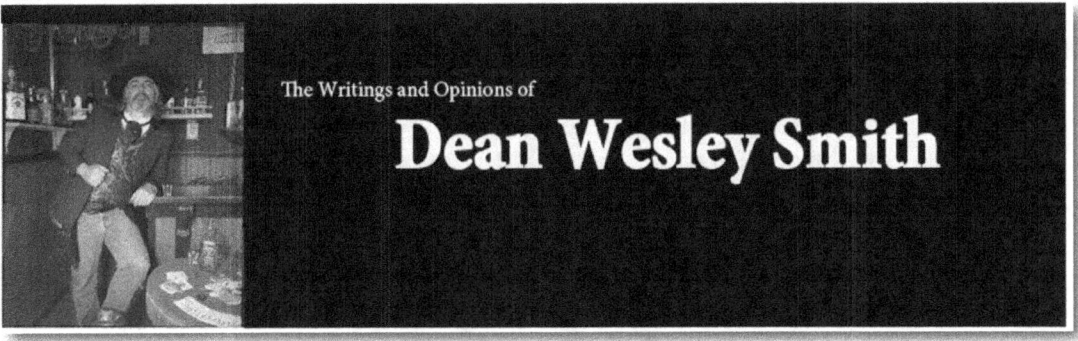

Introduction

WELCOME TO THE CRAZINESS

I'm having a hard time actually believing that I need to write this. The idea of a magazine filled entirely with one writer's short stories, serials, articles, and full novels seems just nuts, plain and simple.

And honestly, with me being that writer, doing almost one hundred thousand words of content every month, it becomes totally insane.

Yet here I am, writing this first introduction.

And honestly, this idea would have been impossible to do just four years ago. But publishing has changed and writing fiction has changed and this magazine is going into a new world.

A crazy new world, granted, but a new world.

So let me tell you just a little about myself first. I'll make it quick, I promise so you can get on to the stories and serials and novel.

I sold my first short story in 1975 at the ripe old age of twenty-five. I had just the year before moved back to Moscow, Idaho to return to college after spending time in the late 1960s and up to 1974 both skiing and playing professional golf. I got back to college in late 1974 and because of an English requirement in my architecture degree program, I took a beginner's poetry class.

The instructor of that class forced her students to send off poems to this national college poetry contest. I was the first student of hers to ever win it or even get into the book. So for a year I wrote poems and mailed them all over the place and got into a bunch of literary magazines with them. Then, as a lark, because I couldn't type, I wrote out this one-thousand-word short story and had a friend type it. I mailed it before I could think twice about it.

It got bought.

So I wrote another one real quick, again the massive length of one thousand words.

The editor purchased that story as well.

Then for the next seven years I bought into every myth in publishing and wrote slow and rewrote everything to death and sold nothing. Nada. Zip. (Thankfully, all those stories burned up in a house fire in 1985.)

Finally in 1982, after dropping out of law school in my last year because I didn't want to be a lawyer, I started to study how other professional fiction writers that I admired did it. Duh. Wish I had thought of that seven years earlier. So I started to follow the advice from Heinlein and Bradbury and Ellison and Block.

And I started selling and never looked back.

Since then I have sold well over one hundred novels to traditional publishers and hundreds and hundreds of short stories. I also worked as a publisher and as an editor. I wrote over twenty *Star Trek* novels, the only two original *Men in Black* novels, and a bunch of movie novelizations including *The Tenth Kingdom* with my wife, Kristine Kathryn Rusch under the name Kathryn Wesley.

I wrote scripts, movies, and comics along the way as well. Anything a professional writer would do to keep the money flowing. I wrote under upwards of fifty or more pen names over the years as well. I have only worked as a fiction writer and in the publishing world since I left my last real job in 1988. (Wow, that's a long time.)

So last spring I was doing a ghost novel for a New York publisher because the writer was too sick to write it and they needed it and they tossed more money at me than was decent. I couldn't talk about the novel itself, but on my blog I detailed out each day of the ten days it took me to write the novel. It seemed a lot of writers and fans really loved that, even though I couldn't tell them anything about the book.

So in July, 2013, as I cast around for a new challenge for myself and my writing in this new indie publishing world, I came upon the idea of doing a series called "Writing in Public." Every day now on my blog at www.deanwesleysmith.com I put up a post about what I managed to do during the day, including details about my day.

Far more information that most people want, but alas, I started it, so I'm keeping going now into the second

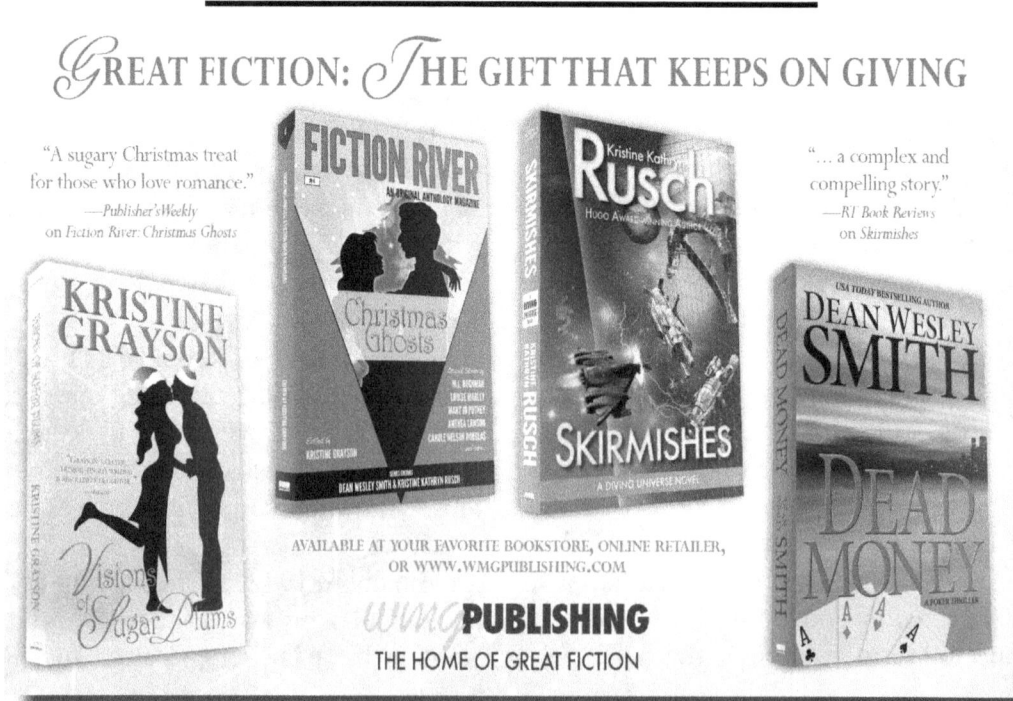

month. And people tell me they enjoy it and are reading it. Even my wife finds it entertaining and she lives in the same house with me. She tells me that now she knows what I do all day.

But if I was going to "Write in Public" starting on August 1st, I needed to tell people where the stories were going and when they would be out. That's fairly easy to do in this indie world, so I hadn't given it much thought past that. Then one day I was casting about for a title to get me started on a new novel when I grabbed one of my *Zane Gray Magazines*.

Right beside that were the *Mike Shayne Magazines*. And on another shelf were the *Asimov's SF Magazine*s and the *Ellery Queen Magazines*. In *Zane Gray's Magazine*, Zane Gray tended to do an entire novel every month. I thought that would be fun, so I mentioned it to my wife on a drive to see some Shakespeare plays down in Ashland, Oregon in June.

I told her I figured I would do mostly new, filling the entire magazine every month, and when I couldn't, I had enough stories in my inventory to keep the magazine going for a very long time.

Surprisingly, she didn't laugh at me. It always worries me when she doesn't laugh at one of my hair-brained schemes.

In fact, she liked the idea a lot and helped me fine-tune the entire thing. And she was the one who came up with the title *Smith's Monthly*.

So now this starts into the new world, with the very first issue of *Smith's Monthly*. It's going to be available in trade paper and electronic. I hope you'll stay with me on this ride.

All I can promise is entertaining fiction. A lot of it, actually.

Every month.

—Dean Wesley Smith
September 6th, 2013,
Lincoln City, Oregon

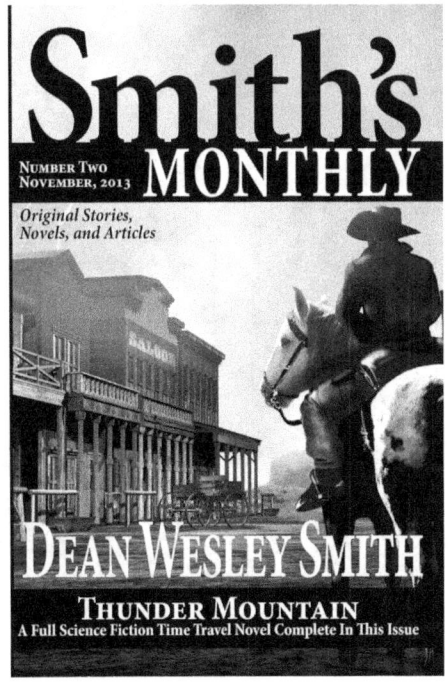

DEAN WESLEY SMITH

the ROAD BACK

A DOC HILL STORY

USA Today *bestselling writer Dean Wesley Smith returns to the world of his acclaimed thriller* **Dead Money** *with a new problem for professional poker player, Doc Hill.*

Doc agrees to help find a missing college student, the son of the Las Vegas Chief of Police. But little did Doc know that such a simple case would turn out to be so large and ugly and dangerous.

"The Road Back" gives readers a perfect introduction to the world of Doc Hill and professional poker.

THE ROAD BACK

When you are short-stacked in poker,
and in life, the road back
to being in contention
often has a very sudden end.

ONE

"DO WE HAVE ANY IDEA where he might be?" I asked Annie over my shoulder.

She had crouched down behind my chair at the no-limit ring game I had joined a few hours before at the Bellagio. I was almost a thousand up and had been enjoying the game as a warm-up for a series of poker tournaments coming later in the week to the Bellagio.

I seldom played regular ring games anymore, only tournaments. But at times it felt right to just sit and play for a time. This hot September afternoon was one of those times to relax in the air-conditioned poker room and drink iced tea and win a little money in the process.

"Not a clue," she said. "Dad's got all the information."

Annie had her long brown hair pulled back and the white blouse and dark slacks she wore accented her perfect body. She was the best-looking *former* Las Vegas detective I had ever met, with brown eyes that could stare through to your soul. Actually, she was one of the best-looking women I had ever met, and also one of most deadly poker players in the modern game.

In the year we had been together, she had taken down a dozen tournaments and won two World Series of Poker bracelets for two different events.

Now she wanted my help to find some guy her dad thought was missing. Actually, her dad, Detective Bayard Lott, also a former Las Vegas police detective, wanted her help and she was asking if I would help out as well.

"You want me to deal you in, Doc?" the dealer asked.

"No, thanks, Al," I said, pushing back from the table as Annie stood and stepped back. I flipped him a twenty-five dollar chip and he tapped it and nodded thanks before slipping it into his tip slot.

I turned and nodded to Ben, the brush in charge of the room at the moment who was headed my way from the poker room desk.

"Cash you out?" he asked.

I flipped him a twenty-five dollar chip as well and said, "Thanks. Just add it to the account."

I had had a running account at the Bellagio for almost ten years now. Made it easier than hauling racks of chips to the cage all the time. And after the two tips, I had five hundred in starting money in my stack and another eight hundred and fifty in winnings.

My chip vanished into Ben's pocket and he worked to rack the rest as I turned and headed with Annie out of the poker room and into the noise and bells of customers filling the slots.

"Dinner?" I asked, realizing I was starting to get hungry as we turned toward the front of the casino.

"Dad's meeting us in the Café."

I laughed, taking her hand. "You were pretty sure I was going to help you, huh?"

"Not really," she said, smiling at me as we wound our way through the people toward the restaurant. "I would have gotten the information from Dad and told you later if you were really interested in staying in the game."

"It was enough warm-up," I said. "More than enough, actually."

"Lucky for those guys at the table," she said, laughing. "You warm-up much more and they would have been broke."

"That's the point, isn't it?" I asked.

She agreed and then waved at her father sitting at a semi-private four-person table off to one side of the café where it looked out over the pool. The smell of hamburgers and steaks drifted from the direction of the kitchen and my stomach rumbled. I really was hungrier than I had realized.

I liked her dad a great deal. He looked pretty sharp for his sixty-three years with short-cut white hair, broad shoulders, and only a hint of a gut around his stomach. He had a wicked sense of humor and his laugh could start an entire room laughing with him.

He and a bunch of his retired detective friends played poker every week in the basement of his house and worked to solve cold cases for the Las Vegas Police Department on the side. They called themselves the Cold Poker Gang. Annie and I helped them when we could.

But from what Annie said, this didn't sound like a cold case. More like a missing person problem. And in Vegas, there were always a lot of those.

For all sorts of reasons.

TWO

I WAS INTO MY RIB STEAK and onion rings, Annie was picking at her hamburger, and her dad was about halfway done with his French Dip before Annie finally broached the subject.

"So who is missing and why are you involved, Dad?"

"Steve Benson Junior," he said between bites.

Both Annie and I glanced at him.

Finally Annie asked exactly what I was thinking. "The son of Chief of Police Steven Benson?"

"One and the same," her dad said. "Chief Benson called me, asked if I would look into it for him."

"He thinks his son is in trouble?" I asked.

Annie's dad shook his head. "Not that kind of trouble. He's a good kid, graduate student at UNLV focusing on Nevada history. But his dad this morning went to meet him for breakfast and Steve didn't show up. Steve's best friend hasn't seen him either."

"And his dad's worried?" Annie asked.

"I would be too," her father said, smiling at her. "Steve is like you in that he calls when he has to cancel something."

"He have a car?" I asked.

"Red Jeep SUV," he said. "About a year old. It's missing as well."

"So he went somewhere and hasn't returned yet," Annie said. "More than likely he's fine."

Her dad nodded. "That's what the Chief thinks as well, but he's still worried. Steve's cell isn't picking up. I think that's really why the Chief called me. He doesn't want this out yet, so he's just calling in personal favors at the moment."

I sat back munching on a crisp onion ring, thinking. My little voice was telling me that something was wrong with this kid. I didn't know him and I didn't know

his father, but this felt wrong for some reason I couldn't put my finger on.

However, when at a poker table, I had learned to trust that little voice when it told me something was wrong with a play another player made. And in life I had also learned to trust that voice. And right now the very same voice was telling me we needed to move on this and fast.

I finished the onion ring and leaned forward toward Annie's dad. "Could you call the chief and ask him if Steve is back yet? And if not, could we go look at his apartment?"

Detective Lott slid the key across the table at me, smiling. "Steve wasn't back five minutes before you two showed up, and I got this key from the Chief before coming over here."

I just shook my head and grinned as Annie patted her father's arm, smiling. It was no wonder the guy had been such a great detective in his day. He was a half step ahead of everything.

THREE

STEVE'S APARTMENT near the university seemed far neater than I would have expected a grad student's apartment to be. And it was clear with only a quick look that there was nothing at all out of place.

Nothing.

The apartment had one bedroom with a living room with only a couch and chair and a large desk in it. A small, clean dining room table with four chairs sat near the open kitchen. There was a bathroom off the bedroom.

There was no sign at all of any woman's touch in here. Everything was standard apartment except the large computer on an L-shaped desk on the left side of the living room and large wall of books on the right side, mostly textbooks that at a glance I was glad I never would have to read. My college days were a long ways behind me now.

However, one full shelf was full of books on various aspects of Nevada history that looked very interesting, from the gold rush towns to railroad history to the founding of Las Vegas.

All of them in perfect order by author.

Annie was looking through Steve's desk. There were a couple of books open on the desk on Nevada place names and another on lost mines of Nevada.

"Can you access that computer?" I asked Annie. "See what he was researching before he left?"

"If it's not password protected," she said, sitting down in the chair and moving the wireless keyboard closer toward her.

Her father came out of the bathroom shaking his head. "This kid is the cleanest kid I have ever seen. Nothing out of place, no sign that anyone else but him even visited here. Not even a hair on his comb."

"He folds his socks and underwear," I said. "His bed is made, even though he slept in it recently. And he washed his breakfast dishes before he left, more than likely yesterday morning, since the dishes are completely dry as is the dish towel."

Annie brought the computer up and then shook her head. "Protected."

"He's going to have a password book," I said. "Upper drawer on the left."

She opened the drawer and pulled out a small notebook, shaking her head. "How did you know that?"

"Someone like Steve is completely predictable. Every move, every detail. It's how his mind works. He has no choice."

"Easy pickings on a poker table," Annie said.

"He'd never sit down at one," I said. "He wouldn't be able to handle the uncertainty that comes naturally with the game."

"Obsessive-compulsive?" Annie's dad asked.

"Borderline," Annie said, nodding. "It goes toward hoarding or being neat freaks."

"We know which way Steve goes," I said.

As Annie worked on the computer and bringing up the history, I went back into the small apartment bedroom. Steve had his shoes lined up perfectly along the bottom of his closet, from dress shoes through tennis shoes to boots. There was an empty spot between a pair of tennis shoes and a heavy pair of boots. That's where he would put his hiking boots.

His shirts were lined up hanging in his closet and there was a clear opening where a light casual shirt had clearly hung. More than likely brown from the patterns of the colors.

I went into the bathroom and opened the medicine chest. There was an empty spot where a tube of suntan lotion would have sat right between a small jar of Vaseline and a tube of blister cream.

I closed the cabinet and went back into the living room with the desk and books. "He's gone into the desert. More than likely yesterday morning. My guess is he was planning on returning before dark last night and something happened."

Annie's dad looked around. "I can see why the Chief was worried."

"Got it," Annie said, moving back through the history of what Steve had last looked at on his computer.

The very last thing was a map of an area of the Nevada desert to the north and west of Las Vegas along Highway 95.

"Skeleton Mountains," Annie said, hitting a button to print up the map just as I was sure Steve had done.

One of the books open on the desk referred to the area as well, and I picked it up as Annie kept going back through the history on the computer.

Seems the Skeleton Mountains were a group of rocky peaks sticking up out of the desert about ten miles to the west of the highway. The article said that no one knew exactly how it got its name. From what I could tell in the book, the rocky peaks had just always been named that.

And they weren't that big, with the largest being not more than six or seven hundred feet off the desert. Compared to the mountains I spent the summer in every year in central Idaho, guiding rafts on the River of No Return, these Skeleton Mountains were nothing more than large piles of rocks.

"He was researching some old patented mining claims in those mountains," Annie said, again hitting the print button. "All of them are long dormant and never produced anything of real value."

"So we know where he went," Annie's father said, nodding.

"Get a search team set up from the Chief," I said to him as Annie printed a second copy of the map of the small group of mountains.

"Where are you going?" Annie's dad asked, as he pulled out his phone.

"Fleet's in town and he loves testing out his new helicopter," I said, and Annie laughed. "He'll get us up there and we'll see what we can see from the air, see if we can spot his car before you and the Chief get there."

I was on the phone to my best friend and business partner, Fleet, and Annie's father was talking with the Chief of Police as we headed out into the hot early evening air and Annie pulled the door to the apartment closed behind us.

FOUR

FLEET LIVED IN BOISE with his family. Annie and I had a house there as well, but unlike Fleet, we were seldom in Boise. Fleet had a wonderful wife and two kids there, but at the moment they were all here, letting the kids have one last vacation before school started up again.

Fleet had decided that our company needed a helicopter to go along with our own private jet. It seemed that over the years, his investments of my poker winnings had made us, as he said, stupidly rich. We gave millions away to charity every year and spent what we wanted and somehow just managed to get richer.

Fleet was that good with business and investments.

My father's death a year ago had just added more millions than I wanted to think about into the picture.

When Fleet bought the jet helicopter for the company, he had decided he wanted to fly it, much to his wife's horror. And in the last year he had become a very good pilot.

On the phone I told him what was going on and he almost beat us to the airport, even though we had a shorter distance to go. Any excuse to take out the helicopter was a great idea as far as he was concerned.

Within forty minutes after leaving Steve's apartment, we were airborne and headed for the Skeleton Mountains, the loud drone of the chopper a constant noise.

"So what do you think we're going to find?" Fleet asked through the communications links we all wore.

Annie was in the co-pilot chair because she had taken a few lessons with the chopper last year. I was behind them, strapped in tight. I wasn't afraid of flying, but I had to admit having my friend from childhood doing the flying didn't instill great confidence, even though he had a lot of hours in the air already.

"Besides rocks and snakes?" Annie asked.

She moved slightly so I could see the wink she gave me.

I smiled. Fleet was deathly afraid of snakes. Any kind and size of snake, actually. And everyone knew it.

"Not funny," he said.

"If we have to land, you can stay in the chopper," I said. "There will be snakes."

Fleet shook his head. "You two sure know how to kill a good flight."

Less than fifteen minutes after leaving the Las Vegas airport, the mountains sort of rose from the rolling desert floor in front of us. They were sure nothing to look at. Mostly rocks and scattered open areas covered in scrub brush. I hadn't been kidding Fleet. Those rocks would be infested with snakes, since it was clear the area got little or no attention by humans at all.

"Come in from Highway 95," I said to Fleet. "See if you can spot a road into those mountains."

Fleet nodded and slowed until Annie pointed ahead.

A bare excuse of a dirt road left the highway and wound toward the mountains.

Fleet banked over it and followed the road, moving slowly as we all studied the area.

There was no place to hide below us at all. Just open desert and scrub.

Up ahead the road started to wind up a small canyon and then seemed to break out into an open flat area before going back into another canyon and deeper into the piles of rocks laughingly called mountains.

Nothing but huge rocks and scrub brush.

"On the right," Annie said, pointing.

It took me a moment, but finally I saw what she was pointing at. A glint of the sun reflected off some metal. At closer look I could see hints of a red car hidden beside a rock and covered with scrub brush. Someone had spent a lot of time in the task of hiding the car and had the car off the road so it couldn't be seen by anyone driving in.

"Someone really wanted that hidden," Fleet said, shaking his head.

My stomach was twisting like my rib steak was suddenly not agreeing with me.

"Same speed," I said to Fleet. "Just keep going straight and off into the desert on the other side of the mountains."

"Like we're on Fleet's tour of the desert," he said and did as he was told.

Annie had her cell phone to her ear as all of us watched the ground below. To the right of our flight path I could see a trail going up to what looked to be an old mine entrance. There was no sign of anyone there, but that meant nothing.

Then, near where the dirt road came out the other side of another rock canyon and started across the desert, I spotted an old pickup truck parked under a rock outcropping. It was brown and clearly dusty and blended in perfectly with the rocks.

"Truck on the right," I said as we went past and out into the desert just as if we were a sightseeing chopper doing nothing unusual.

"Get us away from these rocks and turn back toward Vegas until we are completely out of sight," I said to Fleet.

"Looks like the kid found some real problems he didn't expect," Fleet said.

"Dad," Annie said into her cell. "We found Steve's car, but looks like he's in trouble with someone living in an old mine in the Skeleton Mountains."

She waited for a second. "They hid his car," she said. "Spent a lot of time doing so, actually."

Again a pause as her father said something on the other side of the conversation that I couldn't hear.

"There is," Annie said. "A brown pickup, dirty, also hidden. We've moved away from the mountains to not spook anyone in there."

Then she gave a description of the truck to her father.

This one-sided conversation was driving me crazy. I had a hunch that the longer we delayed, the less chance Steve was going to make it. He had clearly walked into something ugly. You don't go to that much trouble to hide a person's car if you ever plan on letting them leave.

She nodded for a long minute, then she glanced at me, her brown eyes big. Then she said, simply, "Shit."

Then she hung up.

Fleet had the chopper flying low over the desert and had turned back for Vegas. We were out of both hearing and sight of the mountains.

"Dad and the Chief and a bunch of Vegas police and the State Police are all coming hard and silent from all directions. They are going to button up all ways in and out of that group of mountains."

"What did he say?" Fleet asked just before I could.

"A brown truck matching the description of the one back there has been connected to a string of disappearances. Maybe up to a dozen women going back years."

Now the steak in my stomach was really twisting around. Steve really had stumbled into something far, far bigger than he could handle.

"Take us back up to where the road into the mountains hits Highway 95," I said to Fleet. "Drop us off there and then make a wide circle out and around the rocks to the other side and out of sight and watch the road on that side. We don't want this guy getting away before the police get here."

Fleet nodded and two minutes later had us on the ground next to the highway. Then he lifted off and swung back to Vegas, climbing and moving fast.

I had tossed in an older twenty-two Remington saddle rifle from my car in case we needed to take out a couple of snakes and Annie had brought along her revolver. We had both grabbed bottles of water.

The air around us was hot, and there were very few cars passing by on the highway. The sun was low on the horizon, but not low enough to cut off the heat. It would be dark in less than two hours.

As Fleet vanished and the sound of the chopper faded off, Annie pulled out her phone to call her dad.

She told him what we had done and then asked how far out they were. As she listened to the answer, she shook her head.

"They are still a good fifteen minutes out," she told me. "And it will be thirty minutes or longer before they can have the entire place locked down from all sides.

I glanced at the half mile of road between us and the first edge of the rocks they called Skeleton Mountains. I wasn't sure that Steve had that long. If the guy had a police scanner, he would know the police were on the way.

I glanced at Annie and she could read my mind. She nodded and then said to her dad. "We're going in on foot. Warn everyone we're in there. And don't put that on the scanner."

Then before her father could object, she clicked off the phone and tucked it in her pants pocket.

"Up for a jog?" I asked.

"Why not?" she said, smiling as she made sure the clip in her gun was in place and ready. "Seems like a perfect evening for some exercise."

I knew there was a reason I loved this woman.

FIVE

IT TOOK US LESS than five minutes to run the length of the dirt road to the edge of the first rock canyon. It was a tough and hot run since we both had to keep looking ahead and also down at our feet to watch ruts and rocks that could twist an ankle.

We slowed as we entered the shadows of the canyon and walked, both of us drinking from our water bottles.

The rocks towered a good hundred feet over the road that ran up a wash. Annie watched the left side, I watched the right.

And I had been right about snakes. A couple nasty Speckled Rattlesnakes lay on rocks. As we approached, they slipped down into the brush. Both of them were large, far larger than I had seen in some time, actually.

In Idaho, as a guide on the summer rafting trips on the River of No Return, I warned people away from climbing the rocks near the river. The rattlers there were much smaller, but could still ruin a good rafting trip if you cornered them or got too close.

The road came out of the rocks and opened up through an open area a quarter mile across before ducking back into the rocks on the other side. Steve's Jeep was hidden to the right about a hundred yards into that canyon ahead.

We stopped, still in the shadows and both took another long drink. Then we left the bottles beside the road. I had a hunch we were going to need our hands free from here on out.

I glanced at my watch. Eight minutes had passed since we left the highway.

"You ready?" I asked?

She nodded.

Running low, bent over, we headed out into the sun and across the open area. I kept expecting to hear a shot or something, but we made it quickly to the shade of the other canyon, both of us panting.

From there we slowed to a walk, Annie again watching the right walls of rock while I watched the left.

As we got even with where Steve's Jeep was hidden, Annie pointed it out. No one would have ever seen it simply driving this dirt path up this narrow canyon between all the rocks.

We kept moving up the road and within a minute we were at the place where the path left the road through some scrub and up a narrow cut in the rocks toward what looked to be an open mine.

"Got any ideas?" Annie asked as we stopped in the shadows and studied the path.

"Nothing," I said. "Trying to climb these snake-infested rocks to get up there another way would be suicidal."

"Going up that trail won't be very healthy, either," Annie said, studying the trail up to the mine opening a hundred feet above us. "It would be like shooting ducks in a pond for anyone above."

We both stood there, with not an idea in the world between us. The heat of the day had really baked the rocks around us and even though we were in the shade, everything was just radiating heat. I would have bet the temperature was a good hundred and twenty and there wasn't a breath of wind. Sweat dried so fast it left my skin feeling coated in dust and salt.

Annie took out her cell phone, then shook her head and put it back.

Then an idea hit me. "Car alarm."

Annie glanced at me, puzzled and listening. There was no sound at all out here in the desert in these rocks.

"Steve's car," I said. "I'm going to go back and see if I can set off that car alarm. If the guy up there doesn't know anyone is on the way to look for him, he's going to come out thinking a snake set it off or something."

"Good idea," she said.

"Don't let him get back in that cave or Steve is dead."

She nodded and glanced around for a place to hide. I started back down the road and behind me she whispered, "Watch out for snakes."

"You too," I whispered back.

Actually, snakes were my biggest concern with this entire plan. With brush all over that Jeep, there could be a dozen rattlers in there already, both in the car, in the engine, and under it. The car formed a perfect snake cave and I wasn't looking forward at all to wading in there.

I spotted a long piece of brush in the ditch beside the road and grabbed it. It was a good six feet long and sturdy. A rattler needed to get within four feet to strike, maybe more if they were big ones like we had seen coming in.

I glanced at my watch as I neared the Jeep's hiding place beside the road.

Annie's dad and the State Police would be almost into position. If this guy ran, and Annie couldn't stop him, they would.

I just hoped Steve would still be alive if the guy did run.

I took a deep breath of the warm afternoon air and started off the road toward the red Jeep buried in the brush. Then, before I had taken two steps, I heard Annie's clear voice ring out through the rocks.

"Stop! Police. Let him go and put your hands up!"

Then two shots filled the air.

Running low and silently, I headed back up the road, not allowing myself to think about Annie getting hurt.

As I neared a corner in the road that would allow me to see the road ahead and the area where the trail left the road to the mine, I slowed.

Annie somehow had gone up the trail a dozen steps and then climbed into some rocks. Somehow she had managed to stay hidden as the guy holding Steve had come down the trail to the road. He must have had a scanner and finally clued to the fact that they were coming for him.

She now had him basically pinned on the road using Steve as a shield.

Steve looked tired and scared out of his wits in his tan slacks, hiking boots, and tan shirt. The guy holding him was short, about five-four, and wore jeans and a light green T-shirt that was stained by sweat. His face looked like it had a five-day growth of beard and his dark hair looked like it hadn't seen a comb in days.

He had a large pistol pressed against Steve's temple and was holding it as if he knew what to do with it.

Annie saw me and nodded.

"Police!" I shouted. "You are surrounded!"

The guy spun in my direction, trying to drag Steve with him, but Steve tripped. The guy's gun left the side of Steve's head as he fought to get his hostage back into position. In doing so he gave Annie a clear shot.

And she took it.

The guy jerked back from the impact and smacked back into the rocks and brush in the shallow ditch beside the dirt road. His gun flew away from him to the left.

Steve went the other way, tumbling to the ground in the middle of the road.

I came in fast and Annie was almost faster down the trail, both of us watching for any movement in the guy. Annie had gotten him in the right shoulder. He had been holding his gun in his right hand. It didn't look like the wound would be fatal. There was blood, but not enough to cause him any danger.

A huge rattlesnake came out of the brush under him and struck at the guy's left arm. Clearly the snake wasn't happy about some guy landing on him.

The kidnapper moaned and jerked away.

All I could do was laugh.

"That's going to make his recovery a little longer," Annie said, laughing and shaking her head as she turned to help Steve to his feet.

"You all right?" she asked the son of the Las Vegas Chief of Police.

Steve nodded and didn't say anything. He was clearly in shock.

"You dad will be here shortly," Annie said, patting Steve's shoulder. "Is there anyone else up there in that mine?"

Steve shook his head. "No one alive."

Then he dropped to the road and buried his head in his hands and just sobbed. The guy in the ditch moaned and the large rattler slithered off down the ditch, clearly not happy, as I glanced at Annie.

She looked up at the mine entrance and shook her head.

I had a slight desire to see what was in there, but my better judgment quickly got control.

Some things were better just left unseen.

SIX

I HAD MANAGED to go up the dirt road a short distance and get a clear enough phone signal to get word out that it was clear.

Then I called Fleet and told him it was clear and to meet us back at the intersection on Highway 95. But I told him that it might be awhile. He might have to transport Steve to the hospital with his dad before he could take us. We had some paperwork to fill out and a story to tell before we would be released, of that I had no doubt.

By the time I got back to Annie, I could hear two Las Vegas Police cars powering up the road.

They slid to a stop just short of us in a cloud of dust and Annie's dad and Steven's dad both piled out.

"You two all right?" Annie's dad asked.

"Had to put a bullet in his shoulder," she said, pointing to the guy in the ditch.

"And then a snake helped keep him down as well," I added, smiling.

Annie's father just shook his head and studied the moaning man for a moment before turning back to us.

The Chief helped his son to his feet and eased him back toward the patrol car as a number of State Police officers arrived on the scene sending up even more clouds of dust into the hot evening air.

As we watched, two Nevada State Police officers carefully worked to extract the guy from the ditch and made sure he didn't have any other guns on him. Then they flipped him over on his face in the dirt and handcuffed him in the middle of the road, not seeming to care at all that he had been shot and snake bitten.

I moved over to the tall State Police officer who seemed to be in charge and pointed up the trail. "From what the Chief's son said, that cave up there isn't pretty. More than likely a major crime scene."

The guy nodded. "Which one of you put the bullet in this guy?"

"I did," Annie said, coming up and handing him her gun. "Retired Detective Annie Lott."

"Thank you, Detective," the officer said, handing the gun to one officer to put away. He didn't seem to care at all about the rifle in my hand.

Then he motioned for two other officers to follow him up the hill.

Annie's dad, Annie, and I moved into a deep area of shade and stood watching as the three State Police officers went into the cave while another stood near the prisoner in the road.

A short minute later one came out, moved to the edge of the mine entrance, and threw up.

"That can't be good," I said.

Both Annie and her father just shook their heads. In their days I was sure they had seen things I flat didn't want to know about.

A few minutes later the other two came out and came back down the trail, a haunted look in all of their eyes.

The Chief climbed out of the patrol car where he had been sitting with his son.

"Your son is going to need counseling help after what he saw up there," the officer said. "He's going to have a long road back to normal."

"That bad?" the Chief asked.

"Worse," the officer said. "This is going to solve a lot of missing persons' cases. More than either of us care to think about."

I had never seen a police officer look so haunted in his eyes. He also was going to have some trouble dealing with whatever horrors were in that old mine.

Then the State Police officer walked over to the guy lying handcuffed face-down in the dirt and kicked him square in the side of the stomach.

After that, the officer turned and walked away down the road past the patrol cars, leaving the desert silence and heat closing in around all of us.

At that moment I was so glad I had resisted the slight temptation to go up to the mine opening.

The Chief glanced over at us, a look of relief in his eyes. Then he said simply, "Thanks."

"You are more than welcome," Annie said as her father put his arm around her.

"Just take care of Steve," I said.

The Chief nodded and went back to the car to sit with his son.

As the door to the patrol car closed, I turned to Annie's father. "Think all the good feelings will cut down some on the paperwork for us?"

Both Annie and her father laughed, as did the state cop standing near the prisoner on the ground.

"Not a chance," Annie's father said between laughs.

Annie stepped over and kissed me. "You always were a dreamer."

~

USA *Today* Bestselling Writer

DEAN WESLEY SMITH

THE SECRETS OF YESTERDAY

A Poker Boy Story

Former professional poker player and USA Today *bestselling writer, Dean Wesley Smith returns to the world of Poker Boy.*

When Poker Boy senses someone watching him as he stands in his invisible office high over Las Vegas, he knows only trouble lurks. With his boss, Stan, the God of Poker at his side, they go to investigate and what they find gives Poker Boy a glimpse into Stan's past.

A glimpse he did not want to see.

THE SECRETS OF YESTERDAY
A Poker Boy Story

ONE

FROM MY OFFICE floating a thousand feet over the MGM Grand Casino and Hotel in Las Vegas, the city and surrounding area seemed painted in light brown. I could almost see the heat shimmering off the concrete and streets below as the record temperatures continued for a third day.

For a change I was alone in this office that I had designed to look like a booth in a fifties retro diner. All four walls were clear and the red vinyl booth sat in the middle of the room, two fake trees behind it to give it a feel of containment.

I had put in a wooden railing in front of the glass walls all the way around because it felt like I could fall off the edge of my office floor. Before I put those railings in I couldn't even walk near the edge. Just too creepy.

The place was invisible to anyone from below and there were only three ways to get here. You either had to teleport, which I knew how to do, or go through the door from my girlfriend and sidekick Patty Ledgerwood's apartment. But most of the team entered through the secret door from The Diner off Freemont Street in downtown Vegas.

This office looked exactly like a booth in The Diner, actually. We used to meet there when dealing with a problem, so when I built this office, it just felt right to make it look like the old booth in The Diner.

Most everyone on my team except Stan used The Diner entrance. Patty tended to either come with me, or use the door from her apartment.

At the moment I was waiting for Patty and we were going to head to dinner, but she didn't get off work at the MGM Grand Hotel front desk for another twenty minutes.

It felt kind of odd being here alone. Normally at least three or four of the team were with me, talking about one thing or another.

And Madge, from The Diner, was always coming in and out serving us milkshakes and burgers.

At times the room had held up to fifteen people, but Madge had had to bring chairs from The Diner for that. The booth only held eight when we crowded in, and three chairs could be pulled up at the head of the table.

Right now I sat in a chair, my feet up on the wood railing around the room, facing downtown Las Vegas.

What a view. It just didn't get any better.

I felt about as relaxed as I ever could feel as a superhero always chasing down one bad person or another. Usually I only felt this relaxed while playing poker.

Suddenly one of my faint alarms in the back of my head went off.

As a poker player, before I had become a superhero, I had learned to trust those alarms. They warned me when I was up against another player who had better cards or who might be cheating or who was getting angry.

I called the feelings my "super powers" back then. Little did I know that many of them actually were superpowers. All I had done was learn to trust them.

This time my little voice was telling me someone was watching me.

But at the same time I knew that wasn't possible. I was in an invisible office floating a thousand feet over the Las Vegas Strip. No one could see this place.

As Stan, my boss and the God of Poker, told me one day, the office was slightly out of phase with the real world. A plane trying to land at the nearby McClaren airport could fly through the office and no one would notice.

I expect that if I saw a plane coming directly at this place I would notice.

So who could be watching me now?

And why was my little voice considering that a threat?

A God of something or other might be able to see the office.

Or maybe another powerful superhero like me.

But not many others.

In fact, no one else that I could think of.

I stood and stared in the direction of downtown Vegas. The new Rush Tower of the Golden Nugget stood above most of the buildings there, but I still had to look down on it from my height.

My little voice was telling me that tower was where the problem was coming from.

And I didn't like this at all. Not one little bit.

TWO

"STAN?" I SHOUTED UPWARD as I always did when calling my boss.

Stan appeared almost instantly beside me, also looking out toward the downtown area.

He had on his normal gray slacks, gray shirt and sweater and had his brown hair combed perfectly. He was the most nondescript man I had ever known. You could walk right past him in a hallway and never notice him, which was one thing that made him so deadly on a poker table.

I had yet to sit across from him at a poker table, and honestly had no desire to do so any time in the near future.

"You feeling it as well?" I asked as he stared at the downtown area.

"Someone's watching," he said. "And they are not blocking the fact that they are watching."

"That's why I could sense it?" I asked.

He nodded.

"Can you get a spot on the location?"

"Someone's watching," he said. "And they are not blocking the fact that they are watching."

"A suite on the 25th Floor of the Golden Nugget. Corner suite. The person is staring at us?"

"Suggestions?"

"I'm going to jump us there and take us out of time," Stan said.

I nodded and a moment later we were standing in a large suite on the top floor of the Golden Nugget. The place was decorated in brown tones, with a large brown couch and chairs in an area under a large screen television.

A made king-sized bed filled another part of the huge room, with a brown comforter and white pillows. A large vanity with a marble surface faced the bed with a desk and another large flat-screened television.

Someone was in the bathroom to my right, pocket-doors slid closed.

And standing in front of the window facing in the direction of my floating office over the strip was a teenager, not more than sixteen at the most.

He was frozen, his hand holding open the drape, as was the newscaster on the television screen, since Stan had taken us out of time.

Actually, I knew how to do that as well. It was more that he had slipped us between two instants of time, but it had the affect of seeming to stop time for anyone taken out of time.

The kid was dressed like most normal teenagers with jeans and a blue tee-shirt not tucked in. His hair was cut short and he looked like he played sports because his shoulders were broad and he didn't have an ounce of fat on him.

"He's powerful," Stan said, nodding at the kid. "I can feel it."

Actually, I could as well. "Is this unusual for someone his age?"

"Very," Stan said, his voice serious.

"Can he sense us here?" I asked.

"He might be able to."

"I can hear you as well," the kid said, turning to look at us.

His face was angular and his eyes a deep black. And as he turned just about every alarm I had as a superhero went off in my head.

More than anything I just wanted to jump and run. But Stan stayed put beside me and so I did the same, my best poker face firmly in place.

"You were looking for us?" Stan asked, his voice as neutral as it always.

"I was," the kid said, nodding and moving away from the window. He moved past us and sat on the couch. "Actually, I was looking for more people of my kind. Guess I found a few, huh?

That your place out there floating over the Strip?"

I nodded and said nothing more. At this point, I was glad, more than glad, to let Stan handle this.

"So who are you?" Stan asked.

"Jason King," the kid said. "My mom, Bonnie, is in the bathroom. She doesn't have any of these powers I have, or at least doesn't seem to."

"Oh, I do, dear," a voice said as the pocket doors to the bathroom slid back. "I just never let you know about them."

I glanced around.

Stan still held us in a time bubble. The newscaster on the television was still stuck in mid sentence and outside the window I could see a jetliner headed for McClarin just hanging there in mid-air. And there were no sounds coming from the city around us at all.

Yet two people had broken into the time bubble Stan had set as if it were nothing unusual. I couldn't do that and I was supposedly one of the most powerful superheroes out there.

Or maybe no one had taught me how to do that yet.

"Hi, Stan," the woman said as she came around the corner in the suite from the bathroom area.

She was attractive and thin and looked to be about the same age as all the Gods and superheroes, mid-thirties. It seems we all pretty much stopped aging at that point for some reason or another.

She had long brown hair pulled back off her face and dark brown eyes. She wore a red summer dress and was barefoot. And she was smiling, but I wasn't sure the smile was reaching her eyes or not.

"Bonnie?" Stan asked, actually sounding shocked.

I glanced at my boss. He was the God of Poker. Even when something shocked him, he never showed it. He was the master of poker faces. But right now he was showing surprise just as any normal human would.

This time the smile actually did reach her eyes. And there was more there. A love, a fondness.

"It's great to see you again," she said, moving over and taking his hands and then reaching up and kissing him on the cheek.

And she was smiling, but I wasn't sure the smile was reaching her eyes or not.

"But I thought... I thought..." Stan couldn't seem to finish his sentence.

"That we were dead," she asked, still smiling. "We were."

"And it wasn't a lot of fun, either," Jason said, dropping onto the couch and putting his feet up on the coffee table.

Stan stared first at Bonnie, then looked at Jason. Then back at Bonnie with a questioning look.

I was reading Stan's face. In the years I had worked for him, that had never happened. Not once.

"Is he...?" Stan asked.

Bonnie nodded. "Jason," she said, turning to her son slouched on the couch. "I would like you to meet your biological father, Stan, the God of Poker."

"So," Jason said, nodding, but not acting surprised or shocked. "He's the guy who killed us."

THREE

THE SILENCE IN THE ROOM couldn't have been cut with a chainsaw.

I moved silently over and dropped onto a chair near the vanity, doing my best to just pretend I wasn't here. I had no idea what was happening, what had happened between Bonnie and Stan, and not a clue why Jason scared me to death.

This all seemed way, way out of my league at the moment. I really, really, really needed someone to spend some time filling me in on the history of all this, including the history of the people I worked with. I had only been a superhero now for a short ten years. I was an open book, but it sure seemed that everyone around me had a lot of history and secrets.

"I didn't..." Stan said, shaking his head, clearly upset and clearly surprised at meeting his son.

"Oh, we know you didn't," Bonnie said, smiling at Stan. "Don't we, Jason?"

"Yeah, whatever," he said, shrugging like any teenager.

Bonnie smiled again, but this time the smile once again didn't reach her eyes.

Every alarm in my body went off again.

I focused all my powers and without saying a word out loud, I shouted the thought, *Laverne!*

Watching. Her voice came back strong in my head. *And no need to shout.*

Laverne was Lady Luck herself, one of the most powerful Gods there was. I felt a lot better with her watching this. Whatever this was.

Stan shook his head and then regained his calm poker face. "If you didn't die, then where have you been for the last sixteen years?"

"Oh, we did die," Bonnie said.

"Buried," Jason said.

I almost shuddered at the very idea, but managed to stay still, tucked off on the side in my chair.

"Buried?" Stan asked. "How can that be? I saw the cabin burn to the ground with you in it. I couldn't get to you and couldn't stop the flames."

"Did you find a body?" Bonnie asked.

Stan shook his head. "The magic in those flames took everything down to fine ashes. I killed Crystal for what she did to you."

Holy smokes. Stan killed someone?

Bonnie nodded, clearly sad. "I know you did. And I know what that cost you."

Don't ask, Laverne's voice said softly in my head before I could even form a thought about asking Stan what had happened later. *Don't ever ask him. Ever.*

Understood.

"I had crawled under the floorboards of the cabin," Bonnie said, her voice soft. "I dug down into the mud and soft dirt, but I still died. And our unborn child, Jason, died with me."

"But how?" Stan asked. Then clearly, as I watched his face, he seemed to understand something. "Osiris?"

Bonnie nodded.

Laverne put in my mind an image of a tall, thin, green-skinned man wearing a white long beard and carrying a black stick. He wore robes that seemed to shimmer in the image. *One of the great old ones. The major God of Death and of Life.*

I didn't know there were great old ones.

Laverne thankfully said nothing to that stray thought by me.

Bonnie went on. "Osiris took my remains while the flames were still hot and put me in an ancient wooden coffin in an old cemetery in Boise, Idaho. The previous resident had gone mostly to dust. In there, in that darkness, Osiris slowly let life come back into my body."

"I was born in that coffin," Jason said, clearly disgusted. "We were in that old coffin until I was five living on worms and grubs and dripping water from above."

Now I actually did shudder. There were many things about the Gods and superheroes I had come to dislike, but whatever had happened to these two topped anything I had learned so far.

Stan's face looked white and he turned away. I had no idea how he was even holding it together. His son had been born six feet underground in a coffin. And had to stay there for five years.

"It took that long before we regenerated completely," Bonnie said softly. "But we are now alive. Osiris accepted us into his world and we live in comfort there. Osiris is training Jason."

I wanted to ask what he was training him for, but then Laverne thought *To replace him as the God of Death.*

Oh.

Stan looked at his son and then bowed slightly to him. "I did try to save you. I had no idea you survived. I owe Osiris a great debt."

Jason just sat on the couch under the window and shrugged like any bored teenage kid would do.

A moment later a very tall, very green man with a long white beard appeared beside Bonnie. He wore a silk robe that shimmered and radiated power like I had never felt before.

Suddenly the suite smelled of a beach fire and rose petals.

Laverne appeared beside him and bowed to him.

Stan bowed to him and I scrambled to my feet and did the same, stunned that Laverne would bow to anyone. Wow did I have a lot to learn about the Gods and this world I played a very small part in.

I so wanted to just jump away from this, but instead I backed up as much as I could and tried to make myself as unnoticed as possible.

Jason just sat on the couch looking bored.

Osiris faced Stan. "I am sorry I could not tell you about your wife and son. I did not know if I could save them or if they would come through the process sane."

"I am very glad you did save them," Stan said.

"We cannot return to you," Bonnie said to Stan, a sadness now in her brown eyes.

Stan nodded. "I understand."

Osiris reached over and took Bonnie's hand and it was clear they were now a couple of some sort.

Stan nodded and smiled and after a moment Bonnie also smiled.

Then something happened that I am sure would give me nightmares for years. Osiris, the God of Death and one of the ancient ones that even Laverne bowed to, turned and faced me directly.

His eyes were a swirling pool of silver and black and he seemed to have a sly grin hidden in that white beard.

"Poker Boy," he said and I swore his voice seemed to echo into all parts of my head. "I have watched you and your team save this world and the gods in it many times. I now ask for your help."

I nodded and somehow said with a slight bow, "Anything you desire, sir."

"In a few years Jason will require training in the arts of discipline and control of his emotions if he is to someday rule in my place."

On the couch Jason just snorted. I did not look away from Osiris.

"When the time comes, I would like you to teach him those arts through the game you call poker. You are the best poker player in the world. Jason will require the best."

I don't think I was breathing, but I did manage to say, "I would be honored, sir."

"Very good," Osiris said, smiling and showing me a mouthful of rotted and yellowed teeth.

He turned to Laverne. "It is always an honor."

"The honor is mine, Great One," Laverne said, bowing slightly.

Osiris then turned to Stan. "I am deeply sorry for your loss."

Stan nodded and then glanced at Bonnie with a smile. "It seems that from the ashes has come some good."

Bonnie smiled back and the smile reached her eyes. And the relief that Stan understood.

Stan was letting her go.

Osiris nodded and bowed slightly to Stan. "You are as great a young god as Bonnie led me to believe."

Then Osiris, Bonnie, and Jason were gone.

My legs gave out and I dropped down onto the chair.

Laverne stepped over to Stan and put her hand on his shoulder like a parent comforting a small child.

Then without a word they were both gone and the sounds of the city outside the suite came crashing back in as they let go of the time bubble we had all been inside.

I was now alone in a plush hotel suite trying to catch my breath. I took two deep, shuddering breaths, working to slow my heart that seemed to want to pound right out of the front of my chest.

I worked to just clear my mind and relax as I had learned to do at a poker table in times of stress.

In a moment I felt better.

I stood, went to the window, and looked out the window at my office floating there in the sky over the MGM Grand. There were still almost thirty minutes before Patty got off work. She'd never believe what had just happened. Or maybe she would.

And then I realized that I had just agreed to give the adopted son of the God of Death poker lessons.

Once again I had to sit down and try to catch my breath.

And that wasn't easy to do.

~

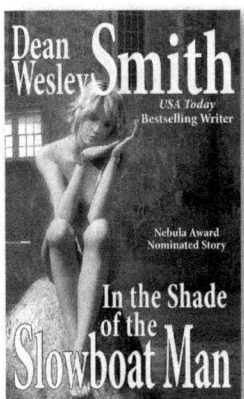

USA *Today* Bestselling Writer

DEAN WESLEY SMITH

THE LIFE AND TIMES OF BUFFALO JIMMY

Chapters 1-3

USA Today *bestselling writer, Dean Wesley Smith returns to his love of the wild west in this ongoing serial story.*

In the west in 1866, Jimmy Gray lives the adventure of his life.

His family dead, his only brother sick, he must uphold the family honor and follow one of the most ruthless men to ever ride the trails.

The very man who killed his parents and who holds Jimmy's future hostage.

Western adventure in a modern new style.

THE LIFE AND TIMES OF BUFFALO JIMMY

Part One
A GREAT LOSS

THE FIRST SHOT RIPPED into nineteen-year-old Jimmy Gray's saddle with a sickening thud, barely missing his right leg.

The sound of the shot echoed over the rolling Missouri hills and died into the clear, sunny afternoon air. His horse reared and threatened to bolt even though the shot had not gone through the thick leather, but Jimmy fought it back into control, spinning around completely on ridgeline covered by prairie grass.

A second shot knocked Jimmy's brother, Luke, off his horse.

Jimmy dove for the ground and cover as a third shot narrowly missed him, the sound of the bullet whistling past his ear.

He lay on the ground, face pressed into the soft dirt and grass, trying to breathe. His heart was racing. He had never been so scared in all his life.

He had never been shot at before. He read about such things in dime novels and in the newspapers, but reading about it and having it happen to you were two very different things.

Jimmy and his family were two days ride from Independence, Missouri. He and his brother had just come over the ridge two hundred paces above their family's wagon. Five men had been down there near the back of the wagon, off their horses, from what Jimmy could tell in the quick glimpse before the shooting had started

He hadn't seen his parents.

That scared him even more than being shot at. He just hoped they weren't hurt.

This was just like all the bad stories he had heard about the western frontier coming true right now.

And was Luke hurt? He had to find out.

He had to move.

Jimmy couldn't believe this was even happening. All Jimmy had wanted to see was buffalo. Since his teacher a year ago back in Boston, in his last year of high school, had told him stories of the great buffalo hunts, Jimmy had been focused on little else. The big beasts had become an obsession, his mother had said. His father had only laughed and promised that Jimmy would see his share of buffalo by the time they reached the Wyoming Territory.

His older brother, Luke, had told him as they rode out of camp that the buffalo were no longer in Missouri in 1866, at least not this part of it. They had all been killed or driven hundreds of miles away from the wagon trail, but Jimmy didn't care. He still had his mind set on seeing a buffalo and proving Luke wrong. For all he knew, there could be an entire herd just over the next ridge.

After riding fast away from the well-worn wagon road for a half-mile or so, they had scared up rabbits. Luke, who was twenty, had the family rifle. He had become a great shot and had managed to get three rabbits with only five shots. Jimmy was an expert shot as well. Once Luke even had admitted he was better than Luke, a real natural with a gun.

Jimmy had helped Luke skin the rabbits and then they had headed back. Luke had been sick since leaving Kansas City and was riding slowly. Jimmy could tell that both of his parents were worried about Luke making the long trip across the country, but Jimmy' father had a job offer at a bank in San Francisco, and had bought a gold mining claim in the mountains near Sacramento, so the family was set on making the trip and starting a new life in the west.

It had been such a perfect, spring day.

Until the shots.

What had happened?

Jimmy scrambled on all fours through the grass, his head low, until he finally managed to reach his brother.

Luke was pushing himself up slightly on his elbows and blood was streaming from his leg. "Get the rifle off my saddle," he said through gritted teeth. "Quick!"

Jimmy glanced around.

Luke's horse had only gone about twenty paces back from the top of the ridge and then stopped. Keeping his head down, Luke ran for the horse, grabbed the rifle from the saddle and brought it back.

There were no more shots at him coming from their wagon, but off his horse, Jimmy couldn't see the trail over the edge of the rise, which means the men doing the shooting couldn't see him.

Luke had torn off the bottom of his shirt and wrapped it around his leg, but it didn't look to Jimmy as if the bleeding had slowed much.

Luke grabbed the rifle from Jimmy, cocked it to make sure it was loaded, then staying low, hopped the few steps to the top of the ridge, dragging his bad leg behind him.

Jimmy stayed beside him, and at the top of the ridge they both lay down in the grass and crawled the last few feet so they could see the trail below.

Jimmy was shocked at what faced them. He wanted to jump and run, but somehow stayed beside Luke.

Two men on horseback were riding up the hill toward them, guns drawn. Three other men were pulling things from the wagon and scattering them on the ground. Jimmy had no idea where his parents were.

He and Luke were going to die, Jimmy was sure of that.

This was just like all the bad stories he had heard about the western frontier coming true right now.

His stomach was so twisted up, he could hardly breathe.

"Keep your head down," Luke whispered.

Then, taking a deep breath, Luke pulled down on the men like he was shooting rabbits. The shot exploded in Jimmy's ear, since he was so close to Luke.

The lead man went over backwards off his horse like a trick rider Jimmy had seen at the Circus last year in Boston.

The other man's horse reared up, and by the time he could get turned around, Luke fired again.

He must have missed. The second man took off back down the hill toward the wagon. The man that Luke had shot pushed himself to his feet, holding his stomach, and then half-ran, half-staggered back down the hill.

The three men below had their guns out and were firing up at Luke and Jimmy.

"Keep your head down," Luke ordered again. Then he fired back at the men around the wagon. Jimmy watched one of Luke's shots splinter wood off the wagon bed right beside one man.

Luke shot again and another of the men danced as the bullet kicked up dirt and mud right at his feet.

Luke didn't hit any of the men, but his next shot, and the one after, sent them scrambling for their horses.

Jimmy recognized one of the men.

Jake Benson, the man his father had hired to guide them from Kansas City to Independence.

The three men quickly mounted up and joined the fourth. He had picked up the wounded man and was riding at full speed down the trail toward Independence. The horse of the man Luke had shot grazed on the side of the hill. Clearly, they didn't have the stomach for a fight in the open for a horse with Luke having the rifle and the upper ground and all they had were pistols.

Jimmy watched them go, their dust kicking up small clouds behind them.

It seemed to take an eternity for them to vanish over the distant rise.

When would they be back? The question made Jimmy shudder.

The wagon still sat where Jimmy and Luke had left it when they had left to go hunting. It was sitting just off to one side of the muddy tracks of the wagon road, with their two secondary horses grazing while still in harness. But the lunch fire was smoldering instead of burning, and a lot of their personal things had been tossed out into the dirt and dried mud.

After all the shooting, the silence of the wide-open prairie was broken only by the light breeze through the grass.

Tomb-like silent.

Luke sat up, checked his wound, then pushed himself to his feet.

"Get our horses," he said to Jimmy.

Jimmy turned and ran for their two horses, the fear of what might have happened to his parents twisting at his stomach like a bad belly-ache. He grabbed Luke's horse, then mounted up on his own, the hole where the bullet had embedded in the leather of his saddle a clear reminder of just how close he had come to getting shot.

By the time he got back to his brother, Luke's face looked white, and it was clear that he was in a lot of pain.

"Let's find Mother and Father," Luke said, reaching for his horse's reins.

Jimmy made sure Luke could get back on his horse, then started down the hill ahead of his older brother, working to keep his hands from shaking and his stomach under control while trying to look in a thousand directions at the same time for Benson and his men. They would be back. He had no doubt.

The wind whistled lightly in his ears under his hat, the warm afternoon sun glared in his eyes. He forced himself to take shallow breaths as the ride seemed to stretch into an eternity.

It wasn't until he had moved almost halfway down the hill that he saw what he had feared the most. His mother and father were lying in the mud near the rear wheels of the wagon. Neither seemed to be moving.

Jimmy dismounted ten running steps from the wagon before the horse had even stopped.

An instant later he was on his knees beside his father.

He was dead.

His blood had made a muddy pool, his eyes were staring up, unseeing at the blue sky and light white clouds. He had been shot at least twice.

Jimmy stared at the man who had always been there for him. His father couldn't be dead. He was too strong, too powerful a man to die.

An instant later, Luke was on the ground beside their mother.

Jimmy watched as Luke rolled her over. The front of her pretty blue dress was coated in mud and her own blood.

She had been shot in the back.

As Luke rolled her over, she blinked, then opened her eyes.

She was alive!

For a moment, it was clear she wasn't aware of where she was, but as Jimmy moved closer, she looked up at Luke.

"Mother?" Luke said, his voice shaking.

Jimmy touched her arm, trying to give her some comfort as well. He had no idea what they could do.

"Benson," she whispered. "Hide from him."

"He's not here," Luke said. "We chased him and his men off."

She nodded, seemingly satisfied with that. She coughed, blood coming out of the corner of her mouth. She looked up at Jimmy and smiled, then back at Luke. "Take care of each other."

Jimmy watched as she closed her eyes and her body relaxed.

All the life seemed to leave her.

"Mother!" Luke shouted, his voice

swallowed by the vast wilderness around them.

Their mother was dead.

They were alone.

Part Two
MOVING FORWARD

JIMMY HAD NO IDEA how long he had sat beside the wagon road alternating between staring at his parents' bodies and watching the trail and hills for Benson to come back.

Maybe minutes.

Maybe hours.

He didn't know. But finally, the cold afternoon wind made him realize he and Luke had to move.

Luke had crawled a few feet from the bodies and just lay on his back, the rifle at his side. Jimmy couldn't tell if he had passed out, or was just staring up into the sky. The shirt tied around his leg was bright red with blood.

Jimmy found a sheet one of the men had tossed out of the wagon. He ripped out bandage-length strips, then found a bottle of his father's best whisky and, with a quick check for Benson and his men, moved over to his brother.

Luke didn't protest as Jimmy unwrapped the bloody shirt, tore open his pants a little near the wound and checked how bad it was. The bleeding had mostly stopped and the bullet had gone all the way through. That was lucky, but Jimmy still had to get Luke to a doctor and soon.

He poured some whiskey on the wound, as he had seen his father do when Jimmy' mother had cut her hand.

Luke winced, but didn't say anything. He didn't even open his eyes. Then Jimmy wrapped the wound in the clean strips from the sheet.

"We have to get you fixed up," Jimmy said, his voice breaking the silence of the vast plain.

The wind seemed to pull his words away over the swaying grassland almost as he spoke them.

Luke didn't move.

Jimmy pushed himself to his feet and then, without looking at his parents' bodies, he climbed into the back of their wagon and pulled out two of his mother's favorite blankets, then got the two shovels his father had bought in St. Louis and went back out into the sun and breeze. He tossed one shovel onto the ground beside Luke. Then he covered his father with a blanket, then his mother.

"Luke, I'm going to start digging some graves up on the top of the rise. I should be able to see if Benson and his men are doubling back from up there. Rest as long as you need to."

Luke shook his head. "We stay together."

Luke took a deep breath and pushed himself to his feet, using the shovel to balance on one leg. The sickness he had been fighting since they left Boston had really made him weak, and now getting shot had made him much worse. Even though Jimmy was the youngest, he was going to have to be the strongest until Luke got better.

Together, with Jimmy keeping guard and carrying the rifle, they slowly moved up the hill through the grass, Luke using one shovel as a crutch.

At the top, at a place that seemed to overlook the vast plains, they started to dig through the thick sod and into the wet, damp ground.

It would be a good final resting place for their parents.

Jimmy had no idea how long they had been digging, but every few minutes he kept watch, and finally, he saw something. Three wagons were moving toward them slowly but steadily, coming from St. Louis.

"We have company," Jimmy said. "Wagons. Not Benson."

He felt a little relieved. As his father had always said, there was safety in numbers out west. Benson and his men might still attack them, but with other wagons close by, it wasn't likely.

Luke stopped and leaned on his shovel. He was breathing hard and sweating far more than he should have. Bright red blood spotted the bandages on his leg.

"They'll go around," Luke said, and went back to digging.

Jimmy watched his brother for a moment. They had not made that much headway on the two graves, and Jimmy doubted Luke was going to be able to keep going much longer. If they were going to do this right, and give their parents a proper resting place, and be safe from Benson, they were going to need help.

"I'm going to see if they'll lend a hand," Jimmy said. "You rest."

"I don't need rest," Luke said.

"I don't plan on burying you as well," Jimmy said, turning back to glare at his brother. Then with his sternest voice, he said, "Now rest and I'll go talk to these people."

Luke stared at Jimmy for a moment, then nodded and dropped to the ground. A moment later he was lying on his back, his eyes closed, the family rifle in one hand.

In all his life, Jimmy had never felt so alone.

His parents dead, his older brother injured and sick. He was in charge.

How could he be in charge of anything? He was only nineteen.

He first gathered up the killer's horse, then the two horses that he and Luke had been riding. Luckily, they hadn't gone far and were just grazing near the trail. He tied them to the wagon, constantly keeping watch for Benson and his men.

Then he started down the wagon trail, walking beside the deepest ruts toward the oncoming wagons. The three wagons were spaced a good distance apart, and all seemed to be what was called a "small wagon" with square canvas tops, similar to the one his parents had purchased.

A man about his father's age was driving the first rig, moving a team of four oxen gently forward. A woman and two younger children were walking along to one side of the wagon, and a fifth oxen and a horse were tied to the back. The other two wagons also seemed to have families, but they were far enough back that Jimmy couldn't tell for sure.

"What can I do for you, mister?" the man said, stopping his wagon with the lead oxen about twenty paces from Jimmy.

Jimmy stopped as well. He didn't want to seem threatening in any way.

The woman moved up beside her husband and stared at Jimmy, holding her two younger children behind her skirt.

"We were robbed and my parents were killed, sir." Jimmy made himself go on after that sentence. "By the man we hired to guide us to Independence. My brother and I were out hunting. My brother's also been shot and is not very strong, since he's recovering from being sick. If you might stop for a short time, we could sure use the help in burying our parents."

"Oh, my," the woman said before her husband could get out a word.

"Of course we'll help," he said, nodding. "We'll pull around you and stop." He turned to his wife. "Go back and tell the other wagons what we are doing."

"Thank you," Jimmy said. "Very much appreciated." He turned and walked ahead of the wagons back toward the hill. He didn't allow himself to look at the blankets behind his wagon.

"They're going to help," he said to Luke as he reached the top of the hill, picked up his shovel, and went back to digging. "And with them helping, we'll be safer for the moment."

Luke only sighed and didn't move.

Part Three
INDEPENDENCE

IT TOOK TWO DAYS to make the trip into Independence, following the other three wagons as part of their group. Luke had just laid in the bed of the wagon most of the trip, seemingly getting sicker and weaker by the day, even though one of the women from the wagons had nursing training from the war and had cleaned Luke's wound and got it to stop bleeding.

Jimmy had driven the team, taken care of the horses each night, and done what little cooking they needed. Luke didn't eat much, and Jimmy hadn't felt hungry either. He just felt numb.

Luckily, his father had spent a few hours teaching him how to handle the wagon and the horses, but he clearly wasn't that good, and a few simple stream crossings had almost turned disastrous.

Henry Basker, the man he had first talked to in the lead wagon, had finally, on what looked like a really nasty downhill crossing, offered to take the wagon across for Jimmy and show him how to do it. Jimmy had never felt so relieved in his life.

Every mile of the trip, he kept expecting Benson and his men to come charging in and kill them all. Jimmy had told Basker and the other two men about Benson and his men, so all of the men on the wagons rode with their guns at the ready.

During the first night of camp, with Luke asleep in a tent beside the wagon, Jimmy had dug through what was left of their family's possessions. Benson had stolen the supply money his father planned to use in Independence and his mother's family jewelry. And worse yet, Benson had stolen the gold mine deed.

The entire family had all been excited about that mine when his father first told them about buying the deed. Ever since Jimmy could remember, people had talked about finding gold out west and never having to work again. Now his father had bought them a real gold mine.

The plan was for his father to work in the bank while Jimmy and Luke worked the mine. Jimmy knew he couldn't get the money or jewelry back from Benson. Those would be gone before they caught up with him. But Benson would hold onto that deed, not knowing how much it was worth, and Jimmy figured that if he found Benson, he and Luke could get the mine back.

To make the deed be worth anything, Benson would have to register his ownership of the deed in Sacramento, just as his father had been planning to do. Jimmy and Luke had to make sure they got to Sacramento before Benson, or get the deed back along the way somewhere.

If Benson didn't come and kill them first, that is.

In his search of the wagon that first night, Jimmy was very relieved to find that Benson hadn't found the false bottom of a family chest his mother had insisted they bring along. In that false bottom, his father had put the money he planned on using to buy them a new home in San Francisco.

Jimmy had strapped a third of the money in a cloth holder to the small of his back under his shirt, then left part of the rest in the false chest bottom, and some more in a false bottom in the wagon floor.

By the time they arrived outside of Independence and stopped the wagon with what looked to be thousands of other wagons, it was around noon of the third day since the shooting.

Jimmy left their wagon camped on a wide plain a mile to the north of Independence next to the Basker wagon, then took Luke into town to find a doctor.

Luke was so sick, he could barely ride, and Jimmy had to stop three times along the well-traveled road to let Luke rest.

Independence was far larger than Jimmy had expected, seeming to spread out over two small hills and fill a broad valley. The wide main streets were so crowded, it was hard to even walk a horse up the middle of them. The streets were muddy and smelled of horse manure. The sidewalks were wood and slippery from spring rains and mud tracked up from the street.

The excitement of being in a new place, a vibrant, alive place like Independence was shocking. It felt like a large carnival, with lots of noise, loud talking, and construction sounds. Piano music came from the open doors of dozens of saloons, and men fighting in the mud seemed to be common.

Everyone, no matter what age, seemed to have an intense purpose, and no one noticed the two brothers at all, at least that Jimmy could see.

Jimmy, on constant alert for Benson, went into town from the side, staying off the main streets, and tied the horses off on a side street near a saloon. With Luke leaning on him, he managed to walk along the wooden sidewalk and get into a doctor's office beside a general store.

In town, he felt a lot safer with all the people around him, but he still didn't want Benson to know he and Luke were here.

The doctor, a friendly, older man named Davis, stood about as tall as Jimmy's five-ten, but had a pot belly on him that made him look almost round. He wore glasses and his brown hair was thin and long, combed over to one side.

Doc Davis took one look at Luke, touched his hot forehead, and had Jimmy help him get Luke in a bed in the back of the office, beside two other sick men and a sick child.

"What happened?" Doc Davis asked Jimmy after Luke was resting.

"We were coming with our parents," Jimmy said. "Ambushed by robbers. Parents are dead." He was shocked at how that sounded. It still didn't seem right that they were gone.

"They shot Luke in the leg before we ran them off."

"I'm so sorry," Doc Davis said, putting his hand gently on Jimmy's shoulder.

"Luke and I can get by all right," Jimmy said, taking a deep breath and squaring his shoulders. He pulled a coin out of his pants pocket to pay the doctor. "Will this be enough to get Luke well?" He gave the doctor the twenty dollar gold piece.

Doc Davis looked at it, clearly surprised, then nodded and put it in his pocket. "More than enough. We'll take good care of him, I can promise you that. Do you have a place to stay?"

"I have the family wagon outside of town," Jimmy said. "I'll be staying there."

Doc Davis brushed his thinning hair to one side of his head. "If you need anything, you just come to me. Understand? And I'll let you know more tomorrow on how Luke is doing."

Jimmy nodded. "Thanks, Doctor. I'll be back tomorrow."

With that, Jimmy stepped back out onto the street of the busy western town.

Alone.

His parents dead, his brother sick, and he was alone in a strange town. He had told his friends in Boston he wanted to go west for the adventure.

He just hadn't dreamed it would be like this.

Continued Next Month…

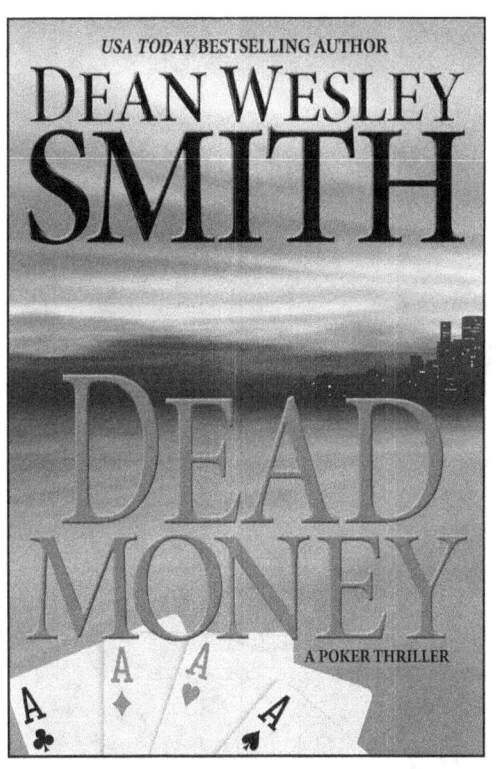

Written in the fast-paced style of James Patterson, Dead Money takes readers into all aspects of poker, from high-stakes private games to one of the largest tournaments of the year at the Bellagio Casino in Las Vegas.

Considered a sport by the courts and television, the prize money given away in major poker tournaments far exceeds the total of golf and tennis combined.

But when one of the greatest poker players of all time dies, the stakes rise even higher.

DEAD MONEY could be the start of a new thriller genre— the political poker thriller.

—Sheldon McArthur,
former owner of
Mysterious Books in Los Angeles

Available November 2013 from any of your favorite bookstores.

USA Today bestselling writer, Dean Wesley Smith twists you into a Twilight Zone type story and then beyond.

A long ways beyond.

Clarice Williams dreams of a fantasy lover, her standards set so high she seems destined to live out her lifetime in Boise alone. Then her dream lover tells her his name.

Real or a dream, she must find out.

THE BIG TICK OF TIME

ONE

CLARICE WILLIAMS LISTENED INTENTLY to the faint hum of her alarm clock.

Outside the pulled shade of her bedroom window, she could tell the sun wasn't even thinking of coming up. And yet she knew, without a doubt, that any moment now that alarm would go off, the annoying sound of a shrill buzz able to wake even the dead across the street in the cemetery.

Yes, she had bought a house directly across the street from the Morris Hill Cemetery, oldest cemetery in Boise. And she liked it that way. Better looking across the grass and through the old trees than at the garage door and scattered kid's toys of another house in some subdivision somewhere.

And she had a high wooden fence around three sides of her large property, so it felt like she actually had no neighbors.

As a senior attorney for one of the largest and most powerful law firms in the state, she could have bought anywhere in town, or up on the foothills above the city. But she liked this old neighborhood and the peacefulness of the cemetery.

She had always liked it, for as long as she had been in this town.

Those people across the street seldom demanded her time and energy or asked stupid questions.

She had sat the alarm for buzz, because she really, really needed to get out of bed every morning and into the office before seven. But no sane person should ever be forced to get up on a cold winter morning at 5 A.M. and at some point she would cut back the schedule, slow down, take more vacations.

She had been promising herself that now for three years. Soon, it would have to happen. This pace was wearing on her.

She burrowed down into the soft cotton sheet and the two quilts and pretended the alarm wasn't about to go off.

Instead she let herself imagine her dream man, the one she knew deep down that in this life she never would meet. She was just too picky when it came to men.

The past had spoiled her, of that there was no doubt.

As one of her friends had once said, no man could live up to her standards.

Her friend had been right. But Clarice did have a dream man who was just perfect. He was six-two, with dark hair slightly long in the back. She imagined him wearing jeans, a dress shirt open at the neck, a duster-like leather jacket, and a dark cowboy hat.

He would smile at her, tip his hat, and then ask her to dance.

And from there, she imagined they made passionate love.

With the help of a wonderful device she had been given as a gag gift one Christmas party, she often felt satisfied for days after those long adventures with her dream man.

Clarice knew that she didn't have time this morning to fire up her special gift before the alarm went off. So instead she just lay there, waiting for the buzzing that would start yet another day that would be like most every other day.

She had never made up a name for her perfect dream man. She closed her eyes and let her mind roam trying to imagine

what he would be named if he actually existed.

In her mind she was now dressed in a wonderful, blue evening gown, tight around her chest, but flowing to the floor in sweeping lines. Her brown hair was pulled up on her head and done perfectly.

Her dream man stood in front of her and she could feel herself tingle just staring at him.

"James Tick Edwards," he said, his voice deep and almost rumbling as fit his look and frame. He tipped his hat. "My friends just call me Tick."

"Tick it is, then," she said, smiling at him.

And her alarm went off.

She sighed, rolled over, turned the alarm off, then slipped out from under the quilt and put on her slippers to protect her feet from the cold tile of the bathroom floor.

Another day had begun.

TWO

AS THE DAY WORE ON, Clarice just couldn't shake the strangeness and the exactness of her dream man's name. Had someone else she had met had that name and she just wasn't remembering and now associating it with her dream man?

James Tick Edwards seemed far too exact for her imagination to come up with, especially so early in the morning.

By eleven in the morning she decided she needed to find out.

With her fifth cup of coffee for the day in her hand, she headed two floors down to the firm's research department. She had done a computer search on her own and found nothing, so she needed better help.

The firm occupied a four-story office building tucked back in the trees near the Boise River and only about four blocks from the university campus. The area was packed with restaurants catering to both the university crowd and the varied office buildings nearby.

Her office was on the top floor with a wonderful view out through the old trees and over the slowly flowing river. Right now the river wasn't much more than a trickle and the leaves were all gone from the trees. A little snow still clung to the shaded areas from the last snow a few days before.

She loved the view, but as a senior attorney in the firm, she seldom had time to turn away from her desk to enjoy it.

The head of research was a young guy named Stanton, not more than twenty-five, who had long blonde hair, solid shoulders, and a tan that couldn't be beat. His passions were skiing and he managed to spend most late afternoons and all evenings in the winter up at nearby Bogus Basic Ski Area.

And in the summer he spent his weekends and spare time on rivers, rafting some of the most extreme water the area had to offer. Every woman who had met him found him fantastically attractive, but sadly for all women, he found men more to his liking and had been with the same partner now for six years. His partner worked at the university.

Stanton was the best person she had ever known with computers, and if something needed to be found or tracked down, he could do it.

When he saw her coming his smile lit up his face. "Clarice, what can I do for you?"

She smiled back, pushing away the wish that she could just jump him once. Totally inappropriate thinking for a senior attorney in the firm.

"I need to see if you can find someone for me?"

"Sure," he said. "Which case do I bill the time to?"

"No case yet," she said. "This is background, so put it to my office."

"Got it," he said, nodding and making a note on his ledger as he was supposed to do. "Who are you looking for?"

"James Tick Edwards," she said. "I have no other information but the name.

He shrugged. "I'll see what I can do."

"Thanks," she said. "I appreciate it.

And with that, she headed back upstairs to her office, feeling silly that she was wasting the firm's time on her fantasy. But she worked enough extra hours for the firm. It could afford a little payback.

THREE

THREE HOURS LATER her secretary said that Stanton was here to see her.

He came in, smiling, a brown research folder in his hand. "Only one James Tick Edwards that I could find in all of history."

"Really?" she asked, her heart suddenly beating harder. More than likely the guy was a five-two bank manager instead of her dream guy, but she had to know.

"You two are neighbors, actually," Stanton said, handing her the file. "He's buried in the old section of the Morris Hill Cemetery right across from your house."

She looked up at Stanton, who was still smiling and clearly not noticing the shock and surprise she was feeling.

"Buried?" she asked.

Stanton nodded.

"He was an amazing man in his day," Stanton said, pointing to the file that she could see also contained printouts of old newspapers. "That was some fun reading."

With that Stanton turned and left the office, leaving the file open on her desk in front of her.

And there, staring out of an old newspaper photo was her dream lover.

"Well, that figures," she said, shaking her head. "So just where did the name come from?"

She stared at his picture. He was the man she had had numbers of wonderful dreams about. He was tall, seeming to tower over other men in the picture. He wore a duster and a dark cowboy hat. He seemed to be looking out of the image at her.

"So, if this was a Twilight Zone episode, he will appear right about now."

She looked up from her desk, but no dream-lover ghost standing there. Her office was empty.

She glanced out the window at the river walk below her office. No one there either.

She felt both relieved and disappointed.

She couldn't believe he was dead.

And buried.

For the guy in that picture, that didn't seem possible. Her dream lover was too powerful, too much to be killed.

The intercom on her desk buzzed telling her it was time for her next meeting, so she carefully closed the file and tucked it in her case to take home.

Maybe she'd read it later tonight, in the bathtub, with a bottle of wine and her favorite Christmas gift.

FOUR

CLARICE DECIDED there was no point in waiting to read the file, so after her meeting she told her secretary that she wasn't to be disturbed for a half hour, then went back and opened up the file, spreading it out on her desk.

Stanton had been right, James Tick Edwards had been an amazing man. An early pioneer to the area, he had owned a large mansion outside of town above the river and had helped in the construction of the capitol building. He had remained single, but was seen regularly with the appropriate ladies of the time, as the articles said.

He supported numbers of good causes, was free with his money and time, but yet remained a private man. No one was sure where his money came from, or where he was from, although there was speculation he was from New York. He left a large part of his fortune on his death to a number of charities and the rest to a young nephew in London.

She stared at that nephew sentence for a moment, then went on reading.

James Tick Edwards died in 1927 at the age of forty-two in a massive house fire. What was left of his body was buried across the street from her in a ceremony attended by the governor and the mayor and many others.

"Wow," Clarice said after finishing the file. "At least I have great taste in fantasy lovers."

Then she stared at the closed brown file in front of her. How in the world had she gotten his name? She must have read something about him somewhere.

Otherwise she really was in a *Twilight Zone* episode.

She clicked her intercom and had her secretary ask Stanton if he could come back to her office when he had a moment. She needed to find the nephew.

She knew without a doubt that until she figured out where she had seen a picture of that man, and gotten his name, she wasn't having any more fantasy dates.

And with her workload, she needed those dates.

FIVE

THE NEXT MORNING Clarice made it in before seven like normal. The sun was barely lighting the winter sky and it would be dark by the time she left the office. Damn she hated winters. At least in the summer she could take a break and stroll on the river walk. Right now it was too cold out there to do any strolling, at least in comfort.

Usually she was the first person in, even ahead of her secretary, because she liked the quiet, but this morning Stanton was waiting for her when she arrived, drinking some sports drink and pacing in front of her secretaries' desk. He had a large file in his hands and an excited look on his face.

"You're never going to believe what I found," Stanton said, holding up the file before she could even say good morning. "I stayed up all night researching this after I got back from skiing. Not sure what case you are working, but this is really something."

She motioned for the excited young man to come in and then she closed the door behind him. She took her coat off and hung it on the coat tree behind her door.

"Okay," she said, "go slowly. Start from the beginning."

He nodded, took a drink from the sports bottle, then placed it on her desk with the folder and started pacing. She left the folder closed even though she wanted very much to open it. But first she wanted to find out what had Stanton so excited about the research on her mystery man. And why he had stayed up all night doing the work.

She moved around behind her desk but did not sit. Instead she leaned against the desk sipping her own Mocha she had gotten on the way in, just as she did every morning. At some point she would have breakfast brought in and eat it at her desk.

"I started with the nephew who inherited all the money in 1927," Stanton said. "He was twenty-two and his name was James Edwards as well. James T. Edwards, actually. I could not find out what the middle initial stood for."

Clarice nodded, but sat her coffee down.

"That James T. Edwards died in a fire in 1947 at the exact age of forty-two and was buried in London. He was never married and gave all his money to a James Edwards from New York. A twenty-two-year-old nephew."

Now Clarice had to pace.

"That's a very strange coincidence," she said, her hands clasped behind her back because she didn't want to let Stanton see them shaking.

"That's what I thought," Stanton said, "which was why I came back after skiing last night. But it gets even stranger."

She nodded and motioned for Stanton to go on.

The file on her desk beckoned her to open it, but she kept her hands off it.

"The nephew died at 42 in 1967, in a house fire. Unmarried."

"And he gave all his money to?" Clarice asked.

Stanton stopped and smiled. "A twenty-two-year-old nephew named James T. Edwards who lived in Australia. He died exactly twenty years later in 1987, in a house fire, unmarried, and he gave his fortune to his nephew, James Edwards from Phoenix."

"And let me guess," Clarice said, her stomach twisting like the morning after a long night of drinking. She couldn't believe this was even possible. "That James Edwards died in 2007 in a house fire, never married, and gave his fortune to James Edwards, his twenty-two-year-old nephew."

"Exactly," Stanton said. "James Edwards of Boise, Idaho. No middle name or initial listed."

That froze Clarice in her tracks and she managed to get to her chair and drop into it before her knees gave out.

He was here?

Now?

After all this time, could he really be here?

Stanton stopped his excited pacing and opened the file and turned it for Clarice to see. On top was a driver's license picture of James Edwards. And he was the same exact man of her dreams, staring into the DMV camera with a slight grin on his face.

"That's either some very powerful genetics or something very, very strange is going on here," she said. But she said that for Stanton. She knew exactly what was happening if she could let herself believe it.

He was here. That thought just kept echoing in her mind over and over.

"Exactly," Stanton said. "I went back and tried to find birth records for any of these men. Nothing. I could find no record of any of them being born. Not unusual for most of them, but odd for the last two."

"But there were bodies in those burned out houses?" she asked.

"Always," Stanton said, nodding.

"Looks like I need to talk to this guy," she said, feeling some excitement about finally meeting the man of her dreams. "Do you have his address and where he works?"

"Careful," Stanton said, suddenly worried. "Are you sure?"

She smiled. "I'm sure there's a perfectly logical explanation for all this. I need to talk with this man about a legal matter, which is why I wanted you to find him, and I'll ask him about his relatives when I see him."

Stanton nodded, clearly not happy. "He works about three blocks from here as a financial investor, even though he doesn't need to work."

That close! Amazing.

She had no idea how that was possible. Why hadn't she seen him, run into him in a restaurant?

She wasn't even sure how she had gotten his name in the first place. She needed answers and she needed them now.

And she needed to see him.

That more than anything.

"Thanks," she said, smiling at Stanton and raising. She moved the file to the top drawer of her desk. "I'll let you know what I discover. And I really, really appreciate the extra work on this. Take the rest of the day off and put your hours last night in as overtime and I'll approve it."

"Thanks," he said, smiling. "You sure you don't want me to go with you to meet him."

She laughed. "No thanks. Let me read up on him first before I go." She pointed to the file. "He has strange ancestors. That doesn't make him a killer."

"Yeah, good point," Stanton said, nodding and smiling. "It's just all so weird."

"That it is," she said. "And I'm going to find out why. I'll let you know tomorrow."

"Thanks," he said and left.

On the way down the elevator a half hour later, her hands were shaking so much, she could barely get her coat buttoned before she walked out into the cold air to meet her fantasy lover.

The very man she could not believe was alive and so close.

SIX

It was barely eight in the morning when she reached the offices of Daniels and Associates, financial investors. But the place looked like it had been going for hours. More than likely there were people here before the stock market opened on the east coast.

She had decided to walk the few blocks up Boise Ave to the two-story office complex tucked back in the trees. The walk allowed her to clear her mind and figure out what she was going to say.

The investment office radiated money and power from the outside, which was what it needed to do if customers were to trust them. She went in through the large wooden front door and then through another inner door.

A large trading floor was to her right behind glass, and a wide staircase led up behind the reception area. There were very plush and expensive couches along one wall with plants. No one was sitting in them.

Clarice walked up to the middle-aged secretary with dark brown hair at the front desk who greeted her with a large smile, more than likely sizing up Clarice's clothing and measuring her for money. Clarice dressed the part of a powerful attorney. That was enough for the woman.

"I'd like to see James Edwards, please," Clarice said.

She managed to sound in control, somehow. Was this going to be even possible?

"Do you have an appointment?" the woman asked, going through the routine she was trained to do.

"I do not," Clarice said, smiling. "But please tell him that Clarice Williams is here to see him. I am a fan of his great, great, great uncle."

Then she slipped the lady her card, which had the name of her firm on it.

The receptionist glanced at it, nodded and stood, moving to the wide staircase that led up to what must be the executive offices above.

Clarice forced herself to take a deep breath and relax. She needed to know how this happened and what it meant and that meant she had to stay as calm as possible.

A moment later the secretary came down the stairs followed by James Edwards.

If he had on a long duster, jeans, and a cowboy hat, he would have been the replica of the man of her dreams.

This James Edwards wore a silk suit like it was the most comfortable thing he had, and he had loosened his tie some around his neck.

He saw her about halfway down the stairs and actually jerked, catching himself on the railing. He paused for a moment just staring at her, clearly not believing what he was seeing any more than she believed he was standing there.

Clarice felt relieved that he was as shocked as she felt.

Finally he regained his composure. As he reached the bottom of the stairs, he extended his hand and smiled that wonderful smile of his.

"James Edwards."

She took his hand and felt the electricity between them. His skin was firm, his hand slightly calloused like he actually did physical work at times.

"Clarice Williams," she said, smiling back, not letting go of his hand.

She stared into those wonderful brown eyes and he stared back, clearly not wanting to let go of her hand either.

Finally both of them came to their senses and he said, "Let's go to my office." He indicated they should go back up the stairs and she shook her head.

"If you wouldn't mind," she said, smiling, "I could use some breakfast and a large cup of coffee."

"I'd love that," he said. "Café right around the corner is wonderful."

"I know," she said, smiling, "I eat there regularly."

"You do? How have we missed each other?"

"I honestly don't know," she said. Then she whispered so that the secretary couldn't hear. "And I understand you own it."

He leaned back and looked at her, then smiled. "How much do you know about me?"

"More than you can ever imagine," she said as they went out the door and back into the cold morning air.

"Oh, I can imagine a great deal," he said. "Don't you remember?"

She smiled. "It's only been four hundred and twelve years since our last few lifetimes together. How could I forget?"

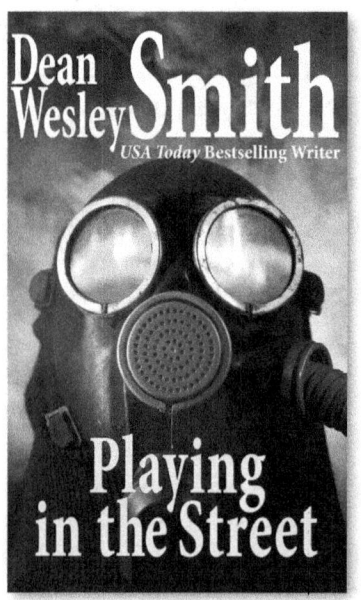

"I was afraid you were dead," he said as they reached the cold air and started through the parking lot. "I've really missed you, but had no real idea how to track you. You cover your tracks well."

"Better than you do," she said, laughing.

He reached over and took her hand.

"I worried about you as well," she said. "And dreamed about you all the time."

"Starting in the last few years?" he asked, smiling that impish smile she loved so much.

"More so, yes," she said, staring up into the smiling face of the man she had loved for centuries, ever since they had first met in an Egyptian Court over three thousand years before.

"Remember Jimmy David?" he asked.

She nodded. "I've run into him off and on for centuries since we met him."

"He's a computer nerd now, one of the best," James said. "He's figured out a way to get in contact with more of our kind, maybe bring a number of us together, help us cover our tracks a little better in this new information world."

"He put your name in my head?"

James nodded. "Among other things. He's been working on this special linked communication thing for three years now, trying to pull us all together. I'm funding him. He even guessed you might be in this area six years ago if you were still alive, which is why I came back here."

Then her fantasy lover smiled and looked into her eyes. "Was it good for you, having me in your mind?"

She laughed and squeezed the man of her dreams hand. "Better than you can ever imagine."

"Show me after breakfast?" he asked, laughing.

"With pleasure," she said, smiling at her no-longer-fantasy lover. "With pleasure."

~

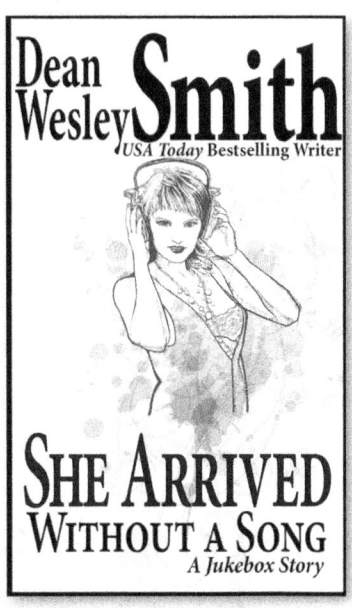

DEAN WESLEY SMITH

THE ADVENTURES OF HAWK

Chapters 1-3

USA Today *bestselling writer, Dean Wesley Smith takes us on a thrill-ride adventure in some of the world's most exotic places.*

In search of his missing father, Danny Hawk must survive against all odds and a long ways from home.

In 1970, Egypt breeds danger for Hawk and his friends. Hawk's only hope to find his father rests in staying alive and ahead of the dangerous men chasing him.

Sometimes only a half-step ahead.

THE ADVENTURES OF HAWK

CHAPTER ONE

August 16, 1970
American University, Cairo, Egypt.

NINETEEN-YEAR-OLD DANNY HAWK held his breath and tried to listen. He had moved to a position near an open window in the old palace-like building that housed the science department of the American University in Cairo. Outside the window was a concrete ledge six inches wide. He could move along that ledge, three floors above the ground, if he had to.

From what he could hear, two men were threatening Professor Davis in the outer office. The professor was pretending that he had no idea what the men wanted, even though Danny knew that was a lie. The men were after Danny's father's records, just as Danny was.

"He's not going to tell us," one man's voice said. "Kill him and search the place. They have to be here."

There was a sound of scuffling and then a muffled gunshot.

Danny managed not to gasp or make any noise at all, but he wanted to be sick. It wasn't possible that Professor Davis had just been killed.

He couldn't be dead.

Danny's entire body felt like it had turned to Jell-O, but with more noise from the outer office, he made himself move.

And move quickly.

He climbed out the window and stood on the narrow ledge. Holding on to the rough wall as best he could, he pulled the window silently closed behind him. The only other exit out of that back office was through where the professor had just been killed, and Danny certainly wasn't going that way.

The late-evening Cairo air was hot and dry. A slight wind whipped at his loose pants and shirt as he stood with his back against the stone wall. His long black hair blew around his face as he edged inch-by-inch along the stone ledge. He had spent a lot of time climbing rocks back home in Idaho and he had no fear of heights.

But his life also hadn't been threatened in any of those climbing expeditions.

And none of them had been on the side of a building.

He forced himself to concentrate on what he was doing and try to not think about what had just happened inside.

The lights of the massive city of Cairo spread out in front of him. From the ledge, he had a good view over the palm trees and buildings, and in the distance, the Pyramids at Giza were lit up. There was so much light in the downtown area, he felt like there was a spotlight on him. The last thing he needed was to be seen from below and attention drawn to what he was doing.

The door slammed open to the back office and the men's voices got louder.

"Search it and make sure you don't miss anything."

Danny glanced back. Through the edge of the window, he caught a glimpse of a man with a red hood wearing the traditional Arab robe. Except for two eyeholes, his face was completely covered, but Danny caught a glimpse of one of the man's hands. His skin was so pale, he

couldn't be Arab. And he had a tattoo on his hand that looked like something with a snake.

Danny glanced away from the window at his path of escape ahead. This wall of the American University Science Building was long, with evenly spaced windows along the ledge. He didn't dare try for the corner. That was too far, and would risk him being seen from either the men in the office or someone on the ground below.

Either would likely get him killed.

The next window to a dark office was locked. Danny glanced back. If one of the men happened to open the window and look outside, he would see Danny.

Danny stepped up onto the windowsill and pressed himself against the glass and the corner of the stone wall. He was a solid five-foot-eight, and people called him husky. But luckily, the windowsill opening was just barely deep enough so that he wouldn't be seen if one of the men looked his direction.

Now Danny just hoped no one below noticed him.

He kept himself perfectly still, using some of the techniques his Native American grandfather had taught him to stay calm.

"Like a stone," his grandfather would say. "Breathe in so slowly, no one can see you, exhale slowly, never stopping. Keep repeating to yourself: No one can see you."

Over and over, Danny did that, keeping himself pressed against the ledge and the glass, breathing as he had been taught.

Not moving.

I'm invisible. No one can see me.

Danny had never been so afraid in all his life.

His father had gone missing a month earlier, and now Professor Davis was killed because of Danny's father's notebooks.

What had his father found that had caused so much trouble?

Why did these men want that work?

Why was it so valuable?

And what was in the notebooks?

Danny had no answers to any of those questions. The last couple of years, his father had been gone so much, they hadn't talked.

But whatever it was in those notebooks to make them so valuable, if Danny wasn't careful, he would be killed as well for it, before he had any chance to find out what was going on, or what had happened to his father.

His mother insisted that his father was still alive, that she would know in her heart, in her very soul, if he had been killed. And Danny trusted that special connection. His father was being held somewhere. Maybe close by in this very city, as far as Danny knew.

That's why Danny, his best friend, Craig, and his Uncle Steve were in Cairo. The authorities didn't seem to care what had happened to Danny's father, so now he had to go in search.

Danny had expected his father's notebooks, left with Professor Davis days before his father disappeared, might give him a clue to what had happened.

He never expected the notebooks themselves to get someone killed.

Finally, he heard a clear voice from Professor Davis's office. "There's nothing here."

"Wipe up the blood," another voice said. "Wrap the professor in his rug. We'll haul him with us and make sure his body is very lost in the desert."

The sound of movement echoed out over the night, then one of the men asked the other.

"What do we do now?"

"We trail Hawk's kid," the voice said. "He'll lead us right to the notebooks. His father must have told him where they were. Of that, I'm sure."

Danny was startled at the mention of him. How did these killers know he was in Cairo?

He forced himself to stay perfectly still, to breathe regularly. The last thing he needed at this point, on this ledge, was to panic.

"The kid's here in Cairo?" the other man asked.

"Yeah, he flew in this morning with a friend and Professor Hawk's brother. No reason for them to be here except to find the professor and get his notebooks. Those three will be easy pickings."

Danny was stunned breathless.

Whoever those two men were, they had just confirmed that they were after his father's notebooks. And they knew that Craig and Uncle Steve had come with him to Cairo.

The other man laughed. "Yeah, who knows, we might not have to even kill the three of them."

"Don't count on it," the man in charge said.

CHAPTER TWO

August 16, 1970
American University, Cairo, Egypt.

DANNY HAWK WAITED long enough on the ledge to make sure the men had gone, then when the area below the window was clear of late-night walkers, he eased along the ledge and back inside Professor Davis's darkened back office.

He didn't dare turn on the light. His eyes were accustomed to the dark anyway, so he pulled the window closed and locked it, and then moved quickly over to where Professor Davis had hung his suit coat on the inside door of the closet. Luckily, the coat was still right there.

In the dim light, the room didn't look like it had been searched. Clearly these men were professionals.

Danny wanted, more than anything, to just take his uncle and Craig and head for the airport, go home and forget all of this. Whatever his father had found had gotten him either killed or taken captive. And now it had gotten Professor Davis killed as well. And there was no telling how many other lives had been lost.

Danny knew, without a doubt, that he was in far, far over his head. And there was no one to turn to, no one to trust. The only contact they had had in Cairo had just been killed.

Now it was up to him to get his uncle and Craig to safety and quickly. If there was a safe place anywhere in the world.

The professor's suit coat was the reason that Danny had been in the back office in the first place. The professor's car keys were in his suit coat pocket, and Danny, on Professor Davis's instructions, had gone to get them just as those men had burst into the front office. The professor had told Danny that the notebooks were in the trunk of his car in the faculty parking garage.

Danny searched the pockets of Professor Davis's suit jacket, feeling very odd that he was searching through a dead man's clothing. He pushed that thought back and finally came up with the keys.

He put them in his pocket and moved silently toward the door to the outer office. He opened it carefully, and silently, only a crack. The office was empty, the lights off. It looked cleaned and everything in place.

There was no body.

The rug that had been under Professor Davis's chair was missing. Otherwise, everything looked to be in order. Someone coming in would think the professor hadn't been here. It would be days before anyone reported him missing, since he wasn't married.

Danny moved over to the phone and started to call his uncle at the hotel. Danny couldn't go back there, and he now had to get his uncle and his best friend, Craig James, out of there as well without them being seen.

Then, before he had finished dialing the number, he stopped and put the phone back in the cradle, looking at it as if it were a snake that might bite him at any moment.

"Think," he said softly to himself. "Come on, think."

He forced himself to take two slow, deep breaths, let his mind clear a little.

"Those men are professionals. That phone could be tapped."

He took a few more deep breaths just as his grandfather had trained him to do, and tried to put himself into the mind of a criminal who didn't want to get caught. He'd read enough mystery novels, that he should be able to do that.

And right now, he and his uncle and best friend needed to completely vanish from all sight in Africa's largest city.

And quickly.

Danny looked around the dimly lit office. What had he touched?

He took a couple of Kleenex tissues from a box on the professor's desk, then wiped his fingerprints off of the phone. And along the edge of the desk. Then he went back into the inner office and wiped down anything he might have touched in there, including the window. If the professor's body was discovered, there was no point in being connected to this in any way. And since he had an Egyptian visa, he had been fingerprinted when they entered the country.

When he finished, he made himself stand in the center of each room and look around, going over all his movements. He didn't dare miss anything.

And right now, he and his uncle and best friend needed to completely vanish from all sight in Africa's largest city.

"Look carefully," he muttered. "Very carefully."

He then made sure that any surface he might have even accidentally touched was wiped clean. Except for the outer doorknob of the office door, he was finally convinced that he had cleaned off every trace that he had been in the office.

He went out into the hallway and finished the doorknob, then put the tissue in his pocket.

The hallway had very high ceilings and was as wide as some streets. The floor was marble and polished. He walked silently along the empty hall, acting as if he were just a student here who had come later in the evening to see a professor, even though his heart felt like it wanted to explode out of his chest.

So much for the old Indian ways in keeping himself calm. Now he wished he had spent even more time with his grandfather before he died and learned more about self-control. It just never seemed like he would need it. At least, not like this.

He used the wide staircase in the old building and went down to the second floor. An empty receptionist desk filled a large area near the wide marble staircase. A public use phone sat on top of the desk and Danny picked it up and was quickly connected to his hotel.

The hotel was massive and modern. It looked out over the Nile River. Even their room had a river view. They had all been excited getting to it after the long plane flight. Now they were all going to have to run from it, and fast.

His uncle, Steve Hawk, answered the phone. Uncle Steve was the exact opposite of Danny's father. He was friendly, liked to stay at home, and wasn't very smart. Even he admitted that when they had passed out the brains between him and Danny's father, he had got a half serving.

Craig and Danny had the room next door to Uncle Steve's room. Craig was much taller than Danny, standing just over six feet. He had blonde hair and a smile that never seemed to quit. He lived in the same small ski town in central Idaho and his father tried to run a restaurant for tourists, but he drank more than he worked. During the summer for the past few years, Craig had helped Danny and his uncle on their tourist boat on the big mountain lake just to get away from his father.

To Danny, Uncle Steve had been there for him far more than his world-traveling archeologist father had ever been. And even when his father was at home, he was always up north at the University of Idaho, doing research and getting ready for his next trip.

"Uncle Steve," Danny said quickly when he answered the phone. "Don't say anything, just listen to me. I need you and Craig to meet me at the south entrance of the U.S. Embassy. Go down a back staircase and out a hotel back door. Make sure you are not followed. Bring your luggage and what you can of my stuff as well. You're never going back to those rooms. If I'm not there beside the embassy, wait for me without being seen. Move fast. Your lives are in danger."

Then Danny hung up without giving his uncle a chance to argue. More than likely, the call had just scared the poor man half to death. And that was good. After what Danny had just been through, they all needed to be scared if they were going to have any chance of surviving.

Danny forced himself to take another deep breath and think about staying calm.

The seemingly empty old building loomed around him. He had read that a long time ago this building had housed the University of Cairo, before that school moved across the river to larger grounds. It had been some sort of ancient palace before that.

He stood silently, working to calm his racing heart. No one seemed to be listening, to even know he was there. But after what happened to Professor Davis, he could never completely trust that feeling again. He was going to have to be careful every moment and try not to do anything too stupid.

What he really wanted to do was call the police and then just curl up behind the desk until they arrived. But he couldn't do that either. He was in Egypt. A country that was going through a change of government and unrest. Nassar, the leader since 1952 had just died and a man by the name of Sadat looked like he was going to take control. The last thing Danny needed was to get involved with the Egyptian police at this point. Instead of trying to find his father, he might spend the next year in a jail cell even though he hadn't done anything.

Danny had no doubt at all that the three of them were very much on their own. And next what he had to do was take a huge risk and get his father's notebooks out of the trunk of Professor Davis's car. Those notebooks were the only chance he had of finding out exactly what was happening.

And why his father had disappeared and Professor Davis had been killed.

CHAPTER THREE

August 16, 1970
American University parking garage, Cairo, Egypt.

DANNY MOVED SILENTLY into the two-story parking garage and up to the second floor where Professor Davis had said his small red sedan was parked. The car was tiny compared to American cars, but after spending only a half-day so far in Cairo, Danny understood why all the cars here were small. The streets were jam-packed and, except for the main boulevards, as narrow as an alley. You had to have a small car to even get around.

He stood to one side of the garage in a deep shadow and just watched and waited.

Nothing was moving at all.

But he didn't trust that.

He stayed there, silently in the dark, watching, listening, breathing slowly and deeply as his grandfather had taught him.

No movement.

Nothing.

Finally, he stepped forward as if he belonged there, walking with the gait of someone who was heading to his car to go home.

The key fit perfectly in the trunk of the car, even though Danny's hands were shaking.

The trunk looked empty.

Danny's stomach twisted. Oh, no! Had he heard the professor wrong?

Or had someone else gotten to the notebooks first?

He dug in the trunk, moving first an old blanket and then the spare tire. In the well under the tire, was a dark blue backpack, blending into the bottom of the trunk.

Danny recognized his father's brown notebooks inside. Six of them.

He replaced the tire and blanket, made sure the backpack was securely closed, then put it over his shoulder.

He finished his search of the trunk, finding nothing more that belonged to his father.

Using the tissue still in his pocket, he wiped off his fingerprints from everything he had touched, including the trunk lid, then unlocked the front door, wiped off the keys as well, and tossed them in the tray between the seats.

He quickly locked the door again, closed it as silently as he could, and then turned and walked away toward a side entrance.

He was sweating, his hands were shaking, and his breath was coming fast and hard. What he had taken from the car belonged to him, his father's notebooks, and Danny had had permission to get into the car. Yet, it still felt as if he had just robbed something.

And with Professor Davis dead, Danny would have a very hard time proving that he hadn't robbed the car.

Or, for that matter, killed the professor. Who would believe his story of a red-hooded man?

This garage in Cairo, Egypt was a long ways from the tree-covered mountains of central Idaho where he had grown up, and the tourist boat his mother and Uncle Steve ran.

In two weeks, he was supposed to start back at Boise State University in his second year, and even though he got good grades, he didn't work hard at it. He was much more worried about what was going to happen in two years when he graduated with a degree in English. He didn't really believe in all the fighting and killing going on in Vietnam, so for the moment staying in college was the best thing he could do.

All of it seemed so overwhelming to face.

At least, until his father had disappeared and the next thing Danny knew, he was trying to stay alive in a parking garage in Cairo, Egypt. Worrying about being drafted into the Vietnam War suddenly seemed very tame.

At the edge of the garage, Danny opened the door to the staircase, then let it close without going through. He stayed in the shadows, listening, watching for any movement at all in the garage. He needed to know if he had been followed out of the main building.

He stood perfectly still, his jeans and dark shirt blending into the shadows.

Nothing was moving.

The warm wind blew strange city smells through the garage, and in the distance, sirens cut through the night sounds.

Finally convinced that he hadn't been followed to the car, he walked down the curling ramp to the ground level and out the main entrance, turning toward the U.S. Embassy.

He kept one hand on the backpack strap as he turned south on a wide boulevard, trying to keep his pace the same as the few other walkers out this late at night. He knew he looked like a tourist of some sort or another. His long black hair and dark complexion from his Native American heritage helped him blend a little, but not much.

He forced himself to keep an eye on everything as he walked.

No one seemed to be paying him any attention, but he had to be sure. Even though the American University was in the same general area of Cairo as the U.S. Embassy, he still had almost a mile to walk. Cairo was a huge city, the biggest in Africa. And Craig and his Uncle had a good mile to travel from the hotel to the embassy as well, coming from the north along the river.

He stopped two blocks from the embassy, ducked into an open restaurant and then stood out of sight near the front door, making sure no one was following him.

No one was, at least that he could see. But he was convinced that someone with real skill could be following him easily, and he would never know it.

If that were the case, he was as good as dead.

Finally, after waiting long enough to give himself a little confidence that he was alone, he went the last few blocks to the south side of the U.S. Embassy.

Craig and his Uncle were standing hidden from the street between a fruit stand and a dark alley.

Danny walked up in front of them, then pointed at the street as a black and white taxi approached. He had been told that was what he needed to do to catch a cab in the city, but he hadn't tried it yet. The taxi slowed, its window down.

"Airport!" Danny shouted at the driver, and the driver pulled over to the curb quickly.

Danny kept the backpack on his shoulder while, without a word, his Uncle and Craig loaded the bags they had brought into the trunk and back seat of the small Fiat taxi.

Danny slid in beside the driver, indicating that no one should say a word. In broken English, and what little Arabic Danny knew, he and the driver worked out a fare by the time they were halfway to their destination. Six Egyptian Pounds, or Les. That was just under two dollars U.S. Danny knew that was high, but at the moment, he didn't care.

He had the cab driver leave them at the international terminal, then Danny led the way inside and to a hidden restaurant off to one side of a large concourse.

After they were settled at the table, Uncle Steve turned to Danny. "All right, you want to tell us why you scared us to death and brought us here?"

Danny took a deep breath and let himself relax a little for the first time in the last two hours. He figured he might as well tell them the important detail first, then fill in the rest later.

"Professor Davis was killed tonight by two professional killers looking for my father's notebooks."

Both Uncle Steve and Craig stared at him with their mouths open. If it hadn't been so serious, it might have been funny.

"They're going to come after us next to find them," Danny said. "And they will kill us to get the notebooks. Actually, more than likely, they will kill us anyhow."

"Oh," Uncle Steve said, his face suddenly drained of any sign of color.

"And we have them?" Craig asked.

Danny patted the backpack he had on the floor beside his chair. "We have them."

"Oh, great, now what are we going to do?" Uncle Steve asked, his face white.

"Get on an airplane and get out of here," Craig said. "I'll even buy the tickets."

Craig stood up and reached for his wallet. "I think I have enough money."

Danny shook his head. "Nope."

Craig dropped back into his chair. "How did I know you were going to say that?"

"We're not leaving?" Uncle Steve asked, his voice cracking.

"Nope," Danny said. "We're going to find a safe hotel and hole up while we read my father's notebooks. Then we're going to do what we came here to do."

"Find out what happened to your father," Craig said.

"Exactly," Danny said. "And besides, we can't go home. They would just go there and kill us, and maybe my mother, and there is no way I'm putting her in danger."

He looked around at the three of them. "I heard the men talking about when we arrived in town and how easy we would be to deal with. These people are very real and connected and they seem to have eyes everywhere. We have to find out what they want and why. We're the only hope my father has at this moment."

"So we're committed to this search," Craig said.

"Very," Danny said.

Uncle Steve didn't say anything. He just looked like he might be sick at any moment.

Continued next month…

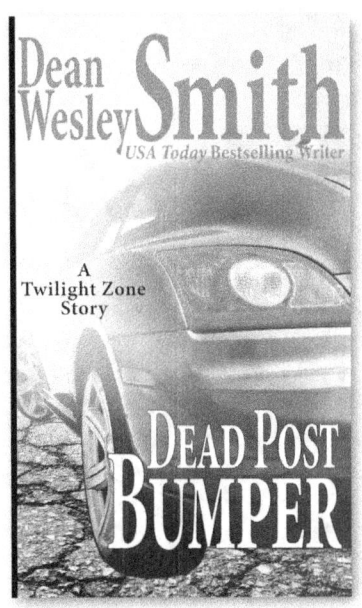

USA *Today* Bestselling Writer

DEAN WESLEY SMITH

THE CASE OF THE DOG-BIT ARM

A Pilgram Hugh Incident

USA Today *bestselling writer, Dean Wesley Smith asks you to once again climb into Pilgrim Hugh's famous limousine, this time with a new assistant in training.*

The case? Possibly a murder.

A human arm found by a dog their only clue.

And the real test? The new assistant.

THE CASE OF THE DOG-BIT ARM
A Pilgrim Hugh Incident

ONE

PILGRIM HUGH SEEMED TO THRIVE on strange phone calls. He got a lot of them from all over the Portland area, asking for his help with one thing or another. Almost always the calls came from police departments stuck on an odd problem of some fashion or another.

The call that came in on this fine, warm September morning was no different. Just flat strange, plain and simple. And yet interesting enough that he took the call.

The day was one of those perfect days that often happened in Oregon in the fall. Cool morning, warm afternoon, no real humidity. In September the kids were back in school and the world to Pilgrim just seemed to be at peace with itself as people went about their lives and jobs.

Except that Pilgrim was in a very foul mood. Carrie, his best friend and assistant, was leaving him next week to go back to school and the very idea of that just depressed the hell out of him, even on a perfect day.

He had on his normal jeans and a blue t-shirt that said simply, "Don't Ask."

So far no one had. And that suited him just fine.

He was peddling slowly on a stationary bike while looking out over the city. He felt at thirty-two that he needed to start doing something to keep in shape. His doctor said he was in great shape and at the perfect weight, but Pilgrim still felt like he needed to do something. He called it his "Portland Rich Guilt."

Pilgrim was so rich, he really didn't need to work at any job. His grandmother on his mother's side had left him more money than he knew what to do with just two months after his one and only divorce. At that point he had been out of law school for three years and pretty much hated working corporate law. His stint in corporate law lasted almost exactly the same amount of time as his marriage. Two years.

He had been good at corporate law and really bad at marriage. And had hated them both.

Somehow, after the money had arrived and he drank and traveled for a year, he had managed to start a law firm and hire great lawyers who liked working in law a lot more than he did. And then he had gone back to school and gotten his private investigator's license because it sounded like fun.

After a short time he sort of combined the law firm and the private investigation firm into what was now one of the largest and most powerful law firms in the state.

Hugh and Associates now occupied five floors of a downtown high-rise that Pilgrim also owned. His office and the entire private investigation section filled the top floor. The four floors below were the legal part of the firm. He had started out rich from his grandmother's money and now was even richer by hiring the right people and taking the right cases and buying the right buildings.

Carrie, Pilgrim's assistant, limo driver, and best friend since grade school, would be heading off to law school this fall for her third and final year before joining the legal side of his firm. He secretly hoped she would come back and remain on the investigation side of the business. They were a great team and he was going to miss her while she was down south in Eugene at school.

But he knew she was never coming back to be his assistant. Unlike him, she discovered she had a passion for the law and loved it.

And that thought of her not returning to be his assistant had him depressed. They would stay friends, sure. But he had loved all the time she had worked with him.

When the morning's strange call came in from the Tigard police chief, Pilgrim listened to the story while working at a Diet Coke and exercising on his stationary bike and looking out over the city and the Willamette River, trying to let the beautiful fall day brighten his darkening mood.

Everyone in this city rode bikes. Riding a stationary bike sort of made him feel a little more like the rest of the population. Carrie thought he was just fooling himself and had warned him a few times that to get any benefit from being on the bike, he actually had to peddle it faster and sweat a little.

He saw little point in that. Especially today.

From what the Chief of Police of Tigard told him in the call, it seemed they had a body.

A dead body.

Sort of.

Actually, they only had a male arm and a right hand that a dog had brought back to the dog's home in a neighborhood of Tigard. The Chief wanted Pilgrim to come and see if he could make any sense of it and try to help them figure out where the rest of the body was located.

It seemed the dog was being of little help.

Pilgrim told the chief they would be there in thirty minutes, then climbed off the bike, took a damp towel to his face even though he hadn't been sweating at all, and headed out of his office door.

Carrie was as tall as his six feet and today wore tight white short-shorts and a green t-shirt from the University of Oregon. As normal with Carrie, her outfit left little to the imagination.

> *She could walk down a sidewalk and cause car wrecks from both men and women staring at her.*

She could walk down a sidewalk and cause car wrecks from both men and women staring at her.

Beside her stood Donna Marks, the assistant Carrie was training to take her spot this year. And, as Carrie reminded him, to take her spot permanently since after graduation Carrie was coming back and working with Ben two floors down in the corporate legal department of the firm.

Donna was shorter than Carrie, maybe five-six, and today she wore jeans and a blue blouse tucked-in. She had short brown hair and wide brown eyes that made her seem far more innocent than Pilgrim figured she was. She was thirty and divorced and had a smile that could light up a room when she used it.

Carrie loved her and said he would as well given time.

He would see about that. At the moment he didn't want anyone but Carrie.

"Did you get all that?" he asked as the three of them headed for the door to the office suite. He had always told Carrie to listen in to all his phone calls on cases. The practice just saved him time in explaining things to her and she often heard things he missed.

"We did, boss," she said. "The Case of the Dog-Bite Arm sounds like it's going to be interesting.

Pilgrim just moaned and shook his head.

Carrie always named all their cases like they were old detective books. Pilgrim liked that habit, he had to admit, even though he always made snide comments about it.

He glanced around at Donna as they reached the elevator. "So what's your take on this?"

Donna had a small notebook in her hand on top of a small tablet. She also had a pen stuck behind her ear.

"I think this is a case of one hand not knowing what the other is doing."

She actually said that directly to Pilgrim without looking away and without breaking into a smile.

Pilgrim laughed and shook his head, then looked at Carrie who was smiling. "You found one like you?"

"She's better," Carrie said as they got into the elevator.

"I am," Donna said, smiling at Pilgrim. "I'm faster on computers, been trained in high-speed driving and car chases, and I am an expert marksman on ten different categories of guns."

"Are you going to decide to go to law school on me?" Pilgrim asked as the elevator doors closed. He had known all that about Donna before Carrie decided to bring her on board. But it was nice to see her stand up like that for herself with humor. On some of the things they did, she was going to need it.

Just putting up with him every day she was going to need a really good sense of humor and patience.

"Already been to law school," she said, smiling. "Dropped out before the last finals of my third year because I hated the idea of being a lawyer."

Now that hadn't been on her resume, so he turned and faced her. "So now you decide to come to work for a law firm?"

"I want to work as a private investigator and you're the best in the business."

He turned and smiled at Carrie. "I'm starting to like her."

"Good thing, Boss," Carrie said. "Because I'm not coming back. Remember?"

"Something I'm trying not to think about," he said, his mood suddenly foul again.

TWO

DONNA WAS DRIVING and pulled the limo up to the curb in front of a brown house in a quite neighborhood in Tigard, Oregon, a suburb of Portland about five miles to the south of the downtown area. The area was built on rolling hills covered in large pine trees.

Three Tigard police cars blocked the street in both directions and one had had to move to let them through.

Carrie sat in the back with him, but they hadn't talked much on the way out, thanks to his mood.

The stretch limo served as their office and had more high-tech computer gear and surveillance equipment than Pilgrim could remember. A bunch of it Carrie had had installed over the years. And she knew how to run it all. He was good on computers, but not as good as she was. He hoped Donna was as good as she said, otherwise, this beast of a vehicle was just going to be a very expensive limo and nothing more.

The Tigard Chief of Police came down the sidewalk from a 1960s style ranch house to greet them. The house looked well-kept and had a fence around the backyard, more than likely to keep the dog in.

Chief Danny, as Pilgrim liked to call him, had red hair, far too many freckles on his face, and brown eyes that seemed to see everything. He was at least fifty, but looked younger unless you actually got close.

He extended his hand to Pilgrim and shook the firm, calloused hand. "Thanks for coming."

The Chief nodded to Carrie, who then introduced Donna as Pilgrim's new assistant and he nodded to her as well before turning back to the house to explain the situation.

Around them the wonderful day was starting to warm up just slightly, but in the shade of the large trees it felt perfect to Pilgrim. The neighborhood was an older one, the trees all grown, the sidewalks cracked with tree roots. The Portland area was full of perfect family neighborhoods just like this one. Sometimes he wondered why he didn't live out like this instead of in a penthouse condo in the Pearl District downtown.

"Dog came from that direction," the Chief said, pointing up the street. The dog dropped the arm on the back porch. You want to see it?"

"Pictures would be enough," Pilgrim said.

The Chief nodded to Carrie and said, "I'll have someone send them along in a moment."

"Thanks," Carrie said.

"So you have men searching the park at the top of the hill?" Pilgrim asked.

"We've already been all over it and up and down every alley around here. Nothing."

"Fingerprints?"

"Nothing on file local," the chief said. "We're searching larger data bases now."

"Send those fingerprints along as well, would you?" Pilgrim asked and the Chief nodded.

"Any identifying marks on the hand or arm?" Carrie asked.

"Besides a dog's teeth marks, nothing," the chief said. "No ring or ring mark, no tattoos, no scars, nothing."

"How was the arm removed from the body?" Pilgrim was starting to get an idea of what they were dealing with here, but he still needed more information.

"The bone and skin looked like it was cut cleanly right below the shoulder with a very sharp blade."

"Before or after death," Carrie asked a fraction of a second before Pilgrim could.

Donna just stood taking notes.

"The guy was dead when the arm was cut off," the Chief said. "And at one point the hand and arm had been cleaned and put on ice."

Pilgrim nodded. He knew exactly where the arm had come from and why. He was surprised no one on the force had clued to it as well.

"Give us five minutes. But do send those pictures and fingerprints as soon as possible."

Carrie handed him a card with the e-mail address on it as Pilgrim turned back to the limo and crawled in. This was going to be an interesting case for Donna to start on.

A great test.

He took a can of Diet Coke from the fridge and then sat in his normal chair near the back of the limo's large passenger area. He flipped a switch hidden under his seat. Two computer screens appeared out of the side and a desk with a keyboard swung up out of the floor and clicked into place in front of him.

Carrie crawled in behind Pilgrim, grabbed a bottle of water, and took her normal spot up behind the driver's seat. She punched a hidden button and a computer console and two large screens wrapped out around her, making her look like she was suddenly in more of a command chair than a limo seat near a wet bar.

Her fingers instantly went to work on the keyboard.

Pilgrim looked at his screens and didn't bother. Carrie or Donna would find the information far faster than he would. So he just left the computer screens in front of him sit idle.

"You going to miss this?" he asked Carrie as Donna climbed in and pulled the door closed.

Donna sat facing the wet bar in the middle of the limo and in a moment was also surrounded by keyboards and screens as well.

"A little," Carrie said. "Not so much the private investigation cases, but I'll miss being around you all the time."

"A very nice thing to say."

THREE

CARRIE TURNED TO DONNA who was typing faster than Pilgrim had ever seen anyone type before. "So, you know where the arm came from?"

Pilgrim knew generally where the arm had come from, but not how the dog got it. He liked how Carrie was using this to test Donna as well.

"Oh, sure," Donna said as her fingers flew over the keyboard. "Just trying to get the address now."

A moment later Donna hit one last key, studied the screen for a moment, then smiled. "Three houses up the street on the same side of the street as the dog's home."

Carrie actually seemed slightly surprised. "And how did you get that information?"

Donna shrugged and looked at Pilgrim. He was doing his best to keep a straight face.

"Easy," Donna said. "The arm was clearly from a medical school here in the area. More than likely a student took it home for study, so I did a search cross-referencing this neighborhood with all the medical students at all the universities in the entire Willamette Valley and southern Washington and included the teaching hospitals in the area."

Donna twisted a screen around so that both Carrie and Pilgrim could see the picture of a young woman with black hair smiling for her student id.

"Peta Edwards," Donna said. "Part Native American, part German. Perfect grades. She lives here with her parents to save money."

"Shall we go tell the poor girl about her missing homework?" Pilgrim asked, punching the button that retracted all the computer equipment around him.

Donna and Carrie both did the same and then Donna went out into the wonderful, fall afternoon air first.

Pilgrim followed carrying his Diet Coke can and motioned for Chief Danny

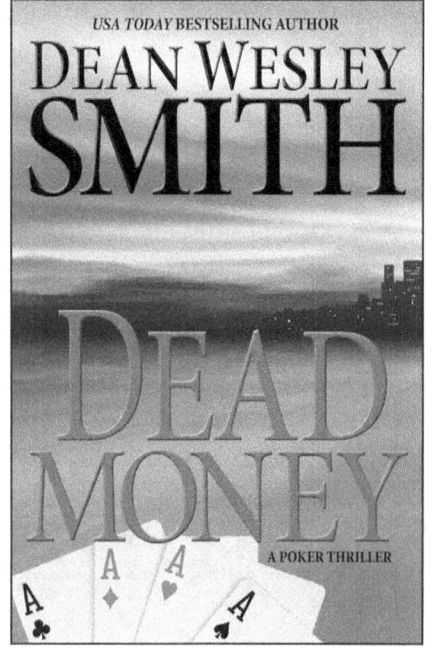

Written in the fast-paced style of James Patterson, Dead Money *takes readers into all aspects of poker, from high-stakes private games to one of the largest tournaments of the year at the Bellagio Casino in Las Vegas.*

Considered a sport by the courts and television, the prize money given away in major poker tournaments far exceeds the total of golf and tennis combined.

But when one of the greatest poker players of all time dies, the stakes rise even higher.

to follow them up the sidewalk as Carrie got out and locked the limo.

As they walked, Donna explained to the chief where the arm had come from.

"And you figured all that out in two minutes in that limo of yours?" the Chief asked, clearly surprised and happy he didn't have a murder on his hands.

"Actually," Pilgrim said, "Donna got the address of the student. And I'll bet you'll find an empty medical school cooler on the back porch. More than likely the poor student doesn't even know the arm is gone yet."

The Chief laughed as the four of them turned up the sidewalk toward the front of another 1960's ranch-style home nestled in among the trees. This one had no fence around the backyard.

"Chief," Donna said, "I kind of feel bad for this poor girl. You're more than likely going to have to write her instructor an official note."

Pilgrim moaned softly and looked at Carrie, who was smiling from ear-to-ear.

But Chief Danny didn't see the next thing coming at all and Donna was keeping a perfectly straight and serious face. Pilgrim was going to have to remember his new assistant could do that, or he would walk into a few of these traps as well.

"Why's that?" the Chief asked, stumbling and falling into Donna's punch line.

"Because no one's going to believe her when she says the dog ate her homework."

Chief Danny just shook his head as he looked at Donna who was still holding a perfect poker face.

Then he turned back to Pilgrim. "Where did you find this one?"

Pilgrim pointed to Carrie, trying to look innocent. "She found her."

And then as the chief turned away to knock on the door, trying to contain his laughter, Pilgrim mouthed to Carrie.

"Thank you."

~

DEAN WESLEY SMITH

USA *Today* **Bestselling Author**

the First Tee Panic

AND OTHER VERY REAL GOLF STORIES

Former PGA golf professional and USA Today *bestselling writer Dean Wesley Smith walks you step-by-step, club-by-club from your car to the first tee and beyond in a laugh-out-loud style that not only teaches, but entertains.*

Any golfer recognizes the fears, the patterns, the downright horrors of the first shot of a round. Ever topped that first shot just off the front edge of the tee box? Or worse yet, whiffed it completely?

Come on, admit it. It happened. Remember?

The problems with that first shot don't start with the swing. Nope, the problems start in the parking lot. And this book will get you flawlessly from the parking lot, through the clubhouse, onto the driving range, over the putting green, and finally successfully off the first tee with a smile.

THE FIRST TEE PANIC
And Other Very Real Golf Stories

Part One:
HELP! I DON'T WANT TO WHIFF THE FIRST SHOT

IT'S A HORRID NIGHTMARE. For some reason, I have it just about every time I play in a golf tournament, or have a big game lined up with friends or other professional golfers. I've heard that other golfers have nightmares like it, but no one seems to deal with the dreams and the nightmares that come along with the game. I'm not going to either, but I am going to talk about what causes my nightmare.

The first tee shot. (Sound effects here of those four words bouncing around in a massive echo chamber, then fading into the distance like a bad horror movie.)

My nightmare goes like this: I'm standing on the first tee, the morning sun is just breaking over the rocks and cactus of the Scottsdale desert. The dew is still thick in the heavy rough, but the fairway is a green, freshly-mowed road stretching impossibly narrow in front of me.

In the nightmare, I always feel great, muscles loose, mind focused, hands warm. My three golfing companions have all hit their first tee shots, all perfectly down the middle of the fairway, and they are now waiting for me.

The group behind us has arrived at the tee and are sitting in their carts also waiting.

Here goes. I step to my ball, take a mighty swing...

...and miss.

A clean whiff. A fly could have made a larger impact on that ball by simply landing on it. Not even the wind of my club passing shook it.

My *Titilest 1* ball with the "1" underlined stares up at me.

Suddenly, I'm sweating in the cool morning air. My playing companions are snickering, two guys in the group behind us are shaking their heads, the other two are trying unsuccessfully to not laugh.

I try to laugh with them. I make a lame joke about a practice swing, take my stance again, another mighty swing, and another clean miss.

It's as if the ball isn't where it's supposed to be.

I've been playing the game of golf since I was three, been a professional for decades. Yet there sits the ball.

Titilest 1 mocks me.

My friends are sitting in the carts, laughing, making ugly snorting noises. The players in the group behind are laughing so hard, one of them falls to the cart path. Even the starter is laughing.

It is *not* funny. Trust me.

I swing again.

Miss.

Again I swing, this time even harder and faster.

Another miss.

I can barely breathe. My arms feel trapped, pinned against my side. I go to kick the ball, but my feet won't move. The wonderful day of golf has turned into a swirling, sweating nightmare of laugher and humiliation.

Then, thankfully, right at that point, I always wake up. Usually, I've twisted the sheets into a tight mess around myself, pinning my sweating body to the bed in a pile of sheet knots that would earn a Boy Scout a merit badge. After I get untangled, I glance at the clock. It's usually about ten minutes before the alarm is supposed to go off.

Ten minutes before I'm supposed to start getting ready for a beautiful day of golf. A beautiful day, that is, if I can manage to get off that first tee.

Now, understand, this dream doesn't come from any real event. No, my imagination has done this all by itself. Not once, not ever, have I whiffed a golf ball on a first tee, yet that reality doesn't help kill the fear. The little voice, deep in the back of my head whispers, "There could always be a first time."

Am I the only golfer who has this type of nightmare, these kind of waking fears? Nope. Almost every golfer I've ever talked to has something like it. And almost without exception, every golfer has a deep fear of the first shot on the first tee, even if they don't have nightmares that twist sheets into rags.

Think about how many times you have heard a touring professional golfer talking to an announcer on television. The conversation always goes something like this:

Announcer: *"How was your round?"*

Professional tour golfer: *"Once I got off the first tee and got settled down, I played pretty well."*

The first tee scares the hell out of touring professionals. Trust me, the last thing those players on the big tours want is to roll their tee shot along the ground in front of a million people on national television. They think about it, have nightmares about it.

Yet it never happens.

Why? Because they also know how to deal with the fear, how to make sure they don't send a ball bouncing down the fairway to stop close enough to the tee that the television networks don't even have to change a camera position.

The pros and better golfers have methods of getting ready for that first shot, little ways of making sure they at least make contact with the ball. I'm going to detail out some of these methods, these tricks of the game, right from the moment you get out of the car to the mighty first swing.

Step by step, I'll get you from the bag drop and safely off the first tee. Trust me, it can be done without a nightmare of humiliation, just like the professional golfers manage it.

I might not be able to help you hit the fairway, but sometimes the goal of the first tee isn't to hit it straight, but to simply get the ball in the air and as far away from you as you can manage. Second shots are a whole lot easier if you're still not standing on the tee box.

Trust me on that as well.

Part Two:
HELP! WHAT DO I DO WHILE A BAG BOY UNLOADS MY CLUBS

MAKING SURE YOU make contact with the ball on the first tee actually starts when you arrive at the golf course.

Golf is a mental game. Keep repeating that.

Golf is a mental game.

To safely get that big driver's club face on that tiny little white ball on the first tee, you have to start thinking like a golfer. From the parking lot to the bar after the round, you're a golfer. The day job is gone, the family and all the chores around the house are forgotten completely. You

arrive at the course, ready for a great day of golf.

So getting ready, getting yourself in the right state of mind is important right from moment one. And that moment is when the bag boy is unloading your clubs from the trunk of your car.

I'm assuming a big golf game on a big country club, on golf courses that cover deserts like those around Phoenix or Palm Springs, or beautiful tracks that wind through pine-tree-covered hillsides like those in Sun Valley or outside of Chicago or New York.

You're a golfer, a privileged member of the working class. You've bought the most expensive clubs, got new head-covers for your birthday from your kids, practiced after work and on weekends. You even make empty handed practice swings while in elevators and in front of mirrors. You're ready, you've carved out the time, and you've finally driven or flown a great distance to a top golf course. You have the right to be there, you've paid for it, and you don't want it spoiled by any first tee missteps, so start thinking like a golfer as you enter the gates of the club.

If you're like most of us and are used to just grabbing your sticks from your trunk or your locker at your local muni course, the first thing you're going to notice different about these big golf resorts and country clubs is a sign as you drive up the landscaped driveway.

Bag Drop.

If you've never, ever been to one of these types of golf courses, just follow the sign's arrows and stop your car when you see some well-dressed, smiling young man or woman approach as if they know what they are doing. This is not where you will park, but it is the first step in getting to the course.

Sometimes, this bag person is the lowest assistant professional at the course, but more often he or she is just a college student who loves golf. Either way, their job is to greet you with a friendly smile, make note of your arrival through some hidden and high-tech communications system, get your clubs out of your car and put them on a cart.

Don't even think about walking the course and carrying your own bag. These top courses won't allow it. The cart fee is required and is part of the massive amount of money you're going to pay when you reach the pro shop.

A small tip of a few dollars to the bag person is in order, combined with a thank you and a respectful attitude if you hope to see your clubs again before the round starts.

One side note about timing. For years I played socially with a group of other top golfers. We would often go to Phoenix and Scottsdale to play golf in the dead of winter. Our goal while there was to play as much as possible, so we often had the earliest tee time allowed by any golf course. This bag boy stuff works fine and dandy for anyone scheduled at a moderate time after sunrise. I can't tell you how many times I headed down a first fairway and the sun was just pretending to light the sky, let alone peak over the nearest cactus. Bag boys don't exist at that hour and don't expect them to be there.

Also, let me say that playing golf before the sun comes up just isn't fun most of the time and should be left to only the extreme golf fanatics. If you do tee off before sunrise regularly, seek help.

So, what do you do to get ready for that first big shot on the first tee as the bag boy unloads your bag from the trunk of your car, cleans your already well-cleaned clubs, and straps them to the back of a cart?

You could stand there staring. Or sit in your car waiting for the trunk to close, listening to the morning news. Or you could use the time to do something you're going to have to do first thing anyway.

Put on your golf shoes.

There is no reason to carry a pair of shoes down into a club house locker room, then store your street shoes in some corner or in the cart while you play. Your time before the round is better served in other areas of preparation. So, while the bag boy is doing his or her thing with your expensive golf clubs, sit in the open door of your car and put on your golf shoes.

But one warning. You still have to drive your car to the parking lot. Diving with your golf spikes on can get tricky. I don't think the Federal Transportation Board has any figures on exactly how many car accidents are caused by wearing golf shoes while driving, but I would wager the number is pretty high. And we won't mention that little dent in that Porsche at the Palm Springs Country Club back in 1973. I left a note before I went out to play.

Honest.

Part Three:
HELP! HOW DO I ACT LIKE A REAL GOLFER IN THE PRO SHOP?

AT THESE BIG country clubs, the pro shops are major businesses, large rooms filled with a massive number of golfing attire, bags, clubs, and balls. The main desk is usually a beautiful, wood-carved monster of a counter that three or four people can fit behind without even touching. It's usually elevated so that the professionals behind it look *down* at the customers.

Or so it seems to me. Maybe I just slouch every time I go into a major pro shop. The places, for some reason, are just not that comfortable, and I've spent my share of years working in them, standing behind those elevated counters. The problem is, the last thing any of us need in our quest to get the ball airborne off the first tee is added nervousness caused by the giant, looming monster of the pro shop.

But you can't avoid the place. The pro shop is like the narrow part of an hourglass, with the outside world filtering down through the pro shop to emerge out on the golf course. Luckily, on the way back to the real world, you don't have to make a return voyage through the pro shop. The bar, maybe, but not the pro shop.

So, let me suggest a routine to get you safely through the pro shop and outside again into the crisp morning air.

First off, find the right entrance.

Sounds simple, right? Nope, often this is a lot harder than it sounds. These big country clubs have *Members Only* areas and really fancy restaurants with tiny little signs warning you and your golf shoes away. Problem is, those little signs are so small, the only way you're going to see them is if you know they are there. I've missed many of those signs and ended up in a swank dining room, on expensive carpet that was never meant to see a golf spike.

Trust me, making this kind of wrong-turn-blunder can really set you back, especially when some waiter has to lead you firmly, but oh-so-politely back the way you came.

Once you are safely in the pro shop, the first thing you want to do is pick up a putter out of the two hundred putters lined up along the wall on a rack. Pretend to be considering buying it by making a few pretend putts.

For heaven's sake, never hit a ball in these practice putts, even though there will be some hanging around a practice ball return. Banging a ball off a display case and under a rack of woman's blouses is not the way you want to start your day. The thought of that kind of putt will haunt you on the third green.

Just pretend putting. Got that? Act cool.

Of course, you have no intention of spending five hundred bucks on a new putter right before a big round when your old twenty-six dollar yard-sale-special is working just fine. But pick one up and look at it seriously anyway.

Next, find the ugliest putter in the bunch, the one with a club head bigger than a toaster, and make a joke about it to the nearest person.

That person will always respond with a joke in kind, unless you happen to be talking to the representative for the putter company. Early in the morning, there is little chance of that happening.

After a few laughs, head directly for the counter to check in and pay for your upcoming round. While there, spending the big bucks on the green fees and cart rental, go ahead and buy a sleeve of golf balls with the club's name on them. Yes, I know you brought enough golf balls along in your bag. These new balls are only for emergencies and if not used, take them home as a reminder of your great day and how much you spent for one round of golf. Sort of like a Disneyland set of Mickey Mouse Ears, only you don't have to wear the golf balls.

Don't ask the pro what kind of balls are the best. Just buy *Titalist* or the new *Nike* ball because Tiger uses them. The country club will have their logo on either type.

And when you ask for the balls, ask for an exact brand. For example, say, "Oh, and give me a sleeve of the *Titlest Professionals*." Or whatever they are called these days. Don't say, "Give me the gold pack." Not golfing cool and might get you looked-down-upon by the professional even more.

Then, and this is critical, ask about practice balls, or participate in a conversation another player is having with the professional about practice balls. The pro will tell you how to get them and where the range is at that point.

Thank him or her, but never tip them. I saw one man in California try to tip a golf professional in his golf shop and I thought the professional was going to take a driver to the side of the guy's head. You tip bag boys, cart boys, waiters, and bartenders. Never golf professionals, unless they give you a really good lesson on the driving range that you have already paid a bunch of money for. Then just add in a little extra.

But never in the pro shop.

So, you have paid, you have the knowledge of where to get the practice balls. Mission accomplished.

Now, without another look at the putters or drivers or six thousand sand and flop wedges, head for the door with a sure stride of a person with purpose.

You're going to go hit practice balls.

Repeat that thought in a very deep-voiced way. *You're going to go hit practice balls.*

Practice in golf is a very serious thing, especially right before an important round, so act the part. It's time to go to work, to get ready to get that first shot off the first tee and into the air.

Just make sure you take your new sleeve of recently purchased golf balls with you as you leave the pro shop. Turning around and going back to get them can really break a serious practice mood.

More tips next month on what to do next to get to the first tee…

A TRUE STORY FROM THE FRONT LINES

How I Didn't Play with Bob Hope (and Lived to Tell About it)

March, 1973. Palm Springs, California.

I WAS A YOUNG golf professional, just fresh into the big world of golf. I had gotten very, very lucky and had been hired the previous fall as the assistant professional by one of the greats of the game of golf, a top player back in the thirties and early forties named Zell Eaton. In his back office, Zell had framed wonderful newspaper articles about how he won this or that tournament, or how he beat Ben Hogan two up, or how he took Byron Nelson to the last hole before winning in a playoff. I used to love standing in front of that wall of framed awards and articles and just read.

Why such a great of the game picked me, a kid from Idaho, to be his assistant, I'll never know. I was cocky, untrained, and not that good of player compared to what I ended up being a few years later. I thought I was good at the time.

Oh, boy, did I have a lot to learn.

For some reason, Zell decided he was going to teach me. And his lessons didn't just include him sitting patiently in a folding lawn chair on the driving range while I hit thousands of golf balls a day, many of them by the lights of my car after we had closed up the golf shop. He did that, often. But in fact, many of his lessons concerned making sure I knew just how good I was, and how much better others around me were. Those lessons were humbling, to say the least, but they did as Zell figured they would. They made me practice harder and harder. And thus get better and better.

And the harder I practiced, the more I showed the drive to learn, the more he wanted to help me.

One big lesson concerned the fear that this book is talking about. By the spring of 1973, Zell had no doubt that I wanted to be good, that I wanted to learn how to play, but he also had no doubt I had no idea what it was really like to stand on a first tee of a major tournament. Now, understand, I had won my share of amateur tournaments up to this point. He figured, rightfully, that they didn't count.

By that March, I had yet to play as a professional, and Zell figured it would be good for me to start slow. Sort of, anyway. He wanted me to work up to some of the tournaments I planned to play that summer up north.

So start small it would be. No real money on the line. Just a charity fund-raiser for the Heart Fund. The idea the charity had was that one local golf professional and one local celebrity would team with two rich players who had paid a lot of money to the charity to play a round of golf.

So, as our course representative, he sent me. When he told me, I felt bad for the poor rich people who would be stuck playing with a lowly assistant from Westward Ho Country Club. Zell, in his way, just smiled and said, "Don't worry. They'll get their money's worth."

Somehow, he had arranged for me to play with Bob Hope.

In my very first professional golf tournament.

I didn't know this until I was standing on the practice tee the next morning at Desert Island Country Club.

I didn't pass out when the starter told me who my "local" celebrity would be, but I'm sure it was only the training of making myself breathe that saved me from that fate right there.

Now, a couple of things transpired to change what I visualized was a coming disaster. First off, the starter saw my panic. This was years and years before I developed any kind of poker face. Besides, when he told me, I'm sure I went pure white, then turned shades of gray. It would have been hard to miss.

"Problem?" he asked.

"Just first professional tournament shakes," I said.

The guy laughed and said, "Yeah, Zell told me that was the case. Don't you like Bob Hope?"

I had grown up in Idaho, sitting watching Bob Hope specials on a black-and-white television before color was even thought of. Did I like Bob Hope? How do you answer a question about a god like that?

"I sure do," I think I managed to say. Right at that moment, I was sure I was going to pass out on the first tee and be one of Bob Hope's jokes in his next television special.

Or I would throw up and then pass out, making everything so bad, they would do a skit about what happened. A really funny skit.

At that moment, fate decided to take a hand and spare me. A rain drop hit the starter. Rain might have hit me, but trust me, at that moment, in my state of fear and panic, I wouldn't have noticed.

It doesn't rain that often in Palm Springs, but this was still winter, and it was a cold morning.

The starter nodded to me and said, "I'll be right back." Then he headed down the practice tee box where Bob Hope was entertaining about a thousand people that were going to walk with him. That guy could really be funny. A little crude in real life compared to his television specials, but really funny.

I turned back to the remaining practice balls and tried to put two thoughts together. I think the two thoughts were, in this order.

"Oh, my, I'm going to play with Bob Hope."

And then, "Oh, NO! I'm going to play golf with Bob Hope."

I am sure I repeated that sequence of thoughts through about twenty practice balls.

I went to taking deep breaths trying to calm down, but all I could think about was that first tee and whiffing that first shot and then passing out. I was having that nightmare back then and at that moment it seemed very real and very possible.

It started to rain even harder, and Bob Hope and most of the crowd at the other end of the practice tee headed for the club house, just leaving a few of us on the tee box.

I started hitting some easy shots, taking deep breaths and forcing myself to calm down. I could do this.

Zell wouldn't have put me in this situation if he didn't think I could do it.

Bob Hope was only a man. I could play with him.

It started raining harder, so I got out my rain gear and kept hitting balls. Rain would help. Slick grips are always a great excuse for missing a shot.

Then they called the group ahead of us to the tee.

I hadn't even hit a putt yet, so I made one slow, smooth swing, as Zell had been teaching me to do all winter, then headed for the practice green beside the first tee.

As I reached there, the starter came out of the club house and walked up to me. I remember his words well.

"Bob's decided to wait out the rain and maybe just play nine. You want to tee it up with McLean Stevenson instead?"

Lt. Col. Henry Blake of *M.A.S.H.* One of my favorite characters on one of my favorite shows.

I think I nodded. But at that moment, I was so relieved to not have to play with Bob Hope, the starter could have told me I was playing with the President of the United States and I would have been happier.

"Great," the starter said. "You're up next."

I ended up riding in the cart with McLean. He was as funny and as nice in real life as he seemed on television. And we had a blast.

And I hit my drive perfect off the first tee.

But the story doesn't end happily right there.

By the seventeenth hole, the weather had cleared and I was really enjoying the day. I also had it two under par with only the last hole to play. Bob Hope's crowd had gone out on the back nine ahead of us, and not more than a few dozen people had followed us around, with McLean entertaining them.

At that time, the last hole of Desert Island Country Club was a fairly short par four, with water all the way along the left side. I hit a perfect drive and was within an easy wedge from the green, over a finger of water to a mostly island green.

Not a problem. I hit a perfect second shot that I remember McLean cheered for while the ball was in the air, telling it to go in the hole.

The shot looked that good.

The ball hit about ten feet short of the pin, bounced once toward the hole, then spun back and kept rolling all the way back down into the water.

The twenty or so people around the green moaned so loudly, I could hear them across the water.

You think that kind of thing doesn't happen? Watch the Master's Golf Tournament some time.

You can also see this same shot on the golf movie *Tin Cup* where Don Johnson's character hits his shot onto the green on the last hole to have it spin back. Of course, for that silly movie, he was hitting a wood and in those days, you couldn't get a wood to spin backwards if your life depended on it.

In real life, with McLean Stevenson sitting in the cart, I hit a perfect wedge and it spun back.

McLean tossed me another ball from my stash in the cart as I laughed.

He made a joke which was actually funny and relaxed me. At that point, it didn't much matter. I had survived the day.

So I dropped another ball over my shoulder (as the rules said we had to do in those days) and hit another perfect wedge. The ball mark was about ten inches beyond the first ball mark in the green, right in front of the hole.

The ball hit, bounced once, then spun back into the water.

It looked exactly like the first shot.

Now I'm really laughing because those two shots were so perfect, but as can happen in golf, the end result really sucked at the same moment.

The groan got louder from around the green.

"I think you need more club," McLean said to me, laughing. He tossed me another ball out of the cart, I dropped it, and hit a shot that McLean again said was perfect.

The ball hit six feet short of the pin, just two strides away, bounced forward so close to the pin that people around the green shouted for it to go in the hole.

Yeah, right. Only in the movies. My shot, with an amazing amount of spin, took off for the front of the green like it wanted to come back to the cart. It hit the water so hard, I thought it might actually skip like a stone.

The moans got really loud at that point.

McLean fell out of the cart laughing.

I kid you not.

He was a pretty good and very avid golfer in his day, and he knew just how insane this was. And how good the shots were I had hit.

I knew how insane this was.

Now we both had the giggles.

A young golf professional and a seasoned actor giggling in the middle of a fairway.

Not a pretty sight, I can tell you.

Go ahead, try hitting a golf ball with someone like McLean Stevenson making jokes and giggling. It was damn near impossible, but after a few minutes, I finally stopped laughing long enough to make a swing.

The next shot, as you might imagine it would, sailed clear over the green and the only thing that stopped it from going in the water behind the green was a bunker. I blasted out and made a decent putt for a ten on the hole.

I got cheers from everyone watching and McLean bought me a drink in the bar where Bob Hope was telling jokes to friends.

I went from two under to four over in one hole, and didn't care. I had played one of the most enjoyable rounds of my life with a wonderful man and a great actor.

And I didn't end up playing with Bob Hope.

The next day, on the range, Zell Eaton spent two hours teaching me how to hit a wedge shot without spin. I just wish he had gotten to that shot a few days earlier in the lesson plan.

More golf stories next month...

Poems by DEAN WESLEY SMITH

He Went Out

My great-grandfather, he went out into space,
traveling faster than any human before,
gone fifty-two years, for a eight light-year round trip.
Ninety-six years passed on Earth while he was gone.

I teach history,
my great-grandfather is part of the history I teach.
Thirty people started with him, sixteen lived.
They said the rest died of boredom, and accidents.

My mother showed me pictures of him,
his dark hair, his old-style glasses, his adventurer smile.
I wondered as a kid what happened to him,
and why he had left his wife and family.

Now I'm thirty, teach history, have two children.
He's part of the history lessons I teach,
Marco Polo, Captain Cook, Magellan,
Lewis and Clark, Armstrong, my great-grandfather.

They found a Mars-like planet. No life.
"It wasn't worth it," he told me,
just before leaving
to visit his wife's grave.

But he's wrong.
It was worth it.
I know.
I teach history.

DEAN WESLEY
SMITH

USA TODAY BESTSELLING AUTHOR

Dust
and Kisses

A NOVEL OF LOVE, HOPE, AND A FUTURE

USA Today *bestselling writer Dean Wesley Smith weaves a tale of love and survival in a devastated future world.*

When Carey Noack returns to the ruined Portland, Oregon, hoping to meet other survivors after three years of living alone. She doesn't expect the man of her dreams.

At first, Matt Ladel, the only person living in the old city, thinks he imagined the beautiful woman weaving through dead cars. Then he finds the reality behind the fantasy.

Suddenly, the two experts in survival and living alone must learn to work together, and trust again, in the face of an even greater danger.

DUST AND KISSES
A Novel of Love, Hope, and a Future

For Kris, always the love of my life.
And Janis Ian and Mike Resnick,
two great writers who sparked this novel.
Thanks.

PROLOGUE

IF SHE HAD THOUGHT ABOUT IT, Carey Noack would have figured that the world would end in a big build-up, with lots of panic and time to say good-bye to loved-ones in tragic scenes of crying and hugging like it always was in the movies. But she had never thought about it. None of her friends read science fiction, and the closest thing she had come to an end of the world thought was worrying about how the Greenland ice cap might melt.

So Wednesday morning, when the world did end, she wasn't expecting it. No one was, actually. But she did remember the exact moment it happened, right down to the second because her job that morning was to stare at scientific measuring instruments and a clock while taking notes about the readings every fifteen seconds.

At 23, she had gotten lucky in life, and she figured in love as well. A post-doc in astrophysics from the University of Oregon, she had landed a plum job working in Portland, Oregon for the famous Dr. Canfield, a man she both admired and hated, often in the same breath when talking to her friends and family. She stood at five-foot-two, a good sixteen inches shorter than Canfield who looked like a cross between a bad Dicken's character and a stretched Santa Claus because of his white beard. She had long, brown hair and brown eyes that everyone said were "fiery" whatever that meant.

Canfield had gotten the habit of patting her on the head like a child every time he was pleased with her, and if she didn't need the job working with him so much for her career, she would have just broken his hand in about a dozen places. If he caught her on the wrong day, she still might. Screw the career.

Her fiancée, Paine Kennedy, worked as an assistant coach at the University, and even though with her working for Canfield in Portland, the two-hour drive down I-5 between the cities didn't stop them from having a wonderful relationship, one they both planned on turning into a marriage next year. This morning, she had kissed him good-bye at seven while he tried to grope her to get her to come back to bed. As much as she wanted to rejoin the man of her dreams in that bed, she didn't dare be late for work. So she had left him to go back to sleep with a promise she would see him at lunch.

Lunch didn't happen.

At 10:18 and seven seconds on Wednesday morning, the world ended.

At 10:18, she was sitting in a protected steel vault watching the "control" readings for an experiment Canfield was doing in another room. Canfield's hope was to get some variance between two readings, hers in a protected control vault and his in the open.

At 10:22, as planned, she logged in her last readings and the exact time and opened the vault door.

Dr. Canfield lay sprawled on the floor of the lab, his eyes rolled up into his head.

For an instant, the sight shocked her. Then she quickly moved, grabbing the phone on the desk above Canfield and jabbing in 911.

"Don't you die on me now!" she said to the thin man.

While it rang, she tucked the phone under her chin and knelt beside him, feeling for a pulse.

Nothing that she could find.

She quickly flipped him onto his back and went through the quick procedures she had learned in her first aid class three years before. With the phone still ringing in her ear, she started pumping on his chest.

"Come on, damn-it! Answer!"

She kept at it, working to keep her pace steady, her pressure solid on his chest, but not too hard.

No answer. The phone just kept ringing.

After about a minute, she knew she couldn't wait any longer. She needed help. No one was coming into the lab to give her help. She needed to go find help if Canfield had a chance of pulling through this.

Leaving the phone connected to 911 and ringing, she checked for a pulse on Canfield, then ran for the door, heading down the lab hallway and out onto the street to get help from someone.

She burst through the exterior door and took two staggering steps before stopping on the hot sidewalk between two tall buildings.

The sound hit her first.

At least a hundred car alarms in the surrounding blocks of the city were going off at once.

She looked around, trying to grasp what she was seeing. The morning promised a hot day ahead. Two blocks down the hill was the Willamette River, two blocks to her left was Burnside, a major arterial through the city. The buildings around here were ten to thirty stories tall. Canfield's lab was on the main floor, tucked to the back of the building.

An intersection with a streetlight was to her right about fifty paces, and parked cars lined the street.

Everything was so familiar. She had seen it all every day for months.

Then her mind suddenly let her see what was wrong.

Nothing was moving.

Bodies lay crumpled in piles along the sidewalk going in both directions from her. Cars had crashed into other cars, their drivers slumped against their seat belts, heads rolled to one side or the other.

She ran to the nearest woman on the sidewalk and checked her.

Dead.

She checked another woman.

And then another.

All dead.

She could see hundreds of bodies around her, all seemingly dead.

Bio attack? Terrorist attack? What had happened?

"Help, someone!" she shouted, but her voice was drowned by the massive wave of noise from the car alarms and running engines.

No one was alive to hear her.

Then the smiling image of her fiancée flashed into her mind and she screamed "Paine!"

He was fifteen blocks away.

She turned and headed for her apartment in the northwest section of town at a run, jumping over bodies, trying not to look at them, trying to ignore the dead staring at her from their still running cars.

The nightmare had begun. The world had ended.

She was still alive.

And very much alone.

CHAPTER ONE

THREE YEARS FROM THE DAY the world ended, Carey Noack stood on the abandoned freeway overpass and wondered exactly where she was going to stay that night.

In front of her, the gray of the dead city of Portland, Oregon, filled the hillside for miles in all directions. Beside her, the deep blue of the gently flowing Willamette River moved silently past. She figured she had every building in the city to pick from. Apartments, houses, hotel suites, and those really nice condos she remembered being down on the river. For all anyone would care, she could set up camp right in the middle of the old city hall. She doubted anyone was left alive there. From what she had understood of the old city politics, there hadn't been much life there before everyone died.

Actually, there were two places she wasn't going to stay. Her old apartment and her parents home out in Beaverton. Both those places weren't options because the bodies of Paine and her mother were still there. But just about every other building was, unless she actually found someone else alive and living here.

She hoped for that. Dreamed about that.

Didn't expect it.

It had been exactly three years ago to the day that the city and almost everyone in it, and in the world, had died, sending her running eventually to the Oregon coast to get away from the smell of a million dead.

Now, on today of all days, like celebrating some sick birthday, she was back, facing the city again. Facing the nightmares of having everyone die around her.

"Such a brave little girl," she said aloud, then shook her head. As a child, her mother said that to her all the time, every time Carey started to feel sorry for herself. Over the last three years, she had repeated that saying a lot to keep from going completely crazy.

Carey leaned her backpack and rifle against the edge of the overpass, then levered her short frame up onto the concrete guardrail so she could get a better view of what was ahead.

It was a good fifty feet to the surface of the freeway below her. The warm wind coming from the direction of the Columbia River Gorge jostled her, so she spread her feet for a better stance. She worked and exercised so much; she didn't have an extra ounce of fat on her body, and often felt a good wind could turn her into the Flying Nun without even having to wear a stupid-looking hat.

Her light-brown hair, left long and pulled back out of the way, whipped at the side of her head and shoulders. She had let her hair grow long mostly because she didn't feel like she had the skill to do anything else with it. Besides, who else was going to see it?

She glanced down at her arm to make sure she wasn't burning in the hot sun. Her skin was light, with freckles, and she had smothered it every day on this trip with lotion. At times, she had so much lotion on, she felt that if she fell down, she would slide like a kid on one of those old Slip-and-Slides her dad bought for the back yard. He'd only tried it once and instead of sliding, did a belly-flop, cracked a rib, and hadn't bothered to try again. Carey remembered her mother hadn't stopped laughing for days.

She slid her hand along her arm. She was greased up like a Thanksgiving bird, enough so that at the moment there was no sign of burning. Good.

She stood there on the overpass, hands on hips like Superwoman, staring into the dead city. For her grand entrance back, she had worn a black sleeveless tee-shirt, jeans, and her favorite tennis shoes. As she was looking into a mirror this morning, the old worry of being under-dressed in the big city came flooding back. It was amazing how old habits died hard.

She glanced down at the wreck-strewn freeway below the overpass. "Man, Carey, how stupid is this trip?"

Her words echoed against the pavement and vanished into the silence of the warm wind.

Stupid. She knew the answer.

Shaking her head, she jumped back off the railing and grabbed a small towel from her pack to wipe the sweat from her face and arms. The weather had turned out to be one of those typical Oregon late-summer days, where the bright sun and clear skies made the air feel hotter than it actually was. And on top of that, the wind from the Gorge was sweeping in even warmer air from the state's central deserts, heating up the valley and the city of Portland like an oven.

She couldn't say, standing there in the center of the freeway overpass, that she had missed that dry, brittle wind during her years away. It seldom got above seventy degrees where she lived overlooking the beach and the waves of the Pacific Ocean. She loved the coolness, the constant pounding of the surf, the fresh, crisp air. But she had also loved this city three years ago.

And right now, if forced, she would admit she still missed it.

She finished wiping off her arms, put the towel back in her pack, and grabbed the water bottle. She was going to have to be careful, make sure she didn't push too hard. The last thing she would need would be to get heat stroke.

She leaned against the concrete side of the overpass

Her biggest, "ugly fear," as her mother would call it, was what someone else would do if they found her.

and let her mind drift back three years. She didn't remember much about those nightmarish last days she had spent in the city, and the trip escaping to the coast. The overriding memory was of the bodies everywhere, the smell of death growing by the moment, and her desire to run as far away as possible.

The house she had found on the coast was just north of a little town called Depoe Bay. The house sat on a rock ledge jutting out into the ocean, and sprawled over three floors, with windows on all levels facing the empty sea. The breezes were always off the water, and seldom did the smell of death reach her.

Nothing to see, nothing to smell, nothing to remind her that almost all of the human race had suddenly died.

Also, the house was hidden from view of anyone who *might* be left alive, and who *might* be moving along the coastal highway. That distance from the road gave her a sense of safety. She knew there had to be others who survived besides her. She didn't know how many, or where they were. But if she had survived, others had as well.

Her biggest, "ugly fear," as her mother would call it, was what someone else would do if they found her. The safest way to get around that fear was to not push the question. Her old, and now dead friends had called her "plucky." But being plucky didn't defend her from someone who wanted to rape or kill her. Being smart did, and the house allowed her lots of smart options.

So, she had a nice, safe, *smart* place there to live. Why, after three long years of living alone, safe, on the coast, was she back in the dead city risking her life?

Was she really that lonely?

Did she really think that there might be a group of survivors living here?

Maybe. Maybe not.

She should just turn around and go back to her cats.

Damn, she missed her cats.

She hoped she had left enough food for them to make it until she got back. Since she had nothing else to worry about beside herself, she tended to be over-protective of her two cats. Centaur was a yellow tabby with one bad eye, and Princess a small female with pure white fur. She really missed them. Maybe she should head back and forget this stupid exploring.

"Such a brave little girl," she said out loud, staring at the dead city. "You've come this far, see this through."

She studied some of the details around her. Windows in nearby buildings were covered with dirt and film, weeds were growing thick in the cracks of the sidewalks, and nothing was lit. She had seen parts of the city look like that when it still had hundreds of thousands of people in it.

No power to be seen, and she hadn't expected any. The power on the coast had gone down the first winter, and nowhere along the way from the coast had she seen any place with power. The stoplights at the end of the overpass were now nothing more than dead eyes hanging over deserted streets. It gave her a sudden feeling that someone was watching her.

Could that be possible?

She studied the area around her, turning slowly. Nothing moved besides the leaves on the trees and the weeds blowing in the wind.

She did a second slow circle, staring at the blank windows, the dead cars scattered everywhere, the overgrown weeds.

Nothing.

No one was watching her. There weren't that many people left alive who could.

She shook off the feeling, took a second, long drink from the bottle of water, and stood on the overpass, just staring at the city down the hill. She still had to figure out where she was going to stay the night. She didn't want dark to catch her without a safe room.

The feeling of being watched again twisted her stomach.

She had to be careful. She had to be smart. There was no telling what waited for her ahead.

CHAPTER TWO

MATT LADEL WOKE with a start as the alarm from his computer security room beeped loudly, echoing through his penthouse apartment.

At first, he couldn't figure out exactly what he was hearing. He had been dreaming about waking up in the morning in his old college dorm room, to his old alarm clock, and the dream had morphed into a nightmarish feeling of the alarm clock going off forever while he searched and searched for it under ten foot deep piles of clothes and stacks of books that seemed to stretch to the ceiling. He couldn't find it, no matter how hard he tried.

And the stupid ringing kept going and going.

He had lived that damned dream more times than he wanted to remember back in his college days. Now, years later, the dream still haunted him.

He needed to wake up, get out of the nightmare.

The reality of its high-pitched, quick-beat alarm slowly replaced the old ringing alarm in the dream. He opened his eyes and stared at the white ceiling and wood beams over his head.

College was long over, a thing of the dead past.

Something had triggered his security alarm again.

"Damn deer," he said, tossing aside the sheet, and standing. He was nude, but since the morning seemed hot and bright outside the windows, he didn't even bother to slip on his robe or slippers. He moved across the soft carpet toward the computer room, trying to push the sleep and the dream back completely.

College was gone, his friends were gone, and he was one of only a few people left alive. And if he ever found that old alarm of his from college, he'd smash it into a hundred pieces, just with the hopes that stupid dream would stop.

Outside the expanse of tall windows in his penthouse apartment, the sun had already cleared off the summer haze, and he could tell without even going out that the air was hot and dry. In the distance, Mt. Hood towered into the sky, snow still covering most of its peak. To his left, Mount St. Helens was smoking again. It had been doing that off and on for years, rebuilding itself from the huge explosion back in the eighties.

The penthouse apartment covered the entire thirty-second floor of the Baxter building. He had set it up to cater to his every need. It had soft, rich carpet, big expansive rooms, and an island kitchen in the center of the main room with bright lights and every appliance known. He loved cooking, and used the kitchen almost more than any other area.

He had picked the apartment because it was a completely defensible place to live. He had locked all the staircases and they could be easily blocked at three different levels. He had gotten an elevator working and he controlled it as well from the top floor. He had even installed a tight cable from his roof to the roof of another nearby building to use as an escape if something trapped him in the building, like a fire.

He had furnished the living room with a deep, comfortable recliner placed directly in front of a large screen television. He had also brought in a couch for the times he wanted to just lay down.

To the right of the living room, he had put together a weight and exercise room to keep his six-foot frame in top shape. He lifted weights every day, and ran on a treadmill facing the windows. He figured that he would never know when being in top shape would save his life.

Another recliner sat in front of a massive picture window overlooking Portland and the Willamette River. It matched the one in the living room only because there had happened to be two of them in the furniture store the morning he had been looking, and they both fit into the bucket of his little tractor that he used to haul things around.

He loved just sitting in that chair with a drink in his hand staring at the mountains. Sometimes, he sat in the chair and read when it rained, watching the patterns of the water on the glass between chapters. When the rest of humanity had still been alive, he never would have been able to afford a place like this. Now, he figured he deserved it.

Besides, who could tell him no?

The loud beeping of the alarm continued, drawing him toward the computer room he had installed in the west corner room of the big penthouse. He had been an electrician before everyone had died. He had installed security cameras for a living for River Drive Security and Alarms. In fact, he had been installing a bank camera with his boss and two others the day everyone just keeled over dead. He and Jenkins had been down in the vault when suddenly everything went silent on the comm link with the boss in the truck.

Jenkins had gone up to investigate, leaving Matt in the vault. Matt had never seen him again. Matt had no doubt Jenkins was alive somewhere, but where was another question.

By the time Matt had given up waiting, left the vault open, and went to investigate, Jenkins was gone, and everyone else was dead.

Everyone.

Just killed instantly in the middle of whatever they were doing.

Matt had freaked, to say the least.

At first he thought it was something airborne that had killed everyone, and it would soon get him, so he had gone back inside the bank. But after a short time of staring at dead bank customers and tellers, his brain kicked in and he knew that staying in there was stupid. If it were something airborne, he would have been dead with everyone else.

Clearly, something about the big bank vault had protected him and Jenkins. He just didn't know from what.

For most of that first day, he had wandered the streets in shock, staring at bodies, not really heading anywhere in particular. After a while, he took to turning off the idling cars, reaching past bodies to yank out keys.

Slowly, as the day wore on, and no one came into the city to start rescue operations, and no planes circled overhead, it began to dawn on him that maybe he, and Jenkins, wherever he had gone, were the only ones left alive in a very large area.

Then, as Matt was turning off an idling car that had ended up against a light pole, he thought of his parents in the resort town of Bend. Had whatever caused this been larger than just the Portland area?

Suddenly, it had become important to him to find out just how widespread this disaster had been.

Bend was a little resort city over the Cascade Mountains at the foot of Bachelor Ski Area. He had managed to make the normal six-hour drive to Bend in just under twelve hours, using four different cars. When he came upon areas of the road that were so jammed with wrecks that he couldn't get around, he would simply leave the car he had been using, and hike until he found another usable car on the other side of the blockage.

He had hoped that his parents had been outside the influence of what had happened, but the closer he got to their home, the more he knew that they had not.

He found his parents both dead, as well as everyone else in the small town.

For an hour that night, he had sat in the middle of the main intersection, with the light changing from green to red over his head, honking a car's horn.

The sound seemed impossibly loud, echoing off the buildings and the pine-covered mountains.

No one came and told him to stop.

He knew right then and there that he was alone. Really alone, and the thought scared him more than he had ever been scared before.

The next few days were only a blur of memory and nightmare.

He had somehow managed to bury his parents next to his grandparents in the cemetery. Then he had gone down to his favorite bar and dragged all the bodies out onto the sidewalk and sat them at tables he had put there, posing each body as best he could in positions of drinking. He had figured if they died drinking, then they may as well spend eternity drinking.

Then he had gone inside, alone in the empty bar, filled the top of the bar with bottles of booze from the bar's storeroom, and sat down on a stool. That day, and for a number of days after, he had gotten so drunk he couldn't think.

Finally, a nasty hangover and the smell of death drove him away from the small town and out into a cabin in the Cascade Mountains. He stayed in that cabin, pretending everything was just fine, for a long winter.

When he hiked back into Bend the next spring, he knew for a fact he could no longer pretend it all hadn't happened. He hadn't been dreaming and he hadn't gone crazy.

It had happened.

For the next year, he had wondered the Northwest, going from Seattle to Boise to Salt Lake, over to Sacramento, and then back up, looking for anyone else alive. He had run across a number of people, all coping with the death in one fashion or another. None of them were the types of people he wanted to stay with, even though some of them were friendly and happy to see him.

Finally, he had returned to Portland two years ago and set up his penthouse apartment.

Now his computer alarm kept beeping, getting louder as he entered the room he had set up for security.

"All right, all right," he said, "I'm coming. Damn deer, anyway."

He expected to see nothing on the monitor, and to have to rewind a recording to see what had triggered the alarm. He had set up the system of motion detectors two years ago right after moving into the penthouse. The sensors triggered cameras, and ran off of batteries that he exchanged and recharged every six months. He recorded the camera feeds in a bank of recorders here in the apartment.

He had installed the system when he realized the lights from his apartment could be seen for miles around the city at night. In fact, from across the river, his place stood out like a beacon.

He figured it would be better to know when someone else alive was getting close enough to see him. The cameras, waiting with motion detectors, guarded over twenty different ways into the main area of the city, and the entire area around his building.

"Stop it, already," he said aloud, dropping his nude body into the chair in front of his monitor command screens. He punched off the loud, annoying alarm, sighing at the sudden silence around him.

Then he glanced at the big control board map of the city. It filled one entire wall of the room. He had green and red lights showing the location of each of his motion detectors and cameras. A red light showed on the old Interstate 5 headed south in the Twiliger Curves area. Deer often went through there, since that area was between the hills and the river. And every year, since the disaster, the deer seemed to be getting more plentiful.

He flicked up an image from a camera he had hidden on a pole, expecting to see either deer, or nothing at all. The sight of a woman, standing on an overpass shocked him to his very core.

His fingers fumbled over the controls for a moment before he brought up the zoom.

A woman standing there by herself.

A very attractive woman.

It wasn't possible.

Yet there she stood.

CHAPTER THREE

THE HOT WIND WHIPPED around Carey, brushing the trees nearby, drying the sweat to her skin as she walked down the freeway on-ramp and moved around some wrecks, working her way toward the center of the city.

"I sure don't miss this heat. How can anyone live in this?"

She laughed. "Oh, yeah, I forgot, no one does."

These days she talked a lot to herself and her cats. It broke the silence. Often she had tapes and CDs playing while she worked or read. But mostly, she just talked to herself.

Sometimes, she actually cracked herself up. There sure wasn't anyone else to laugh at her stupid jokes.

So far, she had been traveling for three days from her home on the coast. She might have done it a little quicker, but she had been careful, taking her time and doing a little exploring along the eighty-mile trip. She hoped to be back to the coast within ten days total, which meant three days into the city, three back, leaving her four days to explore her old hometown. She had figured her cats would be all right for ten days.

She sure hoped they would be. They had enough food for a month, yet she worried about them.

Twice between here and her home, she had come across other live people, all from a distance. One man and a woman had sat on their porch and just watched her walk by, the man holding a rifle across his lap. Those two had looked the sanest of the people she had seen so far, and she had had no desire to talk to either of them.

Once she had had to hide from what appeared to be an insane man, walking along talking to himself. She could smell him from a hundred yards. Granted, civilization was gone, but bathing was something still easy to do. In fact, it was one of the more enjoyable things to do.

She could spend hours in a hot bath with a good book and a glass of wine.

She used to cover the same eighty-plus miles between the coast and the city in a car in two hours. Back then, she would have never dreamed of walking that route. Of course, back then she would have never imagined doing some of the things she had done over the past three years to survive.

Mostly, she hadn't let herself think about the day everyone died. No point. Now, being back here in the city, she pretty much didn't have that choice. She was going to walk right back into the middle of those horrible memories.

Purposefully.

"Such a brave little girl," she said, and then laughed.

At times, she had trouble wrapping her mind around the fact that the world really was gone, yet she was one of the few still here. Back when she had lived and worked in the city, she had thought nothing of jumping in the car and heading to her parent's small beach home on the coast for a weekend, or even just dinner and a show at the casino. But now, for this trip back to the city, it had taken her a year to actually get up the nerve to leave the beach.

Damn, she missed her cats.

She adjusted one strap slightly so that it didn't rub her shoulder too long in the same position. The backpack contained enough water to get her by for a few days, changes of clothes, food for a week, and extra ammunition for her rifle and the pistol in her belt.

She had spent a good amount of time over the last two years learning how to fire that pistol and rifle quickly and accurately. The need for it had come clear one afternoon when she had gone down to the closest grocery store to haul out another load of canned food. Before she had gotten there, she had heard a man laughing. Then he had started firing round after round from a pistol into car windshields in the parking lot.

The guy had been clearly crazy, and Carey had managed to stay hidden and watch him for most of the day until he headed north on the coast highway.

That afternoon, she had found herself a pistol, and the next day the rifle. Now she considered herself a good shot with them, but had no way of really knowing, and she sure didn't want to test the theory on anything living.

As she moved in and around wrecked cars, she still couldn't shake that feeling of being watched. There was someone out there, of that she had no doubt. Whether or not they would show themselves was another matter.

She did a quick check to make sure the rounds were in place in the rifle, and then snapped a bullet into the chamber.

Her hope, and her fear, was there *would* be other survivors in the city. Hope for a community of them, with enough good people to have conversations. Fear that all the people she would find would be in a gang of thugs who would try to take her and make her a slave or something movie-horrid like that.

She had had the discussion between hope and fear many times over dinner with her cats. She was convinced that a normal, sane person would have given up hope of a real society reforming by now, but still, here she was today, standing on the edge of the city, ready to look for one.

Her hope, and her fear, was there **would** *be other survivors in the city.*

Risking her life in the search.

Did that mean she was insane like some of the people she had seen alive? She didn't want to think she might be, even though she always talked to herself. She didn't feel insane, but then, does an insane person know she is insane?

A question for the century.

She would sometimes lay awake at night listening to the waves pound the beach and rocks below her home and worry about the answer to that deep question.

And then she would worry that wondering about such a question made her sane or insane.

The cats offered no answers.

On still other nights, she would lay in bed thinking of people, and how nice it would be to talk to someone, or even listen to someone. Just have companionship. Those nights often ended up in nightmares, or no sleep.

Other nights, after a long hot bath and a few glasses of wine, her mechanical, battery-powered friends helped her fall asleep. She liked those nights the best since the dreams were often of her old fiancée Paine and his wonderful smile on a naked Brad Pitt body.

But during the day, the constant question about being the only sane person left alive haunted her like a ghost.

She knew how to be alone, how to live alone. Actually, she had gotten very good at it. But for some reason, the thought of dying old and alone scared her a great deal.

That final argument was what had gotten her out of the house and on this trip. The fear of dying alone and the desire to find people to talk to were the reasons she was here. She just had to keep that firmly in mind.

The memory of Paine's face flashed back to her, and she found herself smiling as she walked. Paine had been the man she had hoped to marry, spend the rest of her life with. He had been funny and had had a grin that could make a person just laugh at its silliness.

And he had loved her, something that made her feel lucky every day they had been together.

Even with everyone alive, she had been a loner of sorts, and except for Paine, and his wonderful smile, and green eyes, she might have stayed a loner, surrounded by millions of very-much-alive people. So some of this desire to find others made no real sense for her.

Still, even a loner needed company at times. It seemed, now was one of those times.

Around her, the dead city closed in on the freeway as she got closer and closer to the downtown area.

Nothing but the wind and the dust moved.

Oh, yeah, she was going to find Mr. Right here.

She laughed.

Sure thing.

CHAPTER FOUR

OVER THE LAST FEW YEARS, the only women he had seen at all had been with rough-looking men. Three different couples that he knew of lived in the surrounding areas around Portland, but none of them Matt wanted anything to do with, and he was sure they felt the same about him.

This was not one of those women.

This woman wore a black, sleeveless tee shirt, jeans, and tennis shoes. She had long brown hair pulled back tight, light skin, and a clearly muscled body.

He leaned forward, trying to get closer to the screen. He couldn't take his gaze off of her. In the last two years, he would have never expected to see a beautiful woman.

Hell, any single woman.

He watched as she jumped back off the concrete railing and dug into her backpack.

He stared as she wiped down her face and arms and then put on more suntan lotion. Clearly, she could sense that he was watching her, as she kept looking around her at all times.

He suddenly realized that she was a woman he would have been attracted to when everyone was still alive.

How was that possible that she was now standing there on the freeway?

Alone.

He had had a number of steady girlfriends before everyone died. He had just broken up with Sunni the week before everything happened. Sunni had been a short, blonde Swedish-type from Southern California. They had met in a bookstore out in the Tigard area. She was working for Hewlett Packard, doing something she could never quite explain to him.

After six months, they had both just grown tired of each other, even though the sex had been great. He had no idea if she had survived. The chances weren't good, and it hadn't occurred to him to even go looking for her body where she worked.

He had kept the idea of ever meeting a decent woman again so tucked away in his mind, he wasn't sure yet if he was still dreaming. He had to be dreaming; yet he knew he wasn't.

Yet he had to be.

"Wake up, Matt old buddy!"

His voice echoed off all the equipment.

All right, he was awake. That meant that woman out there was real. Very real.

As he watched, she put a water bottle away, picked the backpack up, and slipped it on her shoulders. Then, with the rifle in her hand, she headed off the overpass, walking with the assured gait of someone who had confidence to spare.

"Wait!" he shouted at the screen. "I'm right here. "Don't go!

He wanted to watch her some more.

He wanted to meet her.

He wanted to talk to her.

It took only a moment before she was off the overpass and headed down the freeway toward town and out of that camera's range.

The moment she disappeared, he felt a jolt of panic go through him. "Oh, damn."

His hands scrambled over the massive control board he had set up for the security cameras. Finally, he managed to activate the next camera covering a section of the old Interstate 5 south of town.

For a long moment, he thought he had lost her. Then she came around a large pile-up of wrecked cars and kept walking, right at him, as again the motion alarm for that camera started to ring.

She was too good to be true.

An impossible dream.

Small, strong, confident, and good looking. Something had to be wrong with her.

He flipped off the alarm, sitting back in silence as he watched her stride toward him. She had the walk of someone in control, of someone not afraid of where she was heading. She was a survivor who looked like she lived alone.

This could not be happening.

Almost all of the human population of the planet seemed to be dead, yet here was a woman walking right into his life.

Or maybe through his life.

That thought scared him again. He couldn't just let this dream walk by. He had to do something.

But what? He had no idea where she was headed, what her experiences were over the last few years, if she even wanted to talk to anyone else.

And just like all the women he was attracted to back in his college days, he had no idea how to meet her.

The rifle she carried with ease seemed to grow bigger with every second. The way she handled it, and by the way she had a pistol tucked into her belt, she knew how to shoot.

She might just kill anything that came close to her and wonder why later.

He had no idea how to approach her.

At least back in college, trying to meet a girl didn't mean risking getting shot.

But as he stared at this woman's face as she got closer to his camera, he had no doubt that getting shot was a risk he was going to have to take.

CHAPTER FIVE

CAREY KEPT HER PACE SLOW and easy in the hot sun as she headed down the freeway, moving in and around wrecked cars. In every car the driver was still strapped behind the wheel, smiling skeleton-smiles at her. Human skeletons were just so much a part of the landscape; she had stopped noticing them a couple years ago. With skeletons and human bones being everywhere, they seemed unreal, almost plastic and sometimes comical, like bad special effects of an old movie, even though she knew deep down inside that every one of them had been a real person, with a real life.

Now, the worry she felt about going back into the city today had her noticing everything, and looking at everything with a cold eye of reality, including all the bodies.

"This ain't no movie, Carey. Stay alert."

He voice echoed off the hot concrete and then was taken by the warm wind. She stared ahead at the big overpass and the signs directing traffic to either the downtown area, or along the bridge and beyond to Seattle.

Seattle.

Wow, that seemed so far away to her. Maybe if there was no community of people here that she could meet, she could take a look in Seattle some day.

Maybe.

"And cows fly."

Her voice again echoed on the hot pavement. Seattle was too far away, too much to think about right now. She needed to focus on the city in front of her.

Portland seemed so familiar, yet so alien, especially walking along the freeway to get into town. She had driven this road a thousand times, but never walked it. No one ever walked along a freeway when the world was still pumping. Not and live very long anyway.

While walking, she noticed things she would never have time to see at sixty miles per hour. Pavement colors, buildings, the way signs were secured to the ground. All kinds of strange and useless things. And even though she didn't have to, she found herself staying to the road's edge more than she needed to, just out of respect for old habits.

On the day she had left three years ago, the city still had a sound of a few car motors running, of stoplights clicking as they changed, of power humming through the buildings and overhead lines.

Today, the city had no sound. Only the wind rustling the weeds and the birds chirping broke the silence. Cities were *supposed* to have sounds. Honking horns, construction noises, and police sirens. Not even in the middle of the night was a city ever really silent.

This city was deathly silent.

"This is creepy."

She could just turn around go home right now. What difference would it make?

She kept walking. Her mother's voice echoed in her head. *Such a brave little girl.*

Sometimes she wished she could get her mother to just shut up.

Carey moved under the freeway sign leading her toward the downtown and riverfront areas. She had better start figuring out exactly where she was heading, at least make the decision as to where she would spend the night. It would take some time to get a place comfortable enough to stay in.

Why hadn't she made that decision, had a plan, before now? Had she figured she would never get this far? Most of the time, her way of dealing with something stressful had been to just not think about it. Clearly, staying somewhere in the city had been one of those things.

She left the freeway and moved down onto Front Street, walking in the middle of the street instead of getting anywhere near the sidewalks. The sidewalks felt too close to the buildings to be safe at the moment.

Ahead of her, a dozen blocks or so, the Marriott Hotel tower rose over the river. She could stay there, in one of the unoccupied suites with a view of Mt. Hood and the river. When living here, she had never had a reason, or enough money, to stay in such a nice place. It would be a treat.

"A reward for finishing a long walk."

Her words echoed off a large pile-up of cars and the concrete of the overpass behind her.

She nodded to herself; glad she now had a plan. She would find a good room there, set it up as a base for exploring around the city. She would stock it with food; maybe even get a portable generator in for electricity. But before anything, she would have to check the water, to make sure the water tanks of a place like that had enough good water to last her for a time. In so many buildings, the water supply had been completely drained. Water would make her final decision for her when she got there. After a day in this hot sun, she was going to need a shower. Maybe two.

With a little work, she could even make whatever place she found permanent.

"Duh, why not?" It hadn't occurred to her until just that moment that she could have a place in the city, a place on the coast, a place just about anywhere in the world she wanted.

Nothing was stopping her.

No one was stopping her.

All she would have to do is figure out a way to move her cats from one home to the next with her.

She moved along Front Street. A dozen more blocks and she would be at the hotel. The grass along the river to her right had turned to weeds; the sidewalks and streets were cracked and growing grass in places. Still, the city had a beauty about it, with the blue river flowing through it, the mountains around it, and the green trees everywhere.

The air smelled faintly of water and fish, and birds chirped and flitted from nests in the branches of the trees along the old riverside park. She could see where birds had stained the edges of buildings and built nests in windows. It was lucky she had come into town on such a beautiful day. Even if this trip was a waste of time, it was at least replacing the images of her last days here with something more pleasant.

Two blocks short of the hotel, something moved out of the corner of her eye. She snapped around, the rifle up and aimed, her blood racing. The feeling of being watched had suddenly returned stronger than ever.

A bird flittered away.

She sighed and lowered the gun.

"All right," she said out loud, letting her voice slow her racing heart, "Calm down and don't go shooting everything that moves."

> *Her words echoed off a large pile-up of cars and the concrete of the overpass behind her.*

"I'm very glad to hear you say that," a deep, rich voice said to her left.

She spun around, the rifle up again.

Every nerve, every ounce of focus was on the rifle and her finger and where she was aiming it.

She found herself face-to-face with a man about her age, with brown, unruly short hair, twinkling brown eyes, and a large smile. He had his hands in the air like he had just been caught robbing a bank.

She tried to take a breath and failed as she stared at him.

He had moved out of the shadows near an office building and now was standing no more than fifteen steps from her. He wore a plain white tee shirt, jeans and new-looking tennis shoes. He had the appearance of having dressed quickly, yet still seemed together and clean.

Very clean.

Tanned.

Healthy.

She bet he even smelled good.

And he was one of the best-looking men she had ever seen, even before everyone died.

It was as if time in the dead city around them froze.

Nothing on the street moved.

The river sounds seemed to drop back to silence.

She didn't even feel the heat, couldn't hear the birds.

She kept her gaze locked on his, the rifle pointed at his chest. She had hoped to find someone else alive and sane, but she had never expected to.

And she had never expected to find someone so good-looking.

She just hoped she wouldn't have to shoot him.

The seconds seemed to go on forever as she drank in this man, memorizing every detail.

"I'm not going to bite," the guy said, smiling. His voice was deep and rich and matched his rugged face.

She was surprised his voice stayed level and didn't shake, even though she could tell he was worried about her putting a hole in his chest. She doubted anything intelligent at all could come out of her mouth at the moment.

He laughed. "Sorry for the cliche. I didn't know what else to say. As you can see, I am unarmed and alone."

Then he shrugged.

She didn't lower her gun, and he didn't lower his arms.

She had to get her wits about her, really find out who this person was, and what she had just walked into.

Was this a trap? Was he the bait to get her guard down so others could overwhelm her?

They stared at each other for a few long seconds, then she decided to try to speak. She swallowed and then managed to get the words out.

"How did you know I was here?"

She was proud that she had made the question sound authoritative, and that not a word broke.

"Security cameras," he said, pointing up at the top of a pole back down Front Street. "I have them on all the main entrances into town. A person living alone in the big city can never be too careful."

He smiled at her, and then went on. "But to be honest, I was also hoping to find someone else alive, passing through."

"And you sit all day and watch your cameras?" she asked, now even more worried that she had run into another weirdo. Why hadn't she listened to her little voice when she felt she was being watched? She should have just turned around, found another way into the city. Mistakes like that could get her killed.

He laughed. "Hardly. In fact, you woke me when you stopped on the overpass. I have motion detector alarms with each camera."

She could feel herself starting to relax just a little, and her little voice wasn't screaming that this man was dangerous like some of the others she had seen alive. She would have set up security cameras like he described if she had thought of it, or known how. Especially living in a big city area where a lot of people would naturally go through.

She kept her rifle aimed at him and forced herself to think, slowly, giving herself time to calm down.

One mistake, one slip, and she could find herself in a very bad situation. He was shorter than Paine had been, but still clearly very strong. She had to be careful, no matter how much she wanted to lower her gun and hug this stranger and talk to him.

"So, where do you live?" she asked.

"Baxter building," he said, indicating with one raised hand the direction of the main part of town. "Been there for two years, in the penthouse. How about you?"

"I've been on the coast," she said, feeling that even that small amount of information was too much. At least she hadn't told him which part of the coast.

He nodded, as if understanding that. "Yeah, I was up in the Cascades, in the forest, until the smell cleared."

"Are you alone?" she asked.

"Yeah," he said.

She was thrilled, for some reason, at that news, but at the same time, it made her even more worried about him. She was going to have to put aside her attraction for this man, and her desire to talk to him, and think clearly.

Hard to do. He was so fantastically good-looking. And those eyes of his just begged to be stared into.

"How did you survive?" she asked.

"I was doing the security system in a bank in Beaverton when all this

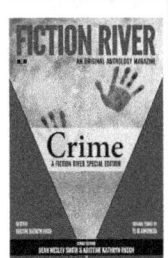

happened. I was down in the vault, but I have no idea why that protected me. Or even what happened to everyone."

"I do," she said.

At that his eyes lit up, and his arms lowered a little. "You do? Why? How? I mean, if you know that, if you would tell me what happened to everyone, it would help me figure out where there are more people alive."

She took her first deep breath since she had been surprised by this hunk of a man, and ignored his question for a moment. Clearly, if he had been watching her, he had known she had a rifle, had known she would get the drop on him, and had risked being shot by introducing himself.

Either the guy had courage, and really wanted her to trust him.

Or he was stupid beyond words.

Or he was working some other trick on her, and had friends helping him trap her.

She glanced around.

Her back was to the riverbank. There was no way anyone could come up behind her where they were standing.

"I'm alone, honest," he said, noticing her movement. Again he shrugged. "I wish I wasn't, to be honest with you. But not many people around here left to talk to these days."

"No groups?"

"None," he said. "A few couples living out on the outskirts of town, but they're not friendly. And the last guy to go through town that I saw was talking to himself, dragging a kid's wagon, and

carrying machine guns. I didn't talk to him."

"So in all of this main part of the city, you're it?"

He spread his arms wider over his head and smiled. "I'm the entire population of downtown Portland, Oregon. And considering my cameras and security system, I would know if anyone else was around."

She said nothing to that, wondering how much she could trust this guy who was clearly trying to show her he could be trusted. Even back when everyone was still alive, she didn't trust too many people, so trust would take a while with this guy. At least she didn't have to keep her gun trained on the only person she had talked to in three years.

She motioned that he should lower his arms, and she lowered the rifle, keeping her finger beside the trigger and the rifle ready to bring back up quickly.

"Thanks," he said. He moved his shoulders around a few times. "I clearly need more reps on those hand-raising isometrics."

She smiled, and he smiled back.

God, she loved his smile. How could one of the last men alive on Earth have such a wonderful smile?

"So, do you have a name?" she asked.

"Matt," he said. "Matt Landel. An actual, native Oregonian, born and raised."

She actually laughed at that, the sound echoing over the river. Being native was something that mattered only to Oregonians. She liked the name, and

He spread his arms wider over his head and smiled. "I'm the entire population of downtown Portland, Oregon.

she liked how it sounded coming from his mouth. So far, she liked a lot about what she saw with this guy. And that worried her.

"I'm Carissa Noack. People used to call me Carey. Also a native, through and through."

It felt strange using her full name after all the years. Strange, and yet somehow normal, as if having and using a full name returned a little civilization to the world.

He smiled at her. "Nice meeting you, Carey."

"Nice to meet you as well, Matt," she said.

Then the silence of the city pounded back in on her as they stood like two high school kids at a dance wondering who was going to make the first move.

"How about I cook us both breakfast?" Matt said, finally breaking the silence with a rushed sentence. "My stomach is starting to sound like an earthquake coming, and I bet you haven't had a good omelet since you left the coast."

"Omelet?" she asked, the word out of her mouth before she had a chance to stop it. She hadn't had anything like a real egg since she moved to the coast. On the hike in, she had seen chickens, but she hadn't been able to get close to any.

"Yeah, real eggs and everything," he said. "Honest."

"How? Here in the city?"

He nodded, smiling as if he were very proud of having eggs. "It seems chickens survived whatever killed everyone. So I went out into the country and trapped some, including roosters, and set them loose in the Rose Garden."

"You're kidding?" she asked. The Rose Garden was the big basketball arena where the Portland Trailblazers had played.

"I'm not," he said, laughing again.

His laugh just made her smile, and relax even more, even though she didn't want to.

"I figured the seats would make great nests for them, plus it's big enough to hold a lot of birds and give them room to move around, but not escape."

She laughed at the idea of The Rose Garden as a giant chicken coop. How perfect. "What do you feed them? How many do you have?"

He shrugged. "Every few weeks I scatter a pickup truck load of grain from sacks I found in a warehouse down by the river. Every month or so I trap some more birds and turn them loose in there. The population seems to be growing, but in a place that size it's hard to count. I try to go get the eggs I can find every few days and there are always more than I can use. I take a bird or two every few weeks for special dinners. I bet I have five hundred birds now, if not more."

"Amazing," she said.

"Thanks," he said, smiling. "I'd be glad to show it to you, right after breakfast. I make a great omelet, honest. And I would love to have someone to talk to while I'm cooking after all these years."

She stared at him for a moment. She had come back into town with the hope of finding someone else still alive. Now she had, and she didn't know what to do. She hadn't expected this, she hadn't expected anyone, let alone a great-looking guy who could raise chickens and claimed he could cook.

She had to keep her guard up, stay alert, watch herself.

And if he turned out to be as nice as he seemed, then she would cross that bridge when it was proven to her. But that was going to take some time.

She was about to agree to go with him for breakfast, like a bad pick-up at closing time in a bar, when her voice in her head screamed at her.

What was she thinking?

She took a deep breath and stared into his eyes. She couldn't just go up into a strange man's penthouse apartment and have breakfast. She wouldn't have done that back when the world was still alive.

Why was she thinking of doing that now? Had three years of being along, taking baths with mechanical toys, made her that desperate?

The answer was yes.

But that didn't matter. The danger was too great.

"I think I'd better wait on that," she said.

The look of disappointment on his face was clear to her, but he nodded. "I understand. I wouldn't trust anyone in these circumstances either. Especially someone I just met. Sorry, don't know what I was thinking."

"It was a nice offer," she said. "Maybe I'll take a rain check."

He indicated the beautiful, cloudless sky above them, and then with a smile said, "I hope you don't decide to wait until it actually rains."

"We'll see," she said, smiling back.

"So where are you thinking of staying?" he asked. "You are staying for at least the night, aren't you?"

She nodded. She could trust him enough to tell him that, since he had cameras and more than likely could follow her anyway. "Marriott," she said. "It seemed a logical place to set up a camp and look around."

"Water's all drained out of the building system," he said, shaking his head. "But the last time I was in the Embassy Suites it seemed to have water. Nicer place, too."

She nodded. The Embassy Suites was the old Multnomah Hotel that had been remodeled years back into large suites. She had been inside it only once, and had been impressed.

"Thanks," she said. "I'll try there then."

"There's a decent hardware store about two blocks west of there that might have some portable generators," he said. "I'll be glad to help you get set up if you like."

They stood there, in the street, staring at each other, letting his question hover in the warm air. She really didn't want to take her gaze off of this man, yet she knew she had to move, give herself time to think, make sure she was safe.

"Thanks," she said. "I might take you up on that. But first I just sort of want to look around. Haven't been here in three years."

He nodded. "You know where I live if you need anything," he said, pointing around and up at the Baxter building. "Just go into the lobby and I'll know you're there."

With that he smiled; clearly embarrassed he had told her that piece of information about his security system.

"How about we meet for lunch tomorrow?" she said, not wanting to have any chance slip past that she would get to talk to this man again. Of course, if she stayed in town, he was the only man or person she could talk to.

"Name the time, name the place," he said, his eyes not hiding the fact that he liked her idea. "I'll bring a picnic basket full of fried chicken."

She laughed at that, wondering just how wonderful fried chicken was going to taste after three years of eating mostly fish.

"How about outside the used and rare room in Powells Bookstore? Have you been up there?"

"I have," he said. "That sounds perfect. Big windows, tables and chairs. I'll even bring a tablecloth and plates."

"Twelve noon?" she asked.

"Twelve noon it is," he said. "Right now my watch says it's just after ten in the morning."

"So does mine," she said, glancing at the watch she'd been wearing for years. She couldn't remember the last time she had actually looked at it for any reason other than to check how long it would be until the sun went down.

"Tomorrow then," he said. "I'm looking forward to it. And my offer stands, if you need help, just come to the lobby of the Baxter building."

"Thanks," she said. "I really appreciate that."

He turned and went back the way he had come, stepping into the shadows of the building and disappearing.

Had she just imagined all that?

Did she really have a date tomorrow?

She looked around at the dead city, the wrecked cars, the skeletons in the driver's seats, and just shook her head.

Post-apocalyptic dating. How much stranger could things get?

CHAPTER SIX

MATT COULD NEVER have imagined, when he crawled out of bed that morning to shut off the stupid alarm, that he would feel so much like a high school kid again.

He walked down the sidewalk, heading back toward the Baxter building, trying not to whistle. Not once, since the world ended, had he felt so good, so light, so positive about any future. Not only had she told him she knew what had happened to everyone, but she had agreed to see him again.

And it had been her idea on how to meet.

He hadn't been this excited, and this scared, for a long, long time.

Back when he was a junior in high school, he had wanted to ask one of the cheerleaders, Betty Rees, to the fall formal. It had taken all of his courage, and some pushing by his best friend, Dave, to finally approach her.

Matt was, as they liked to be called around school, one of the "ghosts." He never really did much in sports, so he wasn't a jock, and his grades were just okay, so he wasn't a brain. And he didn't hang out with any of the known groups such as the science geeks, the band, the skateboarders, or the druggers. He was a ghost, just there, going to school, not really noticed.

Why he had ever thought Betty would say yes to him was beyond imagining now. At least she hadn't laughed at him when he asked.

Then she had done the unthinkable and said, "I'd love to."

It had taken him a moment to realize she had said yes, then for the next three weeks he had worried and fretted about it, especially when she stopped and talked to him in the halls, something she had very seldom done before.

The dance, what he remembered of it, had been fun. Terrifying and fun. She had even kissed him goodnight, since he didn't have the courage back then to kiss her.

That night had made them friends, and they had remained that way right up to the day everyone was killed. Just friends, nothing more, which had been fine with him. She was always a cheerleader in his mind, and very scary.

Now this woman, Carey, had said she wanted to have lunch with him. Just talking to her had made him as nervous as talking to Betty in the hallway, and not because she was carrying a rifle.

Well, maybe a little because she was carrying a rifle.

But mostly because she was a good-looking woman that he was attracted to, in a world where most of the people had died. In this situation, doing the right thing and not making her mad was another level of stakes all-together.

Risking getting shot had been worth talking to her. And even though she had turned down his stupid idea for breakfast, she had asked to see him again.

They had a date.

Noon tomorrow.

Lunch.

Now it felt like he was right back in high school, getting ready for the big dance with Betty.

He unlocked his security precautions in the Baxter building lobby, and used the elevator to get back to his apartment, even though most times he took the stairs because twenty-two flights of stairs gave him some good exercise. This morning he was in too good of a mood to climb stairs.

Even though his stomach was grumbling from lack of breakfast, he headed for the security room, grabbing a breakfast bar along the way. His battery-powered camera network around the city was pretty extensive. He wanted to make sure that if Carey got into trouble anywhere the cameras could see, he would know about it.

Or if she was out of range, at least have an idea where she had gone last.

Plus, he just wanted to see her again. He had to admit that. He wanted to know if she was real, as nice, as friendly as she seemed.

When he left this morning, he had turned off the security alarms, but left on the recording devices for the cameras. On his big board a big bunch of red lights showed where movement had happened.

The area in front of his building, of course, meaning it had recorded him going and coming. And the light on the area where he and Carey had talked was also blinking.

And three other lights in the areas Carey would have gone through in heading toward the Embassy Suites.

He brought up the last section, just in time to see her look both directions along the street, and then go inside the old hotel.

Just the glimpse of her sent his heart racing and his stomach twisting. How could one woman do that to him?

He sat, staring for a moment at the door she had disappeared through. Finally, he said out loud as his stomach grumbled. "Come on, you can't just sit here all afternoon and watch for her."

He reset the alarms and headed for the kitchen. He needed some breakfast. He didn't need to watch for her. His motion sensors would tell him if she left.

Suddenly, he felt guilty spying on her, like he was some sort of peeping tom. He shook that thought off. He could be excused wanting to watch a beautiful woman, wanting to make sure she stayed safe.

Especially since she was one of the last beautiful women left alive in the world.

CHAPTER SEVEN

CAREY MOVED easily along Front Street, staying close to the river, her rifle in her hands. The sweat from her hands made the rifle feel slick, but she wasn't shouldering it until she got to a place she felt safe. And out here, in the open, next to the river, she didn't feel safe.

On each side street she passed that led up into the big buildings of the downtown area, she watched for Matt, expecting him to be pacing her.

He wasn't.

No movement, no sign of him at all.

Or of anyone else.

It took her six blocks of glancing over her shoulder and staring up each street to make sure he wasn't following. Part of her wanted him to, part of her was afraid he would. She was having trouble believing he was what he said he was, yet she had no reason to doubt him. He didn't let off that "danger" signal that she got from some men.

Her mother had told her to learn to trust that danger signal. And a couple times, trusting it had gotten her out of bad places back when she was in college.

Matt felt safe. Good point number one. He was interesting and funny, and incredibly good-looking, in that rugged way.

Good points two, three, and four.

His eyes were full of life, his smile made her smile just thinking of it, and his voice was deep and full enough that she wanted to just spend time listening to him talk.

She had lost count of his good points.

She had felt when meeting him just like she felt back in college, not knowing what to say, or what to do when having to talk to a strange man. Clearly, living on her own, and surviving the end of the world, hadn't given her any more confidence in that area. Actually, considering he was the first person she had actually talked to in three years, she had done all right.

What had amazed her was that he had taken such a risk in just meeting her. She doubted she would have stepped out of the shadows, unarmed, to meet someone she didn't know who had just wandered into her area. Yet he had done that, to make her feel safer. The man named Matt either had amazing courage, or amazing stupidity. From the light in his eyes, she would bet on the courage.

Meeting him tomorrow for lunch was just about as crazy on her part. But since he had taken a risk that she would shoot him on sight, she would take a risk having lunch with him.

She had moved on past the Marriott Hotel without stopping, making her way along the river toward the Burnside Bridge. From there, she knew how to find the Embassy Suites Matt had suggested.

She forced herself to keep her attention on where she was going, what was happening around her, instead of thinking about him. It was hard, but in these times, a daydream could get her killed.

The city was as dead, as silent as it had felt coming in. Only the birds and the warm wind broke the stillness. It seemed that Matt had been telling her the truth, that she really was the only one besides him in this area. She could see no evidence of anything, or anyone else. No worn trails, no looted stores, nothing but a dead city, frozen in time from a morning three years ago.

It took her a good fifteen minutes after her meeting with Matt, but she finally found the old Multnomah Hotel that had been remodeled into the Embassy Suites a decade before. The front of the old hotel faced a fairly empty side street, with a parking garage on the corner. A limo was pulled up out front, the driver still behind the wheel.

The doorman had slumped over a cart full of luggage, and his body had somehow stayed there through the winter storms.

With a quick look in both directions along the street, she decided to go in.

The front door stuck for a moment, then let her into a musty-smelling entrance area that contained five skeletons in different locations around the fairly small space. She went slowly up the two stairs and into the high-ceilinged main lobby area.

The carpet was a rich-looking red, and the artificial plants gave the room a feeling of luxury, even though it was coated with a layer of grayish dust.

The footprints in front of her on the carpet were clear. One of the sets of prints must have been Matt's, since he admitted being in here. Another set, bigger and with a wider stance, was from some time back, before Matt had come in.

There was no sign that anyone else had been in the building, at least through this entrance, at any time in the recent past.

She relaxed a little and slung her rifle over her shoulder, then dug out a flashlight and a water bottle. The room was cooler than outside, making her realize just how much she had been sweating. The light from the front windows was enough in the main room, but if she were going to head down a hallway, or climb stairs, she would need her flashlight.

She stood, looking around, studying the skeletons that slumped in the waiting area near what must have been their luggage. She could still remember waiting

like that for a ride, or a bellman, or for someone to join her from a room. Who knew why these people had been waiting, but they still waited, now forever.

She finished a long drink and put the water bottle back in her backpack, then looked around at the exits. When finding rooms to stay at night on the trip from the coast to Portland, she had made sure she stayed on the main floor. She had figured that was safer. But now, here in this building, it might be safer for her to see what was on the upper floors before deciding. As long as she had two or three good ways out, she would be fine.

She went over to the front desk and crawled up on it, looking along the counter behind the desk for some sort of master key. With the power off, the door key-card systems in these big hotels reverted to a type of punch key that was always kept close by. It took her a minute, but she found it, then slid off the front desk and headed for the back.

She followed what she thought was Matt's tracks in the dust on the carpet to a stairwell, and then inside, she clicked on the flashlight. It seemed to be open all the way up, with no problems.

She used a chair to block open the door into the staircase at the bottom, just in case the door locked behind her. The last thing she needed was to get trapped in a staircase with no one left alive to find her.

Then she realized that wasn't the case. Matt knew where she was going. That thought both eased her fear a little, and worried her. She had spent three years doing just fine on her own. She didn't want to start making mistakes now, thinking she had a person backing her up. She didn't even really know him yet, and certainly didn't trust him.

She followed the tracks in the dust on the staircase all the way to the top floor, seven floors up. She tried to move slowly, carefully, to not kick up any more of the layer of dust than she needed to. The air in the stairwell was stuffy enough without adding swirling dust to it.

At the top, the old footprints went out into a hallway through an unlocked door. The narrow corridor was lit only by the windows on either end, but was bright enough for her to turn off her flashlight.

The footprints went to a window and vanished.

She followed them, then looked out the window. Beyond was a metal fire escape that led both up and down. It looked like Matt had forced the window open, then closed it behind himself after he went through.

The fire escape ladder led down to the top of the building beside the old hotel. This wasn't a way to the ground directly, but it was a good escape. So she had the staircase she had come up, the fire escape through the window. What other ways were there off this floor?

She opened a door labeled no admittance and shined her flashlight into the dark area. Service elevator, but no staircase.

She went back to the elevator and stair area and looked down another side hall. There was another exit sign there, clearly leading to another staircase. She liked that. Three ways down.

She took the master key and faced the guest door closest to the elevator area in the same hallway as the window fire escape. It took her a moment, but the passkey finally clicked something and the door opened.

She took one look inside the large area and pulled the door closed, not going inside. The last guests were still at home, still in bed.

She moved down one door and opened it.

It had a made bed and no sign of anyone staying.

"Wow," she said, letting the door close behind her and moving into the large, multi-roomed suite. She moved across the main room and carefully pulled open the drapes, trying to stir up as little dust as possible while letting the sun fill the space.

The room had high ceilings, clearly left from its days as an old hotel. And from the looks of it, in the remodeling they had combined at least three, maybe four of the old hotel rooms, into this suite. There was a small kitchen area, a large dining area, a business desk, and a room with a bed big enough for three or four people.

"Now the test," she said, moving into the tiled bathroom with old-fashioned gold faucets and a basket of soap. A bathrobe hung on the back of the door with a sticker saying it was free for guest use. This bathroom was larger than her old dorm room in college, and not only had a shower, but a huge step-up bathtub with what looked like special jets.

"Oh, baby, let this work."

She twisted the cold water on the sink faucet. For a moment nothing happened, but she could feel the air being shoved through the system. Then, with a loud sputtering sound, water came out, running dark and rust-colored, spitting with the air bubbles. It smelled like water that had sat for three years in pipes. She had expected as much. But at least it was flowing. Matt had been right.

She moved over to the bathtub and turned the faucet there. It too started running after a moment, filling the tub with nasty looking water.

She started the shower as well, then went back into the dining area and took off her pack. The release of the pressure on her back felt great. She had carried that pack so much over the past three days, it felt as if it were a part of her.

She laid her rifle on the table beside the pack, but kept her pistol in her belt. She wanted to do a little more looking around. She needed to leave tracks into every room on this floor in the dust in the hallway. If she stayed here long enough, she'd clean the dust completely out of the hallway, but for now, if she had been followed, she needed to make sure no one would come easily to this room.

She went back into the bathroom and checked the water. It was still flowing, and a lot better looking. Another ten minutes and she just might have clean enough water to take a shower in.

She looked longingly at the bathtub. If she got a generator up here, she could even heat some water for a warm bubble bath.

She went back out into the hall, blocking the suite door open so she wasn't separated from her pack, then used the master card to open every door and walk into each room on the floor, shuffling her feet as she moved along the hall.

Fifteen minutes of very dusty work later, no one, at a glance, could tell which room she was in. At last, she had a place to stay.

"One problem solved. Now to problem number two. Getting clean."

She went back into the suite, closed, locked, and blocked the door with a chair, then headed for the bathroom. A long, cold shower was going to feel very, very good.

And she did some of her best thinking in showers. After meeting Matt this morning, she had a lot of thinking to do.

CHAPTER EIGHT

MATT FINISHED his breakfast, then checked his security room to see if Carey had moved, even though he knew his alarms would have told him if she had.

Nothing.

Of course, she might have gone out the back. He didn't have security cameras in that area. But somewhere along the way, if she had left, she would trip one of his sensors and he would know.

He hoped she hadn't left, that she was what she had seemed to be, a survivor with a lot of guts, wanting to explore her old home town.

He dropped into his big chair and stared at the security screens showing the empty city around him. Now, the city didn't feel so empty. How one woman could make such a difference, he didn't know. But she sure had.

But now he had a problem. He had promised her fried chicken for their lunch tomorrow, but he didn't have a fresh chicken in his freezer. He needed to get out to the Rose Garden and get some fresh eggs and a chicken. At the same time, he didn't want to leave the security room in case she decided to move.

He wanted to watch her, protect her if she needed it, help her if she needed that.

What happened if she came to the Baxter building while he was gone and didn't find him. How would she trust him after that?

"Get it together, Matt. Leave her a note."

One on the outside door to the building, and another on the main staircase door, telling her where he had gone, what he was doing.

That felt like a silly thing to do, but he had no doubt, he would do it.

He sat, watching the monitors for any movement, planning a very special lunch for tomorrow. He wanted it to be special. After three years, the first meal with someone else demanded to be special.

Fried chicken and a chilled bottle of Chablis from the Willamette Vineyards. He needed to make a lot of chicken. Too much, actually. He wanted to give her pieces to pick from. And maybe two bottles of wine in case the conversation lasted as he hoped it would.

Her smile, the sound of her voice came back to him clearly. He wanted to very much make the lunch last, find out who she really was, let her know that he was safe and a friend.

What else needed to be in a picnic lunch? Fresh rolls. He could bake rolls tomorrow morning with the chicken, just before going.

And, of course, deviled eggs. Deviled eggs always went great on a picnic, especially the ones he made, from his Aunt Rose's old recipe.

It felt like he was forgetting something.

He tried to remember back to the picnics he used to go on when he was a child, usually up on the shores of one of the lakes in the Cascades. His mother and grandmother always made the best picnics, and always brought them in those wicker baskets.

He'd search a few stores on the way back from the Rose Garden, see if he could find a wicker picnic basket. And he needed to bring plates, silverware, and napkins as well.

But he was forgetting something on the menu. He could feel it.

Deviled eggs, fried chicken, fresh rolls, and what?

The memory of sitting on a blanket on a warm July day on the shores of the lake came back strong. His dad had tied up their boat on the sandy beach and his mother was unloading the basket. Life had seemed so perfect back then, and actually, it was. He had had a great childhood, one of the best.

He let himself relive the memory.

First, she took out a big bowl of fried chicken, covered in tin foil. The wonderful smell was always enough to make Matt want to just grab a piece right then. Of course, she never let him, not until everyone was seated on the blanket.

Then she took out a plastic container filled with deviled eggs, then a plastic sack with corn-on-the-cob smothered in butter and wrapped in tin foil.

Corn. Of course, corn and Jell-O. His mom always included corn-on-the-cob and Jell-O. Half the time, the Jell-O had gotten near something that was hot, and had half melted. His mother was always annoyed at that and his dad always just laughed.

Matt didn't much care for the Jell-O, but he could do the fresh corn just fine. It was late enough in the season that his corn in his roof garden had fresh ears on them.

He had it. The perfect picnic lunch. And he would get to Powell's early enough to do a little cleaning up there, wash a window so they would have some decent sunlight, wipe off a few tables and chairs.

The idea of having a picnic with Carey had him so excited, he doubted he was going to sleep much tonight.

"Okay, so much for meal planning," he said out loud, clicking off his audio alarms and leaving the system to record any movement in the city while he was gone. "Time to get everything ready."

He stood and headed for the door of the penthouse, grabbing a backpack to carry the eggs and chicken back in. He also picked up his rifle and a box of shells, slipping the shells into the pack. It was a habit he had always done while leaving, and this morning, being out in the city without a gun had felt damned strange. It had to be the first time he'd done that since moving back to the city.

The risk he had taken to meet Carey was amazing. She could have easily been insane and shot him. He was very glad she hadn't.

He made the two notes to Carey to stick on the building's doors, then started down the staircase, going at a slow but steady clip, thinking about the route he needed to take to get across the river to the Rose Garden.

Usually, he went within a few blocks of where she was staying and walked over the Burnside Bridge, but he didn't want to do that today. He didn't want to do anything to spook her, make her think he was dangerous in any way.

More than anything, he wanted her to show up tomorrow at Powell's.

He went through his lobby and outside, putting up the notes as he went. Then he turned straight downhill toward the river. He would use the Morrison Bridge and go around that way, away from the area Carey was in. A little farther to walk, and harder to get past a few wrecks, but worth not taking any chance at getting too close to where she was staying.

Portland had been a very big city while it was full of people. And a very big place when he was alone. Now, with Carey here, the city seemed frighteningly small.

CHAPTER NINE

THE COLD SHOWER felt wonderful as it washed off the sweat and dust from the long morning hike into the city. Carey had found the hotel's linen closet in the hallway and broke in, getting two fresh towels that hadn't been hanging up and weren't covered in dust. It was interesting how many tricks like that she had learned in the last few days, some from thinking a situation through, others from mistakes.

Learning about hanging towels had been a mistake on her first morning on this trip. She had managed to find a place with running water, taken a shower, then as if the maids had just left the towel on the towel rack, she took the closest one and started to dry herself, finding herself coated in dirt and mud almost immediately.

Gross, disgusting, and downright weird feeling. If it hadn't been so annoying, it might have been funny. Even though she was convinced no one was within miles of her, she had still used the muddy towel to wrap herself in while going in search of a clean towel. She had called herself "Mud Girl" the rest of the day.

She was getting better at picking places to stay as well. This bathroom had a decent-sized window, so there was even enough light for her to see what she was doing. The room she had found on the second night didn't have a window in the bathroom, and she had had to get ready and shower in the almost complete darkness.

She wondered as she dried off and dug out some clean clothes, if agreeing to meet Matt had been another mistake on this trip. Granted, there just weren't that many people left alive and she was hungry for company. And he seemed the same way. But even still, she had to be careful. There were no police, no parents, no friends left to come to her rescue if she got herself in a bad situation.

She finished dressing and moved over to one of the big windows that looked out over the buildings and the river. The room had stayed fairly cool, but she could tell that outside the temperatures were climbing. It was going to be a very hot day. She missed the coast, the cool breezes off the water, the summer fog.

And she missed her cats.

"Well, you made it here," she said out loud, her voice breaking the silence in the room. "Now what?"

She stood, staring out the window at the river, thinking about going to her old apartment. Sam's body would be there, in her bed. She wouldn't mind having a few of her old things from her place, but she just didn't feel up for going there yet.

Or to her parents' house over the hill in Beaverton. Maybe on the way out of town, on her way back to the coast, she would stop and see both places, pick up a few small things to take home, pay her respects to the three people she had loved the most in the world.

Or maybe she'd do that next trip. She wasn't sure if she had the emotional stability to see them just yet.

Some movement caught her eye on the Morrison Bridge. Someone was walking there.

She grabbed her binoculars from her pack and focused in on who it was.

Matt.

Even from a distance, her heart leaped at just seeing him again. He had what looked like an empty backpack on one shoulder and a rifle slung over the other.

So he really had purposely come to see her unarmed earlier.

That made her feel a little better about him, a little safer about their lunch tomorrow. He had been willing to risk his life, something he clearly didn't normally do, just to meet her. Amazing, and a little bit stupid, actually.

She watched him pick his way along the bridge, through the wrecks.

"So, where are you going now, handsome fella?"

Suddenly, the answer dawned on her. He had promised her fried chicken and said his chickens lived trapped in the Rose Garden. He was going to get a chicken for their lunch.

She smiled, watching him move over the bridge and out of sight, feeling disappointed when she couldn't see him any more. She couldn't believe how smart he had been to put chickens in the Rose Garden. It gave him a constant source of food besides a garden, which she bet he had somewhere in the city as well.

Everything about him seemed smart, except his stunt this morning. He appeared nice and was very attractive. She would have thought that even if he wasn't one of the last people alive on the planet.

She was going to have to be careful. Very careful. And go very slowly with him. Clearly, around him, her judgement might not be what it should be.

She searched for him one more time along the far river bank, disappointed that she couldn't see him.

"Okay, better get this place livable," she said, turning away from the window and looking at the high-ceilinged room with its dining table, big soft chair, and huge bed and dresser.

She went back into the bathroom, got two towels damp and another clean towel from the stack she had taken from the linen closet, then slowly started wiping off the dust from every surface.

Then she went back to the linen closet and found clean sheets and a bedspread, taking the ones on her room's bed out and putting them in the service area.

Then she washed the insides of the main window, as high as she could reach. Amazing what a little sunshine can do for moods. Hers was getting better by the moment as she settled in.

Actually, she was almost dancing around doing the cleaning, and it wasn't from the sunlight. The idea of actually having lunch with another person had her so excited, she wasn't sure if she could wait until tomorrow.

But she knew she would.

She downed the last of her bottled water after finishing with as much cleaning as she could do with wet towels. Then she emptied out her backpack, took her pistol and some extra ammunition, and left the rest of her things in the room. She needed more bottled water and there was a drugstore on the corner that might have cases of the stuff.

She went down the other staircase exploring each floor as she went. Nothing out of the usual. And no other tracks in the dust.

She was right about the drugstore, it did have bottled water, along with a large, unopened box of M&M peanut candy. She took twenty bottles and the box of M&Ms up to her room, then eating one pack for energy, she went back out into the heat with a half-drunk bottle of water in her hand.

She was going to see if that hardware store Matt had mentioned had a portable generator, one small enough that she could haul it up to her room. She might

as well try to make her Portland home as much a home as possible.

Otherwise, tonight she was going to be reading by candle and flashlight, and eating a cold dinner. Not to mention the fact that without a generator, a hot bath in that fantastic tub was impossible.

CHAPTER TEN

MATT ALMOST JUMPED out of bed as his alarm clock went off beside his bed. In two years, he hadn't ever had a need to use that stupid alarm clock. But today, he had a date, and he had a lot of cleaning and cooking to do before then.

He took a quick shower, then headed out into the kitchen. Buddy, his gray-haired old cat, looked up at him from the couch, yawned, and then went back to sleep.

"Too early, huh big fella?"

Buddy didn't even move. Matt couldn't blame him. It was early. Really early. The sun was barely coming up over Mt. Hood and the light that filled the penthouse apartment was orange-tinted. A low mist hung along the river and, as always, nothing seemed to be moving anywhere in the city.

He checked his security room, just to be sure he hadn't slept through any alarm.

Nothing.

Yesterday, Carey had made a couple of trips out of the hotel while he was over getting the chicken and eggs. He had recorded her dragging a pretty heavy-looking small generator back from the hardware store and in through the front door of the hotel on a hand truck. He hoped she had decided on a lower floor room, because he knew how much those little machines weighed and he couldn't imagine her dragging it up more than a few flights of stairs.

A couple hours later, just before sundown, she had made a few more trips to nearby stores, clearly for electrical supplies on one trip, food supplies on another.

After the sun had gone down, it was clear she hadn't picked a lower floor. She was on the top floor and that impressed him. No wonder she had survived for the past three years. She was one tough woman.

Lights, for the first time in two years, were coming from another building in the city below him. She had picked a room facing out over the river, away from his building, but he could still see her lights.

All evening, his gaze kept going to the lights. He so much wanted to know what she was doing, what she was thinking, find out more about her. The excitement and worry about the lunch tomorrow made reading almost impossible. Finally, he settled on a movie and didn't notice when she finally turned off her lights somewhere around midnight.

He couldn't believe she was there, that there was another sane person living in the city. At least, he hoped she was sane.

The first thing he needed to do this morning was bread the chicken, get it ready. Then he planned on going over to Powells and do some cleaning. After that, he would take a shower and do the cooking.

As the chicken fried, he would bake rolls and do the deviled eggs. The last thing he would do before leaving was pick some ears of corn and boil them.

The brown wicker picnic basket sat on the breakfast table, ready to be filled, a constant reminder of the hoped-for lunch ahead.

He made himself some quick breakfast, then breaded the chicken, then with cleaning supplies in his backpack, a rifle in one hand and a long-handled squeegee in the other, he headed out to Powells Bookstore.

The morning was cool, the city deathly silent, the streets still in shadow. He figured the best time to do the cleaning he wanted to do in their picnic area was before it got hot. That way, he could also go home and take a shower before cooking.

The area outside the rare book room on the top floor of Powells luckily didn't have many skeletons in it. He used an empty book cart and a blanket to gather the few there were and move them into another room. Then he wiped down one of the big, old wooden tables right in front of the window in the corner. He used the long-handled squeegee to wash the tall windows, and a push broom to move most of the dust out of the area on the hardwood floor.

He stood back and stared at the area. He had loved bookstores before the disaster, had raided a lot of them since. He had more books than he wanted to even count now. This felt like the perfect place for a picnic, and she had suggested it. Did that mean she loved books as much as he did? He hoped so.

He took out a checkered tablecloth he had found in the same store as the picnic basket and spread it on the table. If she got here before he did, she would know he had been here and got the space ready, and that he was coming back.

The sun was just starting to break down into the streets as he finished the last sweeping. He had cleaned them a perfect place to have a picnic and get to know each other.

He hoped the lunch went as well as the place she had picked.

He could feel himself starting to get nervous. He was going to be lucky to get out a word at first. Figuring out what to talk about had always been his problem on dates. He had no doubt that he and Carey had more than enough to talk about, considering what they had both been through over the last three years. He just hoped he wouldn't have to start the conversation.

He glanced at his watch. He needed to get going. He wanted to have more than enough time to get home, take a shower, fry chicken, make the other things, and get back here right on time for his first date in over three years.

He had a date. That was something he never thought he would ever have again.

A date.

He whistled all the way back to his building.

CHAPTER ELEVEN

FOR CAREY, the morning before her first post-disaster date seemed to drag.

She had woken up at the first light streaming in through her east-facing windows.

The bed had been comfortable, the room great. She had opened a few windows just before going to bed to get the cool evening breeze. Now it felt almost cold, a feeling she loved and had missed since leaving the coast. She'd leave those windows open until the day started to heat up, then close them and the

drapes to keep the room cool for later this evening.

She checked her watch. Six in the morning.

Six hours until lunch.

Six hours with nothing to do but shower, get dressed, and walk the fifteen or so blocks up to Powells Bookstore on Burnside. If she stated now, she'd be about five hours early. Maybe she could go a little early and do some cleaning, get the space ready for a picnic.

She liked that idea.

She liked having something to do in her day, something to look forward to. Many mornings over the last three years, she had woken up with no idea what to do for the day. Especially that first year. Many days that year, she had just stayed in bed, cuddling with her cats, only getting up for food and the bathroom. Sometimes she just read, taking her mind away into a made-up world, other times she just slept and lay there, staring at the ceiling.

More than likely, a doctor would have called her depressed. And damn it, she had a right to be depressed. The world had ended, everyone had died, leaving her alone. That would depress a fence post.

During the second year, she had had less and less of those days in bed. This last year, not a one. Just surviving, keeping her home running and food on her table, kept her busy. There seemed to always be something to do, something to fix, some reason to get out of bed.

Today, she had a date.

She lay there, thinking of Matt's wonderful face, his deep voice, his alluring smile. She sure hoped that what she saw was what she got with him.

"Okay, lazy, get up and get going."

Those words often got her out of bed. This morning was no exception. She took a quick, and very cold shower. Cold showers in the morning were a completely different animal than cold showers after a hot, sweaty day of walking. Cold, early-morning showers were just downright painful.

She finished dressing, then decided that the best thing to do was finish setting up her generator in the right place and then, if she had time, set up her kitchen. A decent set of goals for one morning.

The small generator she had managed to bang and lug up the stairs would run a small microwave and some lights at the same time. Last night, she had set up the generator two rooms down the hall, with it venting out an open window. That way, the sound of the motor running didn't bother her and she could still hear if someone was coming.

She had run electrical cords into a dozen rooms from that room, all dead lines. She actually didn't have a cord running through the door of her room. Instead, she had banged a small hole in the wall between her suite and the next and ran the cord through there. It never hurt to be safe, as Matt had said, especially in a big city.

If she did end up making this a regular home that she visited at times, and if she and Matt got alone, she might ask him for help in setting up a security system in the hotel at some point in the future. A lot of ifs there, though.

She went down to the suite with the generator, took the hand truck, and moved the generator out into the hall again. Five rooms down from her room, she found a new home for the generator and again got it vented out the window. Then, using a hammer she had gotten from the hardware store, she banged a small hole in the wall through to the next suite, hiding the hole with a chair.

Thirty minutes later, after a lot of banging out old plaster, she had managed to string an electrical cord through the suites, hiding the cord behind furniture and drapes in each suite. Then she picked up all the decoy cords out of the hallway and other rooms. Now, she felt even safer if someone came looking for her. They would have to trace a cord through five different suites to find hers.

Next, she took a bottle of water and headed down to a kitchen store she had seen yesterday. An hour and two trips later, she had a fully-stocked kitchen, with pans, plates, silverware, serving dishes. If she stayed long enough to store any kind of food, she'd have to connect the small fridge as well, but she didn't plan on staying in the city long enough for that.

Ten o'clock. Two hours until lunch. She had accomplished both of her goals and she still had two hours. She might die of impatience before this date happened.

She went back and took another, slightly longer, cold shower to get the dirt and sweat off her, then put on her last change of clean clothes. She was going to have to do some laundry later today. The bathtub was going to come in handy for more than just taking baths.

Or maybe she could just stop into a store and find some new clothes. After lunch, she just might do that. She had never been much of a shopper, mostly because of the money side of things. Now, it didn't matter. She had even used money one night during the first year to start a fire, just to show herself it didn't matter any more. Didn't help. She still hated shopping.

At eleven, she was ready to leave. She planned on stopping along the way, getting a few cleaning supplies, and getting to

Powells a little early to clean up an area for her and Matt to eat in. It was the least she could do, considering he was bringing the fried chicken and who knew what else.

She moved to the window to shut out the warming air so that the suite would stay cool. But just before she pulled the old window down, she noticed a rumbling sound echoing over the silent city. She leaned out the window, trying to figure out where the rumbling was coming from.

She couldn't tell.

The sound seemed to echo off buildings, one second coming from the south, the next from the north. And it was still very faint.

She stayed at the window, watching for any sign of movement, as the rumbling got slowly louder, seeming to fill every dead street with low thunder.

What could be causing such a sound?

A tank? A large truck pushing wrecks aside? Something massive, clearly, although she had no idea how sounds carried in an empty city.

Then she caught a glimpse of something moving across the river, way down the I-84 freeway toward the old airport.

She grabbed her binoculars. At first, she couldn't see anything. Then finally, she understood what had caused the sound, and what she saw sent chills down her spine.

Bikers.

A fairly large group of motorcycle riders were working their way slowly toward town, weaving in and around the wrecks, coming in on I-84 from the east. From the distance, she couldn't tell how many, but more than she wanted to be around, that was for sure.

Her best friend had been raped by two members of a motorcycle club back in high school.

She hated motorcycles.

She hated bikers.

Suddenly, date or no date, the city didn't seem to be the place she wanted to be anymore.

CHAPTER TWELVE

AFTER MATT got back to his apartment from cleaning up the area in Powells, he saw that Carey had come out of her hotel twice, both for different types of supplies.

Just seeing her working on a place to stay in town excited him. She was as good-looking as he remembered from yesterday. And certainly focused.

He watched her for a moment, then went back to the kitchen and fried the chicken, at the same time baking some rolls. He had just taken the chicken out, and the rolls, and was finishing up the deviled eggs when his alarm went off.

Was Carey leaving already for Powells? He glanced at his watch. It was quarter to eleven.

He left the eggs and moved to the security room, expecting to see a red light on the area outside of Carey's building. But instead, the light was blinking way out on Interstate 84.

He dropped into his chair and flicked up the camera for that area. What he saw rocked him back.

Bikers.

A lot of bikers.

A string of at least two dozen men, and a few women, all on large motorcycles, were working their way slowly through the car wrecks that littered the freeway. A couple of the bikes were pulling small trailers, and every one of the people were dressed in black leather.

Matt hadn't much cared one way or another for the biker groups back when he was in school. He knew that most of them were made up of regular people, folks who just liked riding motorcycles. Some of the main motorcycle clubs were just doctors and lawyers who could afford the pricey Harley Davidson bikes, plus a few mechanics and others who had had the same bike for years and kept it up. In fact, his best friend in college, Danny, had a Harley his dad had bought him. Danny put on his leathers and went for a ride every time he got the chance. Matt had even gone with him a few times, but just never caught the excitement that Danny felt about the experience.

Now, here was a biker group, or at least a group of people traveling together on motorcycles. More than likely, that was the case. And considering all the wrecks along the roads that blocked traffic almost everywhere, using a motorcycle seemed logical. He would have made the same choice if he had decided to go exploring in other cities, and had, at one point last year, even scouted out a few of the motorcycle dealerships in the downtown area, looking for the right equipment.

Matt watched the bikers work their way slowly around a wreck of about fifteen piled-up cars, not seeming to be in any hurry. He took a deep breath and tried to count them, and really look at the faces as they passed a camera he had secured inside a building near the freeway.

Most of them looked dirty, but that could be just from riding. All of them carried rifles within easy reach on their bikes, and a few had pistols stuck in their belts. Twenty-three of them, all but four men.

Suddenly, he remembered Carey.

And their date.

He flicked the monitor back to the camera showing the area around the Embassy Suites entrance. Carey must still be inside, otherwise one of his motion sensors would have activated again. She had no idea what was riding at her.

"Get a grip on yourself," Matt said aloud, letting his voice calm himself down. "These guys are more than likely friendly."

Or maybe they weren't, but until he knew for sure, it was going to be a lot safer for him, and for Carey, to not let the gang know they were here.

He flipped the monitor back to the motorcycle riders. At the speed they were traveling, and the amount of blockage they faced ahead, they wouldn't be into the main part of town for at least another half hour, more than likely an hour.

Maybe they were just heading through, going toward California to spend the winter in the sun, and wouldn't even stop. It was still early in the day. That was possible, but again, he didn't dare take the chance.

And he didn't want Carey to take the chance either. This might be the friendliest bunch of humans he had ever met, but with that many of them, he wanted to be damn sure before he strode up to the front of that line of bikes.

He punched another button and a few moments later a picture of the bikers came out of his printer. It showed at least fifteen of them. He folded it and stuffed it in his pocket.

Then with one more check to make sure Carey had not left the old hotel just yet, he sprinted for the door. On the way, he grabbed a couple of deviled eggs to stop his rumbling stomach, his rifle, and his shoulder belt with ammunition. Then he grabbed his pistol, made sure it was

111

loaded, and stuck it inside his belt behind his back. In three years he had hoped to find more people. Now, suddenly, in just two days, he had gotten his wish.

Just not the way he had expected.

CHAPTER THIRTEEN

CAREY STOOD, almost frozen in the window, watching the pack of motorcycle riders work their way toward her.

"Get a grip, girl," she said. "You got to get out of here."

She quickly tossed all her clothing in her pack, her food, her flashlight and other tools, then made sure the pistol was loaded and ready and stuffed it in her belt.

She did the same for the rifle and slung it over her shoulder. Then she went back to the window. The rumbling seemed to fill everything around her, even though the bikers were clearly miles away. More than likely, when the city had all its people, you never would have heard the bikers from this distance. But now, there just wasn't any other sound on the clear summer day.

Suddenly, from the hallway, Matt's voice shouted out.

"Carey? You still up here?"

She couldn't decide if she should say anything or not.

"Carey? If you're still here, let me know which room. It's me, Matt. You remember, your lunch date? I'd never normally come up here, but there's something happening I think you should know about."

He had come to warn her. That made her smile, even with the rumbling filling the room from the window.

"Open your window and listen if you don't believe me. I have a picture of what's coming up the freeway to show you."

He knew she would be careful, not trust him for barging in like this, so he had brought proof. The guy could think under pressure, that was for sure.

She opened the door, not bothering to take her rifle off her shoulder.

He was standing down the hallway, his back to a wall, his rifle also shouldered. But this time he was carrying one. He looked slightly winded and was sweating. More than likely, he had run from the Baxter building to warn her.

Her stomach twisted at seeing him again. He was better looking than she remembered from yesterday. It was stunning how attracted she was to this man.

"Bikers," she said. "I heard them and caught a few glimpses of them coming in on I-84. I hate bikers."

He nodded, coming toward her, offering her a picture.

She took it and stared. The focus was from the top of a pole along the freeway, and it showed at least ten, maybe more, motorcycle riders working their way past a large pile-up of cars. The picture made her shudder and she handed it back to him.

"What are you planning on doing?" she asked, again stunned at how much she was attracted to the man standing in front of her. She got no hint that he was dangerous. Her mother's voice came drifting back to her. *Trust your instincts with men.*

"Watch them," Matt said. "Just watch them, unless I become completely convinced they are not a problem. Then I wouldn't mind talking to them, but not until I'm convinced they are not dangerous."

"You're not planning on walking up to them, unarmed, with your hands in the air, are you?" she asked.

"Did you look at that picture?" he asked back, his face slightly red.

She smiled at him. "A joke."

It took him a moment, then he relaxed and smiled, his face going to a little darker shade of red. She liked that a lot. A man who could blush. How great was that?

"So what would you suggest I do?" she asked.

He pointed at the shuffled footprints in the hallway. "If they're the type to go looking for people, they'd find you here easily. And worst case, if they are the type to go looking, I don't think you're going to want to be found."

"I agree," she said. "Have I ever told you I hate bikers."

He smiled. "Yeah, think I heard that before."

"Good," she said. "Just wanted you to know."

"I've got the Baxter building completely secured," Matt said. "And enough cameras around the outside of the city to watch these people's movements until we get to know them better."

She stared at him, then glanced down at the image of the bikers working their way along the freeway. She could hear their bikes through the window she had left open in the room behind her, the sounds echoing like thunder on a clear day. She didn't trust Matt completely by a long ways, but she had a hunch he was prepared for something like this.

She could go with him, or she could just head away from the gang, over the hills to the west and back to the beach. But that wouldn't solve the problem she had come here to solve. And the thought of leaving Matt without getting to know him twisted her stomach more than going with him did.

But she also knew he was right. She couldn't stay here in this room. Okay, so choose. She didn't want to head home yet. So going with him, for the moment, seemed to be the best of a bunch of bad choices.

"So, the offer of breakfast didn't work to get me to go back to your place," she said, "so now you bring on a biker gang. Original, I must say."

He looked at her, puzzled for a moment, then she smiled at him again. "Another joke. Lighten up, will you?"

He laughed. "Just not used to anyone's jokes but mine."

"Yeah, I know that feeling."

"I've got most of lunch cooked, if my cat hasn't eaten it all by the time we get back. We can just move the picnic from Powells to my place. From there, we can watch what these visitors are going to do through my security system."

"You have a cat?"

"I'm owned by a cat," Matt said, smiling that wonderful smile of his at her. "He lets me live with him."

"I have two and I miss them a lot right now."

"Cat fix and a fried chicken picnic. That's the best offer I can make."

The sounds of the motorcycles got even louder over the city, almost echoing in the hallway. The idea of facing a motorcycle gang scared her beyond words. But at the same time, she didn't want to just run. She wanted to get to know this man standing across from her. Staying to get to know him might very well risk her life, but as Matt had decided yesterday, coming to her unarmed, sometimes the risks were worth the payoff.

"Best offer I've had in three years. I'll take it."

His face lit up. "Great."

Together, they checked her suite to make sure she hadn't forgotten anything before heading out into the street. For some reason, she had a feeling, she wasn't coming back.

CHAPTER FOURTEEN

MATT LED the way through the wrecks and debris that covered the sidewalks and streets toward the Baxter building. The sound of the motorcycles echoed through the tall buildings like a dangerous storm, sometimes louder, sometimes only distant, but clearly coming.

Matt was very relieved that Carey had agreed to come back with him. At the same time, he was worried. He didn't really know this woman, yet he was inviting her up into his apartment, and along the way, just from sheer necessity, he was going to show her some of his security measures. Not very smart on his part, if she turned out to be a dangerous problem.

Nothing he seemed to be doing around this woman was very smart when looked at from a position of survival. Yet, there was something about Carey that made him want to trust her. He just hoped that instinct was coming from his gut instead of the desire to have companionship after three years. He had learned, early in school, that sometimes his brain migrated to a position a distance below his belt, and when down there made very bad decisions, especially concerning women.

Actually, decisions made below his belt were *always* about women. This didn't feel like one of those decisions. This felt like Carey could be a friend, like

Betty the cheerleader had been. Of course, he wanted more than just friendship, but that would come later, after a lot of trust was built.

But right now, those bikers coming in on Interstate 84 made any slow and easy progress getting to trust Carey impossible. He was going to have to trust her now, if he wanted to help her stay out of the way of that group. And since he wanted to spend more time with her, and didn't want her chased out of town, or even worse, killed, then he was going to have to take some chances.

And on the other side, he knew she was taking some large chances as well with him, chances she probably shouldn't be taking. Clearly the picture and the sounds of those motorcycles had spooked her. Enough that she thought he was the better of two bad options at the moment.

At least she was making jokes about it. She had gotten him a few times already. It was going to take some time to get used to her sense of humor.

He got to the main door of the Baxter building and glanced back at her.

She paused, looking up and down the street. "Aren't they going to be able to follow us in here as well? If they wanted to, that is."

He pointed to the sidewalk they had just walked along.

She nodded. "No footprints. Smart."

"I keep all the sidewalks in a two block radius of this door blown free of dust."

"That has to be a lot of fun," she said, smiling at him.

"If you call digging dirt out of your ears for days later fun. And also I sweep this lobby regularly, along with most of the other hotels in a few block radius. They might figure out someone's around here by the lack of dust, but they won't know exactly where."

She nodded. "Impressive. You've given this a lot of thought and a lot of work."

"I read a lot of science fiction as a kid," Matt said, remembering the large bookshelf in his bedroom when he was in high school. "And I'm more afraid of the human animal than any other. Especially in situations we find ourselves in now."

She nodded at that statement as well, so he went on.

"Besides, before all this, my job was with a security company. After two years with them, this kind of paranoid thinking sort of got in my blood."

"And that's supposed to encourage me?" she asked, smiling at him.

"Sometimes paranoid is beautiful," he said, trying to make a lame joke in return. "Wait until you see the rest of my paranoid delusions."

"I'm looking forward to it," she said.

He headed in through the big glass doors to the lobby of the Baxter building. The lobby had a marble-like floor, with a number of skeletons of people scattered around the large area, including two security guards behind the desk. He had started to clear out the bodies in the lobby one day, then realized that if he did that, he would be leading someone right to him. He hadn't noticed the bodies in a year, but now, with Carey with him, he was seeing everything, as if he was looking through her eyes.

The bodies in the rest of the building he had moved out, laying them all together in a large meeting room in City Hall. It was the best he could do for them, and that task alone had taken him almost two weeks.

She had followed him inside the lobby and was scanning the large area as they walked, their steps echoing in the high-ceilinged space.

"Stairwell doors are locked and bolted," he said, pointing to the staircase he sometimes used. "And I can block the entrances at the top as well so it would take a tank to get through. I also locked all the other stairwell doors in the buildings around this one. Same reason as blowing off the dust."

She nodded and said nothing.

He took a key out of his pocket and inserted it into a slot beside the third elevator call button. Then he touched the button. The elevator door slid open without the customary chime.

He stepped back and smiled at her. "Going up?"

She looked shocked. "You have enough electricity to run an elevator?"

"I do," he said, proud of the accomplishment of hooking up one elevator to an electrical circuit off a series of generators in a maintenance building on the roof. It had been a difficult job, especially triggering extra generators to start when he touched the call button on any floor.

She stared at the open elevator. For a moment, he didn't think she was going to get in, so he stepped inside, holding the door open for her just like he used to do for people in the days before the disaster.

She stared into his eyes for a long few seconds. He could see worry about trusting him, and also intelligence in her eyes as he stared back. She had studied him, just as he had studied her. She didn't like taking this much risk, and neither did he, but for the moment they both needed to.

And clearly, she was as attracted to him as he was to her. He didn't know if that was a good thing or not, but it felt right.

Finally, she nodded and joined him on the elevator.

"Sorry we couldn't have got to know each other a little slower," he said as the door closed and they rode upward in a strained silence for a moment. "I was really looking forward to our picnic."

"So was I," she said.

"I figured you would want to get out of the way of the biker group if you could, and this is the best, and safest place, since you don't have a home and security of your own set up here yet."

"I appreciate the thought," she said. "And if this group turns out to be a nasty bunch, I'm going to be really happy you helped me stay out of their way."

She sighed, then went on. "Actually, when you showed up, I was about ready to run over the west hills and get away from here. I'm glad you talked me into staying."

"So am I," he said as the elevator slowed and the door opened onto his penthouse apartment. "I can't eat all this fried chicken by myself."

She laughed as he stepped out of the elevator ahead of her, dropped his two guns into the rack beside the door, and headed past the kitchen counter toward the security room.

"Make yourself at home," he said. "Water and other drinks in the fridge. Bathroom is off to the right. I'm going to see where our friendly bike riders are. Then I'll work at finishing our picnic lunch."

He didn't even look back. He figured the best way to get her comfortable with his place, and with him, was to take the chance and let her just look around on her own.

He had taken this many chances so far. He just hoped one more wouldn't kill him.

CHAPTER FIFTEEN

CAREY STEPPED off the elevator and stood in silence as Matt dropped his guns on a rack and headed for his security room. She couldn't believe that she was actually in a penthouse apartment with a man she had only met the day before. How stupid was she becoming? She was going to have to sit down and have a good talk with herself when this was over, if she survived it.

And when she got back to the coast, she was going to have to think a lot more about security. The picture of those bikers coming down the freeway had scared her more than she wanted to admit.

Sure, she knew that most people who rode motorcycles were just regular people, and the ones that went on those "runs" were no different. Even most of the motorcycle clubs were just lawyers and doctors and corporate business people having a good time on their weekends.

And she knew it was logical, with the condition of the roads, for people to travel these days on motorcycles. But the image of Diana, one of her best friends in high school, laying in that hospital, beaten unconscious and raped by two bikers from San Francisco, had haunted Carey for years. Anytime she saw anyone in leathers, she stayed away. Didn't matter who or what they were.

She pushed the image of Diana back and looked around at the bright, sun-lit apartment beyond the foyer area.

Matt had left himself clearly unarmed. Again, he was trusting her blindly.

She watched him disappear into the open doorway as the elevator door slid closed behind her. She glanced back at it and then, without thinking, reached over and touched the call button.

The door slid open without a problem, the empty inside of the elevator inviting her to step back in.

She stared at the open elevator for a moment, thinking maybe she should just go down to the street. From there, she could somehow manage to hike out of town and up into the west hills where she doubted anyone on a motorcycle could find her, even if they knew she existed.

But for some reason this man trusted her. Not only to approach her yesterday unarmed, but to leave her alone like this in his apartment. He was doing everything he could to ease her worries, including not locking her in here.

She shook her head. She had come to the city to find other people, see who else was alive. Now she was doing that, and she wanted to run away. How crazy was that?

"Crazy," she said softly.

She had to admit, having Matt come for her today when he discovered the bikers made her feel good. She felt lucky to have met him, actually. Maybe she could get *really* lucky and get to know him even better.

She pushed that thought away, then repeated to herself softly, "Go slowly. Go slowly."

She let the elevator door close again. It seemed she was staying.

She slipped off her backpack and leaned it against the wall beside Matt's gun rack. He had three nice rifles, one was a twenty-two about the size of hers, one clearly was a deer rifle, and a third with a scope that looked like a sniper rifle more than a hunting rifle. From this height, that sniper rifle could do a lot of damage. She wondered how good a shot he was with it. Maybe someday, she'd ask him.

He also had left the pistol he had been carrying, but she didn't recognize its size and brand at all.

She stood her rifle up beside her pack, keeping her pistol in her belt where she could grab it quickly if she needed to. She was taking enough chances, no point in taking any more than she had to.

A large archway in front of her led out of the foyer area and into the apartment. She moved inside, slowly, looking around as she went. High windows and skylights made the entire space seem as if it were as much outdoors as inside. It also smelled of fried chicken like her mom used to make, and fresh bread, something she knew well from her own bread-making at home.

Then something dawned on her.

The apartment was cool.

Oh, my, god, he had air-conditioning. The room was comfortable, actually, even with the sun beating in through the tall windows.

Matt had air-conditioning running. She was almost in love with him now. Any man who could get air-conditioning running on a hot summer's day deserved her respect. She could feel the cool draft swirling on her bare arms. This guy really was good at mechanical things.

She had a hunch, that wasn't all he was good at.

She pushed that thought back hard, then paused and listened for a moment. She couldn't even hear the generators running. He had said they were on the roof. They must be in a silenced room or something.

Power to run a full kitchen, lights, computers, air-conditioning, and elevators. His generator set-up must really be something very powerful.

The apartment had an organized feel to it. And it was clean, very clean. Just standing in the entrance made her realize how dirty and sweat-covered she was, just from the walk across town.

A large kitchen area filled the middle of the space to the left, with hanging pots and just about every imaginable appliance on the counter tops and shelves. Clearly Matt liked to cook, and seemed to know what he was doing, from the looks of the set-up of the kitchen.

The apartment had an organized feel to it. And it was clean, very clean.

A large bowl of fried chicken sat half covered on one side of the counter, and a wicker basket filled another corner of the table. She smiled at that. He had found a picnic basket. He really was one for details.

She walked through the kitchen, touching the countertop, noting where things were. She could cook in this place, that was for sure. It was set up as a chef's kitchen. And right now, she was very hungry. She hadn't really had that much breakfast this morning, originally thinking that she would save herself for the fried chicken. She glanced at her watch. It still wasn't noon, but even still, she was going to need something soon.

A plate of deviled eggs sat near the picnic basket. She couldn't help herself. She took one and the wonderful mustard and egg flavor melted in her mouth. They were the best she had ever tasted, even better than her mother's. If these eggs were any sign of how good a cook he was, she might actually gain weight hanging around here.

She took another egg and the complaints from her stomach eased.

It looked like he had gotten interrupted by the bikers right at the moment he was about to start cooking some ears of corn. His garden must be really good. She couldn't get corn to grow in her garden on the coast. Too damp, wrong climate.

A pile of books sat against the window, and one entire interior wall of the large apartment was covered in books.

There was a couch and a large, overstuffed recliner in front of a giant screen television. And another matching chair in front of a window facing Mt. Hood. Two books were on the floor beside that chair, and another on a small end table. Clearly Matt liked to read. Maybe as much as she did. That was good.

She had almost exactly the same television set-up at home, same big screen and all. The only difference was that instead of one of her cats sleeping on the couch, Matt had a big, older-looking gray cat who was now staring at her, its tail twitching.

"Who are you?" she asked the cat.

The cat's ears went back slightly, and again its tail twitched, as if it were about to bolt. She decided to give the cat some room, so she turned toward a deck area on the other side of a large, sliding glass door. It looked inviting, but hot, so she just stared at it for a moment without going outside, then turned to study the apartment some more.

Off to the right were some private rooms, more than likely his bedroom and the bathroom he had indicated. She was going to have to use it shortly, and wash her face as well.

She stared at the big, gray cat as it stared back at her. She missed her cats more than she wanted to admit. She just hoped they were still there waiting for her when she got back.

"Okay, I won't try to pet you yet," she said to the big cat on the couch. With one last look at the public area of the beautiful apartment, she took two more deviled eggs, one for her, one for Matt, and headed toward the room he had vanished into.

What she found there surprised her even more. Inside what once must have been a large study with one wall of glass was an entire room of computers, recording devices, and monitors. On one interior wall was a map of the entire Portland area, with blinking red lights in different places.

Matt was in a large, high-backed chair, staring at a big screen.

"What are they doing?" she asked.

He started, as if he had forgotten she was even there, then without turning around pointed at the screen. "They are just getting to the I-5 junction."

"These are heavenly," she said, passing Matt one of the eggs, then taking a bite out of the other one.

"Thanks," he said, putting the entire egg in his mouth. "Old family recipe."

She turned and stared out the window. From this height, she could see the opposite side of the river where I-84 ended into I-5. Coming in on I-84 you had to either pick north or south on I-5. The city of Portland was a beautiful sight from that intersection, its tall buildings tucked along the river and against the hills beyond.

"Are these windows reflective?" she asked as she saw something move.

"Perfectly," he said. "But when the sun starts going down, if they are still around, we're going to have to go dark in the main areas." He pointed to the top of the big window. "No drapes."

"Never needed them before, I bet."

"Whoever owned this place didn't seem to think they needed them back when there were people around." He went back to watching the bikers on the screen.

From what she could tell from the images on the screen, he had a camera on something high, directly in the middle of the intersection. There were a couple of car wrecks clogging both directions, but not enough to stop a motorcycle from getting past. She had to admit it made sense to travel on motorcycles. She had considered one for the trip over here, but just couldn't come to make herself learn how to ride one without help.

The bikers looked dirty, which meant nothing in the current world of ruin. It was almost impossible to avoid the dust and dirt that covered everything. She was covered in it as well, and more than likely looked almost as dirty, and that was just from a fast walk across town.

Most of the men had long beards, many of them had their hair pulled back in pony tails. All of them had rifles in their saddlebags and a few carried pistols on their hips.

She could see a few women as well on bikes, which encouraged her. Maybe this was just a group exploring, looking for more survivors, and it was just her old thinking of biker gangs being dangerous that had spooked her. But even if they were friendly, it was a heck of a lot better to be safe and find out first what they were doing.

Matt had been right. This apartment with all his security precautions, felt very, very safe.

And cool. She hadn't needed air-conditioning on the coast. She didn't know how much she missed it here.

"Twenty-three of them," Matt said, nodding as the last one passed under his camera. He tapped his keyboard and the image on the big screen switched to showing the bikers slowly moving south on I-5.

She watched Matt stare at the screen for a moment, admiring his strong shoulders and brown hair. She just hoped this guy was as safe as she felt he was. There was nothing in his apartment that looked odd besides this room. Nothing felt dangerous, nothing set off her warning bells, and that worried her too. No man was perfect. Not even Sam.

"This room is really something," she said. "I'm impressed."

Matt smiled up at her. "Free supplies, lots of spare time, knowledge of electronics, and enough paranoia to fill a small lake will get you a room like this."

"Makes sense."

"Thanks."

"You think those guys saw your lights last night? Or mine?" She didn't tell him that she had gone up to the roof of her building at one point and just stared up at his lights coming from this place. He was right, his place did look like a beacon from a distance.

Matt shrugged. "I doubt it. If they came all the way in on I-84 from the east, then more than likely they camped last night up at Multnomah Falls in the Columbia Gorge. There's food in the lodge there, enough beds for a group this size, and good drinking water. And that would put them in here just about this time, if they started early."

"Makes sense," she said. "I hope you're right."

"So do I," he said.

He glanced around. Suddenly, he must have realized she was standing and he was sitting. He jumped up. "Let me get you a chair."

She held her hand up. "I'll get it. You keep watching."

He smiled at her and nodded. "Kitchen table has a few chairs. Usually I take one and Buddy takes the other."

"Buddy's the cat's name?"

"Yeah, took me six months to get him to trust me," Matt said, dropping back into the big chair. "There were still a few roving packs of feral cats in the city when I came back two years ago. They've all mostly disappeared now. No food. I bet you really miss your cats. I'd miss Buddy if I had to leave him for any time."

"Yeah, I now understand that feeling."

She went back out into the living area of the big apartment and toward the dining table, stopping near the cat. "Well, Buddy, are you going to let me pet you?"

"Careful," Matt called out from the room behind her. "He's got claws."

She laughed. Both her cats had claws that she tried to keep trimmed just enough to keep the points from becoming razor-sharp, but not enough to make the cats defenseless.

Buddy sort of stared at her, clearly not sure what to do. She eased out her hand and he leaned forward and sniffed it. Then he turned his head indicating that she should scratch his ears.

She did as the cat instructed, taking her time and giving his ears a good rubbing. When she finally stopped, Buddy looked up at her and then stood, purring.

"You're just a big softy," she said, scratching his back and then his ears again.

"Now that's something I wouldn't have believed possible," Matt said from the doorway.

Buddy heard his voice and jumped down from the couch, walking toward Matt as if what had just happened went on every day.

"I'm a cat person," she said, smiling at Matt's stunned look before she turned to get the chair. She didn't want to tell him how much simply petting Buddy had done to make her feel better.

By the time she got the chair back into the computer room, along with the plate of deviled eggs, Matt was again in front of the big screen, watching the bikers move south on I-5, heading for the bridge over the river.

Buddy was on his lap, purring as Matt petted him with one hand.

There was just something about that scene that made her relax just a little more. Sitting there, petting a cat and staring at a monitor seemed so normal for him.

And right now, she really missed normal, needed normal, wanted normal more than anything else she had ever desired.

She sat there, staring at Matt and Buddy as outside, the gang of bikers worked their way closer.

CHAPTER SIXTEEN

"**Damn it,**" Matt said, staring at the big screen in his security room. "They're coming into town."

Carey felt her stomach twist into a knot. She was sitting beside, and slightly behind, Matt, with a clear view of the monitor. She watched as the lead two motorcycles, without even a second of hesitation, left I-5 on the I-405 ramp. The two moved slowly around a large pile-up

of cars, then accelerated through a clear stretch of highway.

Blinking red lights on Matt's big board started to flash as the two lead bikers went quickly through two of his motion detector areas. Matt had to jump two cameras ahead to get to a view that allowed him to see the lead bikers on the monitor.

Carey watched, stunned at seeing this many other people alive, and this close, as the motorcycles passed the exit to Beaverton that would have taken them away from the city. They got off at the Chambers Street exit, working their way slowly past a pile-up at the top.

"They seem to all know exactly where they are going," Matt said, shaking his head as he switched the monitor back to the interchange, then to a camera along the way, then back to the two lead bikes.

"It sure looks that way," Carey said.

"The group is spread out for a mile. They must have the night's camp sight planned out ahead. That kind of planning would make sense, considering how many of them there are."

"They are also in contact with each other," Carey said, pointing at the screen. "See the headsets with the microphones?"

"You're right," Matt said. "At least one in every small bunch has one on. This is a very organized group."

Carey wasn't sure if that was a good thing, or a bad thing. After being so alone for three years, it was surprising how dangerous other people felt to her.

Her mother's voice echoed again in her head. *Such a brave little girl.* Carey ignored it. There was a difference between being brave and being stupid, sometimes a fine line difference, but still a difference. And being worried about these new arrivals, maybe even afraid of them, wasn't a bad thing.

"How many cameras do you have in the city itself?" Carey asked.

"Not that many, actually," Matt said. "Most everything I have is on the main ways in. I planned to put up more, but after the first year, there didn't seem to be much of a priority. And I had to go over to one of the stores in Beaverton to get more equipment." He shrugged and smiled at her. "Never really got around to it."

"I'm amazed you have this many," she said. "You climbed a lot of light poles."

He laughed. "It's easy, once you have the right equipment and get the hang of it. I was trained for it in the security job."

Carey couldn't imagine climbing a pole like that, especially with the knowledge that if she fell, there would be no one to help her, no hospital to go to, no ambulance to take her. Over the last three years, thoughts like that had kept her out of many dangerous situations.

The two lead bikers were out of any camera range. Carey wasn't sure why having them in the city worried her so much. She just kept repeating to herself that bikers were just normal people who ride motorcycles. And if you had to travel in this age of clogged roads, bikes were the best way. In fact, maybe the only way to go any real distance. But still, the fact that there were so many of them scared her.

Carey looked at the big board of lights on the city map. "Are we going to know when they get near this building?"

"We will," Matt said, smiling at her. "I have at least two dozen cameras around this building covering the streets in all directions for five blocks."

"Let's just hope they're nice people," Carey said.

"More than likely they are," Matt said, pointing at the screen showing a group of five getting off the freeway on the Chambers Street exit. "The license plates on most of those bikes are Nevada. A couple are Arizona, and I think I saw one Utah plate."

"Nevada makes sense," she said, nodding, thinking about the military establishments there. "A lot of people in Nevada might have survived."

Matt turned slowly to look at her. "How do you know that? You said yesterday that you knew what caused all this. How? And what was it?"

She laughed. "Just like you and all the security stuff, I had a past as well. Tell you what, after we find out where the group out there is going, I'll tell you over that picnic you offered me."

He looked at her, then smiled. "Deal."

She could have just sat there and stared into his eyes for the next ten minutes, but instead she said, "Would you mind if I use your bathroom to get cleaned up?"

"Not at all. It's down the hallway on the left, extra clean towels on the shelf in there. And be careful, the hot water in the shower is really hot."

"You have hot water? I haven't had a hot shower since I left the coast. I think I have found heaven."

He laughed again. "I don't know about heaven, but this place does have air-conditioning, hot water, and a washer and dryer if you want to wash a few clothes. They're just off the bathroom."

She again looked into his eyes. "Thank you, Matt, for the hospitality, and the concern for my safety."

"You are welcome," he said. "It's going to be nice to have someone to talk to over lunch. Besides Buddy here, that is. It's been a long three years."

"For me too," she said.

With that, she got up and headed to get her backpack. She would take him up on his offer to wash some clothes. Washing what she had at this point made more sense than going out looking for new clothes, considering that outside the building, the streets of Portland had people in it again.

CHAPTER SEVENTEEN

MATT WATCHED Carey leave the room, then went back to scratching Buddy's ears and staring at the bikers as they moved through the wreck at the Chambers Street exit and went somewhere into downtown Portland. After ten more minutes, the last one went by and there was nothing left to see.

So far none of the bikers in the city had entered an area of town that he had motion sensors and cameras. So until they did, he was going to have to wait.

He set the loud alarm that had woken him up yesterday morning when Carey entered town. If any of the bikers went into an area where he had a camera and a motion sensor, the alarm would tell him.

He stood, easing Buddy to the floor. "Come on, old guy," Matt said to his cat. "Nothing more we can do here at the moment. We have a guest to finish cooking for." He picked up the plate full of the remaining deviled eggs, popped one into his mouth, and headed for the kitchen.

As he went through the living room, he could hear the faint sounds of the shower running. He couldn't believe that a beautiful woman was in his shower. Maybe he was still in bed and dreaming. Maybe the world really hadn't ended, and he hadn't spent the last three years alone.

Didn't he wish.

He stopped for a moment and listened. The shower sounds were real.

Carey really was in there.

And now he needed to fix her something to eat. Until she had mentioned the picnic, and brought him the deviled eggs he had made, he had been too busy to realize just how hungry he had become. It wasn't often he skipped meals, and his morning exercise routine. Of course, cleaning up the corner of Powells had been some decent exercise. Oh, well, maybe they could use that space another time, for another picnic.

Buddy followed him into the open kitchen area. "I missed your breakfast too, didn't I?"

Buddy banged against his leg and then walked over and sat down at his empty cat bowl.

"All right, you first," Matt said, laughing. He grabbed the half-used bag of cat food from the shelf and fed Buddy quickly.

Then he moved the chicken to the dining room table, along with the eggs and rolls, putting the picnic basket on the floor by the window.

Then he started a pot of water boiling for the corn, added a little butter-flavored powder and some salt to the water, then started to peel the ears of corn.

"That was wonderful," Carey said.

She came out of the hallway from the bathroom carrying her backpack in one hand. "Thank you. I hope you don't mind that I've taken you up on washing some clothes."

Her long brown hair was still damp and hanging over her shoulders. Her face had a red glow to it, as if she had scrubbed it more than once. She had on the same blouse and jeans, and except for the pistol tucked in her belt, she looked more like a college student than a survivor who was still alive three years after the world had ended.

Matt took a deep breath and let it out slowly, trying to get his heart to calm down. She was better looking than he had even thought yesterday morning. Stunning was a better way of putting it.

She dropped her backpack near his gun rack, then took the pistol out of her belt and laid it on top of the pack. Clearly, she was starting to trust him a little more.

She turned and came back toward him. "You're sure on the washing? Water isn't an issue here?"

"No problem at all," he said. "I have filters keeping the water clean in the tank on the roof, and it's good to run more than I use every so often to help the process."

She laughed. "I wouldn't even have good water if I hadn't run a pipe down from a house above where I live. It had a natural well, and I somehow manage to keep the pump going and the long pipes not leaking too much."

Matt nodded. "Pumps can be a problem. I've had to replace two so far that pump water from the main gravity-fed lines under the street to the roof. Took me days to do each one."

"Amazing," she said, shaking her head. "Elevator, air-conditioning, water pumps. I could never keep a place like this going."

He smiled at her nice compliment, then held up an ear of fresh corn. "Corn on the cob with your fried chicken?"

Her face lit up like a kid's on Christmas morning. "Oh, god, that sounds wonderful. What can I do to help?"

He glanced around at the kitchen he was used to being in alone, then pointed at the table. "Just sit there and tell me what you used to do before the world ended. And how you know what caused this mess."

"Sounds like I'm getting the better part of this deal," she said, laughing as she dropped into the chair he usually sat at. He was never going to get tired of her laugh. It had a high ring to it, and just made him want to smile.

"I don't think so," he said. "You know how many times I wished I had someone to talk to while I cooked."

"Actually, I do," she said, her smile fading slightly.

They held each other's gaze for a moment.

How dumb was he? Of course she knew what that was like. She had told him she had been alone the entire time as well. What was he thinking? He nodded and smiled. "Sorry."

She shrugged.

"To the story. I have cooking to do."

She laughed. "Ahh, where to start."

"The beginning," he said.

"Twenty-seven years ago I was born right here in Portland, grew up in Beaverton. My father was a stockbroker the entire time, my mother taught school."

As she was talking, he finished getting the corn ready and dropped it into the boiling water.

"My birthday's in October," he said. "I'll be twenty-seven then as well, also born right here, but grew up in Bend."

"May birthday for me," she said. "Looks like we're pretty close to the same age."

"So where did you go to college?" he asked, assuming that she had. He glanced at the table. Chicken, now cold, corn, eggs, rolls, what more did they need?

"Eugene," she said.

He stopped and stared at her. Eugene was the hometown of the University of

Oregon. "You're kidding? So did I? What was your major?"

"Physics," she said. "I was working on my post-doctorate when all this happened. What was yours?"

No wonder he thought this woman was smart. She was. Anyone who could go that far in physics had to have a brain that was far beyond his.

He laughed. "Electrical engineering. No surprise, huh?" he said, indicating the room with all his equipment in it. "I got a four-year degree and came here to work. Best thing I could find was the alarm company. No regular engineering firm would hire me with only an undergrad degree and moderate grades."

"Turned out to be a great thing," she said, smiling at him.

"Guess it did, didn't it."

He looked up from the boiling corn and into her eyes again. "So how come we never ran into each other at the university? I think I would have remembered seeing you."

She shrugged. "Actually, probably not. I was the shy, bookworm type, stayed in the dorms for the first three years, mostly just studying. I was a freshman at seventeen and never really paid much attention to the party scene. Actually, I was living here three years ago, working on my post-doc in electromagnetics."

"Electromagnetics? What were you doing in Portland?"

"Working at a lab for a Dr. Canfield."

Now he was really impressed. Canfield was a known name, not only in science, but in advisory panels in

No wonder he thought this woman was smart. She was.

Washington, D.C. Matt had even read one of his books during his senior year. "Wow, nice job."

"Actually, it was," she said. "I had a nice apartment up on the hill in the Northwest section, off of Quincy Street. And I made some great money."

"Why didn't you head back to your apartment when you came into town?" he asked, then instantly knew it was a stupid question. "Never mind," he said, waving his hand and focusing on the boiling pot in front of him. "You don't need to answer that."

"No, it's all right," she said. "Paine, my fiancée, was staying with me the night before all of this happened. His body is still there, and I didn't want to see it again. At least not right away."

He looked up into her eyes. He could see there was still a lot of pain close to the surface there. He had topics like that as well. Both of them did.

"I'm sorry," he said.

She nodded and sat back. "Actually, I think the worst of it was that I couldn't bury him, or either one of my parents. I just didn't have the strength to move their bodies very far."

He nodded, remembering his parents and how hard that had been for him to do alone. "Yeah, I managed to bury my mother and father, but it took me most of a day just to move them to the small cemetery in Bend."

This time she looked deeply into his eyes. "Sorry, bad topic I guess."

"I don't think it hurts to talk about it," he said, putting plates, napkins, and some silverware on the table in front of her and in front of the other chair. "Considering that we haven't had anyone to talk to for three years about any of this."

"True," she said, smiling at him, "but not over a wonderful picnic lunch."

"Ahh, good point. Some topics just aren't meant for food."

"So how are we going to know if the bikers get close?" she asked, pointing at the security room.

"I have an alarm set that will tell us when they show up on a camera and set off a motion sensor. Same alarm that woke me up yesterday with you."

She smiled.

"Drink?" he asked. "I have chilled bottles of white wine I was going to bring along, but not sure now that would be a good idea. I have bottled water, Tang, cans of Diet Coke, and that's about it."

"Great thought on the wine," she said. "That would have been nice, but now I agree that this isn't a good time. Just water now."

He got them both bottles of cold water from the fridge, then drained the corn and put it on the table. He uncovered the chicken and rolls and then sat down.

"This smells wonderful," she said, waving the steam off the corn into her face. "I never thought I'd ever have another ear of fresh corn, let alone fried chicken."

She took an ear of corn, then a breast piece, a roll and two more deviled eggs. He watched as she bit into the chicken and her face lit up with sheer joy and pleasure.

"Fantastic," she said, looking up at him. "Thank you."

"No," he said, his smile so big it felt like it might break out of his face, "thank you."

Until that moment he hadn't realized just how much he had missed other people. Other *special* people.

And Carey was, without a doubt, very special.

CHAPTER EIGHTEEN

THE HOT SHOWER, the laundry, and now this fantastic-tasting chicken and corn. Carey would have never thought that such a thing was possible, let alone have it given to her by a guy with looks that seemed right out of a GQ magazine.

And besides the great looks, the superb body, and a smile that would melt a window, he had a wonderful personality, and actually seemed sensitive. He knew instantly when he had asked a bad question about her old apartment, even before she had said anything.

She was amazed that he had been worried enough about her to come and find her when he saw the bikers. He could have just let her go it alone, and she supposed most guys in his situation would have. She might have let him go it alone if the situation were reversed.

But Matt hadn't.

Was he too good to be true? Or was her ability to see another person just warped from three years of never seeing anyone?

She was going to have to be careful. She knew, without a doubt, that she could fall in love with him easily. And that was something she had never dreamed might happen again.

She didn't need, at the moment, to have another loss if he decided he didn't much care for her around. Even with them getting forced together faster than either one of them would have liked, they still needed to go very slowly.

Or at least she needed to go slowly. She had no doubt, that was going to be difficult.

After each of them had taken a few more bites of the wonderful lunch, Matt smiled at her. "So you still haven't gotten to the part of the story where you know what caused this disaster."

"You're right," she said, holding her second ear of corn in front of her mouth, "I'm falling down on my part of this bargain."

He laughed as she enjoyed the bite, then he went to work on a piece of chicken, ready to listen.

"I'm not sure where to start, exactly, so let me back into this a little. For a week before that last day, scientists around the world had been whispering among themselves about what seemed like a cloud approaching Earth. Actually Earth, and the rest of the solar system, was approaching the cloud."

"A cloud from deep space?" Matt asked, a chicken leg halfway to his mouth. "Sounds like a bad movie."

She nodded. "I wish it had been. But it was real. With the speed that Earth and the solar system were moving, and the speed of the cloud's movement, it would flash over Earth for less than five seconds. The problem was, no one was exactly certain what the cloud was."

"You're kidding?" Matt asked.

She smiled. "Actually, the leading theory was the cloud was some sort of energy, visible only because of the light refraction it was causing to the stars on the other side of the cloud. Something out there was bending light, twisting it, ripping it apart, and Earth was going to pass right through that something."

"And no one told anyone this would happen?" Matt asked.

"There didn't seem to be a point. All the scientists believed that no one would notice anything. In fact, even on the night side of the planet, they thought that there wouldn't even be a glow in the sky from the wave."

"And your working with Dr. Canfield got you on the inside of all this information?"

She nodded. "His main lab was down near the river here in Portland. I was scheduled to work with him for the summer, and with luck, the fall semester. It made being with Paine hard at times, since the drive between Portland and Eugene is so boring, but we managed, making our time together special when we had it."

Matt nodded and said nothing. She wasn't sure if mentioning Paine again was such a good idea, but too late now, so she went on.

"Dr. Canfield's belief was that Earth was about to flash through a low-level electromagnetic storm. He had sent out a warning to others on his theory, to give them a chance to protect highly sensitive instruments. Strong electromagnetic pulses, like from an atomic blast, could shut down most modern equipment and destroy computers, but no one thought this wave was strong enough to do that."

"But they were guessing, right?"

"Yeah, we were all guessing." Her stomach twisted at the idea of how many people they might have saved if they had known. But they hadn't and there was nothing she could do about it now. She had already lost far too many nights to thinking about that.

"Dr. Canfield, to prove his theory, designed an experiment with two dozen sets of sensitive electronic equipment, to monitor the effects of the pass-through. Part of the experiment was to have one set of control devices locked in a secure vault, designed to protect anything in it from any kind of electromagnetic pulse. Some banks and some government military installations have such protections, developed back in the days of the cold war. It was easy for Canfield to set one up."

"Let me guess," Matt said. "You were in that vault, just like I was in the bank vault. That's what saved us."

She nodded. "I had worked two long days and nights on the experiments, side-by-side with Canfield, getting them ready. Then during the hour before the storm was to pass over, Dr. Canfield decided I should be closed in the vault with the control-equipment to monitor them."

"No one thought this thing might be dangerous to humans?"

"No one," she said. "Not one scientist in the thousands who were aware of the cloud approaching ever thought it would be dangerous. It was just a big, astronomical curiosity. It would be past Earth in seconds. Papers would be written about it. No big deal."

"Yeah, got that one wrong," Matt said, shaking his head.

"When I came out ten minutes after the cloud had passed, Dr. Canfield lay dead on the floor. From there, for me, as I'm sure it was for you, life became a pure nightmare."

After a moment of silence, Matt asked, "What did you do next?"

"I'm not really sure, to be honest. I think I was in shock. I remember stumbling around, checking for life in almost every body. Once I realized that

was fruitless, I headed home, to my apartment. I found Paine still in my bed."

With that, the silence in the penthouse got very intense. She forced herself to take another bite of corn. Matt was nice enough to not say anything as she let the memory of that moment go past.

"I then made a nightmarish three hour walk over the hill and to Beaverton where I had grown up. My mother was slumped over the sink of our family home with the water still running. She had been preparing what looked like one of my favorite meals, corned-beef and cabbage. I moved her to the couch and made her look as peaceful as possible, as if she had fallen asleep watching television. Then I headed back into town."

"Why?" Matt asked.

"I wanted to find my father," she said. "He was in his office, slumped over his desk, his secretary on the floor in front of the desk. I managed to put him upright in his chair and turn it so it looked out over the city. At least his final resting place would have a view. I wish I could have done more for them."

"It just wasn't possible," Matt said.

She needed to keep going with this story, get it all out. She was amazed she had held her emotions together so far. She clearly was getting strength from Matt, and just telling this story to another human made her feel better.

"Finally, after a day, I managed to gather enough of my wits about me to think about what to do, where to go. I found myself at one point back in the lab. A part of the scientist-in-training in me took over. Since all the data had been recorded, the least I could do was try to discover what exactly had happened."

"Did you actually find out what in the cloud caused this?" Matt asked, sitting forward now, the picnic lunch between them ignored for the moment.

"I did. To be honest, the answer wasn't hard to find. The instruments designed to record and test Dr. Canfield's theory told me that he had been right, the storm was electromagnetic, but it had been resonating at the exact right band to shut down the human-brain's electrical systems."

"Didn't know that was possible," Matt said.

"The military had been working on weapons using electromagnetic pulses for exactly that reason for years."

"Didn't know that, either," Matt said, shaking his head in disgust.

"I double-checked my findings, again coming up with the same answer. All the signals that are sent constantly from the human brain to the heart and lungs were short-circuited and simply shut off. In essence, everyone died before they even knew what had hit them. No one was in any pain."

"That's something good to know," Matt said, nodding. "Makes me feel a little better about my parents."

"Luckily, though, the storm's electromagnetic band had been very narrow. Over the years, I discovered it had killed all dogs, but not small cats. Horses are gone, but not cattle. Rats, mice, most rodents were killed, but not most fish. Deer survived as well. And raccoons. And a lot of bees and insects of different types. I have no idea of the long-term effects the massive disruptions in the food chains will have, and I really

All the signals that are sent constantly from the human brain to the heart and lungs were short-circuited and simply shut off.

have no way of actually measuring why some animal's brains were short-circuited by the storm and others were not."

"Humans just drew the short straw," Matt said.

"They did," she said. "After one full day of doing that research, I had to escape."

She didn't mention to him that she had stopped and visited Paine and her parents on the way out, to say good-bye.

"I headed for the coast and now, three years later to the day, I came back."

"And I'm very glad you did."

"So am I."

Matt leaned back in his chair. "So, as I thought, the bank vault protected me, and the experiment vault protected you."

"Exactly," she said. "The electromagnetic pulse in the wave that hit the planet was weak, but sustained for just long enough to do this level of damage to humanity."

Matt leaned forward and stared at her. "Weak meaning what exactly?"

"Bank vaults would normally not have enough shielding to protect anything from a large electromagnetic pulse. Neither would the vault I was in. That means that just about anyone underground a good distance, or in any kind of military installation shielded for atomic blasts, would have survived. Or even someone behind a lot of metal."

"Oh, wow," Matt said, his gaze looking out over the city.

She watched him as he sat back and let what she had said soak in. Matt was clearly a very smart man and he had a common sense way of thinking that served him well. She admired that, wished she had more of it, to be honest.

"So, there might be a lot of people out there still alive?" Matt said after a few moments. "Which is why it didn't surprise you when I said the bikers had plates from Nevada."

"Exactly."

"After being one of the only people around a city this size for so long," Matt said, "I thought there was no chance of ever finding a large group of humans again."

"Portland didn't have any military protected areas," Carey said. "We don't have subways, or military ships on the river. I'll bet there are more people in Seattle, a bunch more in California, and who knows how many in Colorado and Nevada."

"Subways, like in New York or Washington?" Matt asked. "You think there might have been enough to protect people? Or in submarines, or deep mines. Would any people in those have been protected?"

"Honestly, I don't know," Carey said. "But it wouldn't surprise me that they were. Was the bank vault door you were in open?"

Matt nodded. "It was."

"So even with an open vault, you and your co-worker were protected. I sure don't see why there wouldn't be others. Maybe a lot of others."

His eyes were alert, alive with the excitement of what she had told him. "Don't you want to know how many people might actually be still alive out there?"

"Discovering if people are still alive is the reason I'm sitting here, having this wonderful picnic instead of eating soup with my cats back on the coast."

Matt nodded. "I know you must miss your cats, but to be honest with you, I'm very glad you're here."

She stared at him for a long moment, then she said, "So am I."

CHAPTER NINETEEN

SHE HELPED him do the dishes, putting everything into a dishwasher, something she didn't have in the house she lived in at the coast. She loved his kitchen. It felt perfect for cooking, for conversation, for more than one person to move around another. The light from the big windows made it bright and the air-conditioning kept it cool.

While they worked, he asked her more questions about her job, about why she had become interested in physics, and about her years in college. It felt good to talk about those kind of things again.

Almost normal.

It seemed he craved just normal conversation as much as she did. That made sense after three years. When they were finished with the cleanup, the chicken covered and in the fridge along with the few remaining deviled eggs, she went back down the hallway to put her clothes in the dryer, then joined him in the security room.

She sat in her chair, pulling it up a little closer beside him. It was amazing how, in such a short time, she was really starting to trust this man. And enjoy his company, and being near him. She wanted to get a lot closer than they were, but so far she was managing to not show him that in any way.

He was being equally as cautious in return, something she appreciated.

"No sign of where they all went?" she asked.

"Nothing," Matt said. His fingers moved on the keyboard, showing different views of areas of Portland. All of them were empty. No red light was blinking on his big city map.

"Maybe they had planned on spending the night in the Hilton Hotel. There's also a lot of loft apartments and such in that area that would be easy to get in and out of."

"True," he said. "The old Benson is right across the street from the Hilton. If they're in that neighborhood, we might be able to catch a glimpse of them from the roof."

"You got some good binoculars?" she asked.

He laughed. "The best the stores had to offer. And a couple of telescopes too. One on the roof, one on the deck."

"I bet the stars on a clear night from here are wonderful," she said, standing.

"They are." He pushed his chair back and stood as well. "No lights of the city to get in the way anymore."

"Good point," she said.

He picked up a beeper-like device and held it up for her to see. "Remote alarm, to let us know if they're going somewhere else I have cameras. Or coming close to this building."

"You have all kinds of nifty gadgets," she said, watching him put it on his belt.

"Again, just too much time, an overactive imagination, and no limits on money. The no limits on the money is the key. It's amazing all the nifty devices man had come up with."

She had to agree with him there. Too bad all this invention and originality was now going to be lost in the ruins. She doubted that there was even enough of a population for man to survive, let alone survive in any real civilized fashion.

But she didn't say any of those depressing thoughts, instead she just followed him toward the elevator. Instead of pushing the button, he turned and went to a door off to one side of the entry foyer. "This is a private entrance to what had been a penthouse patio on the roof," he said. "Something extra for whoever lived in this place before me."

He opened the door and held it for her to go ahead.

"You have any idea who that was?" she asked as she started up the narrow staircase.

"Not a clue," he said. "I actually think the apartment might have been between owners, since there were no clothes, nothing in the kitchen, and everything looked cleaned and ready for someone else to move in."

"Lucky find," she said. "I had to clean out an older couple's things from the house I took over. Luckily, they weren't there, but it still wasn't fun."

"I bet," he said.

She reached the top of the stairs and pushed on through the heavy metal door. The heat hit her in the face like a hard slap. It was about noon, much hotter than this morning and even warmer on a rooftop. She wouldn't want to be up here around five in the afternoon when it would be hotter yet. She wasn't sure how long she was going to be able to stand this heat now.

They had come out on what looked like a stone patio, with a number of benches around one side, and what had been some planters, now full of brown weeds, marking the difference between the patio and the rest of the roof. Around her, over the waist-high edge of the building, the city stretched out around her, the river a blue band to her right, the mountains a green forest to her left. The sky was crystal clear, and the snow on the top of Mt. Hood seemed to just glow in the bright sun.

The maintenance building they had just come out of blocked her sight of the city to the south.

"Wow," Matt said. "It's turning into a real hot one today. I better check the garden."

He turned and went around a planter and out onto the gravel rooftop, heading toward the south side. She followed, her steps crunching on the gravel, moving slowly, very glad she wasn't spending the day out in this heat. In more ways than one, she had been lucky to have Matt find her. And being up on this hot roof was reminding her of that. His air-conditioning was a lifesaver.

She went around the corner of the elevator shaft structure and stopped cold at the sight. A lush garden stretched out in front of her, looking very out of place on the gray, gravel roof.

She shouldn't have been stunned by his garden, considering everything she had already found out that he could do. But for some reason, he just didn't seem to be a person who could grow things.

Yet he clearly was.

This guy really was too good to be true.

His garden stretched along the rooftop for a good fifty paces, and was twenty or so rows wide, filling the entire roof between the maintenance structure and the south edge. The planted area was framed by large boards at least a foot deep, forming what looked like a pool-like enclosure filled with dirt. Black rubber hoses of a drip water system ran along each row of plants and kept the ground a dark, rich brown, even in the heat.

"Amazing," she said, moving over and standing near where Matt was checking a water line. "Why did you build this instead of just going out and finding some ground somewhere else and planting a garden?"

"Seemed easier to have everything I needed close by," he said, moving to check a small pump, then working his way down a hose line. "And safer on a day like today."

She had to give him that.

She focused on the plants. From what she could see at a glance, he had about everything growing up here. Green peppers and onions were on the left. There were corn stocks, potatoes, zucchini, and a dozen other types of plants, some she didn't recognize.

"This is really amazing," she said. "It's bigger than my garden, and I have unlimited room. How did you get all this dirt up here?"

"One of those small tractors with a scoop on the front. It just barely fits in the service elevator."

"You're kidding?"

Matt smiled. "Nope." He bent over and checked another water line. Then he stood and smiled at her. "I brought it up here one scoop at a time from a spot down near where I saw you by the river."

She couldn't even imagine the amount of time that must have taken. He must have made a hundred trips at least. Of course, over the last few years, they both had nothing else to do but take care of themselves, so time wasn't an issue.

But having the stamina to do something like this impressed her. Clearly Matt had a level of patience she didn't have.

She walked along the edge, watching him check the hoses, making sure everything was in place. When they reached the other side of the large garden, she was even more impressed. The thing was at least twice, maybe three times the size of her garden, and she knew how much time it took

She stayed right with him, matching him stride for stride all the way to the door.

her to keep it going and alive. She just hoped most of her plants were growing when she got home. Even on the coast, it sometimes stayed dry for long enough to kill a garden.

"Can you grow enough on something this size to last an entire winter?"

"Well, here and on the twenty-first floor," he said, smiling sheepishly at her.

"Twenty-first floor?"

He shrugged. "Yeah, I have an indoor garden there as well, that I keep going all winter with lights. I like fresh vegetables, in case you couldn't tell."

"I guess so," she said, shaking her head.

He pointed toward a telescope sitting near the edge of the building on the north side, then started that way. She followed him, staring out over the city as he picked up the telescope, tripod and all, and moved it toward the west wall of the roof. "I've been trying to learn how to grow some spices down there as well, but not having much luck so far."

"They are tough," she said. "I can give you a few hints I learned from my mom."

"Would you?" he asked, clearly excited at the idea. "Anything to add a little flavor and change to the diet."

"I know that feeling," she said. "I've grown awful tired of fish and clams and crabs."

"Oh, don't I wish," he said. "I've tried fishing the river, but without much luck. Never really knew how to do it."

"Neither did I," she said, remembering those first few weeks of learning how to fish. "Books helped a lot."

"That's how I learned how to garden," he said, putting the telescope up next to the edge of the roof on the west side facing the main part of town and the hill beyond. "Gardening and elevator maintenance, right out of the books."

Just as he was about to look into the telescope, the beeper on his side went off.

He clicked it off, motioned that she should follow him, and headed for the door to the staircase. "Looks like some of them are moving."

She stayed right with him, matching him stride for stride all the way to the door. He opened it and held it for her, then she held the one at the bottom.

The air-conditioning in his apartment felt wonderful, and made her glad they hadn't stayed any longer on the hot roof. She was still not acclimated to this heat after living so long in the cool temperatures.

"Water out of the tap safe to drink?" she asked.

"It is," he said, moving toward the security room, "but grab a bottle from the fridge instead. And one for me if you would. It's colder."

"Got them," she said.

A moment later she joined him with the two bottles of cold water. "What are they doing?" she asked as she dropped into her chair.

"Nothing that I can see," Matt said, shaking his head. "The group downtown didn't set off the alarm. "But this new group did."

"New group?" Her stomach twisted at the words.

On the monitor, she could see another large group of people on motorcycles, slowly working their way through wrecks on the I-84 freeway, heading toward Portland from the Columbia Gorge to the east.

They were dressed basically the same as the first bunch, in leather jackets, logical riding clothes even during hot weather. But from what Carey could see, these were mostly women, and some children. Only one biker in every group of five or so bikes was a man.

A couple of women had doubled-up on bikes, and there were three or four younger kids behind a couple of the men. One bike had a small sidecar with a woman in it holding a baby in her arms. That sight stunned Carey.

She kept staring at the woman and child until they went out of sight behind a large pile of wrecked cars.

"There are more in this group than the first group," Matt said, his voice low and sounding stunned. "Families and kids."

"And one with a baby," Carey said.

Matt nodded. "I saw that. Makes the entire bunch seem a lot friendlier, doesn't it?"

Carey had to admit it did. Seeing families traveling on motorcycles felt completely different than seeing a large gang of bikers in leathers.

"Looks like they're staying in groups of four or five bikes," Matt said, "with one person with a headset in each group, and one guy per group as well. The first group that came into town ahead of this one must be setting up living quarters. These folks are traveling smart. Very smart."

Carey stared at the woman with the baby in the sidecar as they came back into sight, moving slowly under Matt's camera position. "I wonder where they're from?" Carey said.

"Or where they're heading," Matt said.

"You think we should go talk to them later on?" Carey asked.

Just saying that thought out loud scared her more than she wanted to admit, and again she had to remind herself that the reason she was back in the city was to meet other survivors.

Again, her mother's voice echoed. *Such a brave little girl.*

Matt looked up at her. "I think we should wait until they get settled and decide then."

She could tell he was worried about the same thing. Yet she knew that since these were families traveling together, if they didn't take the chance to talk to them, find out where they were heading, they would both regret it later.

Suddenly, she had a thought that scared her even more. What they might be watching right here was the future of the entire human race.

"Good idea," she said, as more bikes came into sight. "No point in rushing into something and taking any extra chances."

Matt laughed. "Yeah, like I did yesterday meeting you. And like you did coming here with me."

She laughed as well, the tension easing. "Yeah, like that."

CHAPTER TWENTY

IN ALL HIS FEARS, in all his daydreams about finding other people still alive, Matt would have never thought it would happen like this, and in the way it was happening. First, Carey walked into town, a beautiful, smart woman, by herself. Then two groups of at least sixty men, women, and children on motorcycles.

After three years of seeing almost no one, this was feeling like too much. A small part of him just wanted the calm, day-to-day existence he had been living over the last two years. But now that he had met Carey, now that he had seen this large group of humans still alive, now that Carey had told him what happened to humanity, and there was a chance that there could be a lot of people left alive out there somewhere, he knew that he could never go back to that loner kind of life. And most of him didn't want to.

Most of him.

He and Carey spent the rest of the afternoon talking and watching the second group of motorcyclists work their way slowly into town. It took them almost twice as long to go the same distance as the first bunch, which explained part of the reason why they were not all traveling together.

But there were clearly other reasons, and Matt was very impressed at the organization and thinking that had gone into moving so many people. One bunch went ahead and set up camp, scouted for food, did what was necessary to find water and decent rooms. The leaders more than likely cleared out bodies from rooms, got water working where they could, found and set up generators, and so on.

The second, larger and slower group, came along as they could, finding a place to stay mostly ready for them when they got to the next stop.

It was also safer, Carey had pointed out. The first group made an imposing sight, and if they ran into trouble with someone already living where they were heading, the first group could handle it, or find a new campsite, without endangering the children.

If Carey hadn't already been there, Matt had no doubt he would have gone down and talked to them the moment he saw the second group coming in. He really wanted to understand better what they were doing, where they were heading, and why.

But with Carey beside him, he wanted to take a few less chances. He wasn't sure what he was feeling for her besides the natural attraction of a beautiful woman after three years of being alone. He was trying to keep that off to one side as best he could.

Most of the time, he was failing, but he was trying.

Carey wasn't making it any easier. She was fun to talk to, laughed easily, and seemed to be attracted to him as well. It was clear that she too was trying to move carefully and slowly when it came to him, which meant that a few times during the afternoon the conversation had been more like a dance.

In the middle of the long afternoon, after the group had completely made its way into the city and out of his camera range, he and Carey moved to chairs at the table, drinking sun tea and talking about their pasts.

He told her that he hadn't had a girlfriend three years ago. He learned about Paine, about Paine and Carey's engagement, and about her dad and mom and what it was like growing up an only child.

He told her about his family, and how his brother was living in New York.

They even told each other about their fears, and how they had coped with being alone, thinking they were the only person left alive, and how they had managed to both survive. Carey seemed very impressed by his travels that first year, and everything he had built here. He was impressed with how she had set herself up a safe home, learned how to use guns, learned many things from books. She had converted herself from a bookish scientist to a survivor and stayed sane. That impressed him a lot.

It was a wonderful afternoon of talking and sharing, one that he would have never dreamed he could have again with a woman.

Or anyone, for that matter.

"You know," he said, glancing at his watch, "it has been over three hours since that lunch. How about I start an early dinner?"

He could see some hesitation in her eyes, as if suddenly the old habits of being polite, not imposing too much had crossed her mind. It was clear to him they needed to talk about the situation of where she was going to stay for the night, get everything out in the open.

He sat back and smiled at her. "Let me tell you how I hope things will go for the rest of the night, then you can tell me what you think."

Before she had a chance to reply, he started. "I would love to cook you a lemon-spiced chicken dinner, one I had planned just for me and Buddy originally. Fresh asparagus, corn, and bread as side dishes. Then, while there is still a lot of light, I'm thinking we might want to go say hello to the city's newest visitors. If we do it together, we won't look like a threat to them."

"Two against sixty," she said, laughing. "We're some threat."

"Good point. So, assuming all goes well with the visit with the bikers, we can come back here, have a late snack, maybe watch a movie. I have a few spare rooms back there that I have only used for light storage. We can set you up a bedroom, since it would seem a lot more logical for you to stay here, where it's cooler and cleaner."

"And don't forget safer," she said. "This alarm system of yours is heaven-sent as far as I'm concerned."

He smiled at her. "Thanks. To be honest, it would be great to have you stay. I've really missed having someone to talk to like we've been doing today."

She stared at him, a slight smile easing the corner of her mouth upward.

The silence in the room seemed to grow as they held each other's gaze. Finally, he couldn't stand it any longer.

"Okay, your turn."

"I would love to have a chicken dinner," she said, "if you allow me to help you cook it."

He nodded. "Deal."

She went on. "I'm scared to death about going down there to meet those people for a reason I'll tell you over dinner. But I think you're right, we need to. A large part of me wants to find out who they are, where they are going, and so on. I would hate myself if I didn't before they left."

"Okay, that sounds—"

She held up her hand and stopped him in mid-sentence. "I would love to come back here and watch a movie as well. But only if you have microwave popcorn."

He laughed and pointed to the pantry. He had boxes of the stuff, and luckily, that stuff didn't spoil very often with time.

"And as far as staying here for the night in a guest room, I would appreciate that as well. I'm not doing too well in this heat, and having a cool bedroom for the night would make me feel a lot more like I was home on the coast."

They stared at each other for a moment.

She was smiling at him, and he could feel he was smiling as well.

He really liked this woman. And the more time he spent with her, the more time he wanted to spend with her. It would have been that way, he was sure, even if the world was still out there beyond those big windows.

Finally, he pushed his chair back and stood. "Dinner and movie it is. And a visit to the neighbors in the middle. Sounds like a normal night to me."

She laughed and stood to help him cook. "Wonderfully normal. Just what the doctor would have ordered if he had lived."

CHAPTER TWENTY-ONE

CAREY WENT BACK to the roof and picked some asparagus sprouts for dinner while Matt cleaned and prepared the chicken. Then she got everything ready to cook the sprouts in a light oil with a little butter-salt flavoring added. It would only take a couple of minutes once the chicken was close to done.

Matt worked on skinning the chicken, then covering the four pieces in some sort of lemon herb sauce he had made. He slid the pan with the chicken into the oven.

"Thirty minutes until dinner. Potatoes next."

She peeled a couple of potatoes and got water boiling for them while he worked on a salad. While all this, they kept talking about anything that happened to come up. Gardening, cats, books they had read. To Carey, it felt wonderful.

She had never thought anything near normal was possible again. And as long as she didn't look out at the dead city too closely, she could let herself pretend they were just an ordinary, *very rich* couple in a penthouse apartment, cooking a summer dinner for themselves.

Right before everything was done, he sent her into the foyer near the elevator and told her to look in a closet there. Inside she found about fifty bottles of different Oregon wines, a couple of which were her favorites. She picked two whites, hoping that one would still be good after three years. Reds tended to last, but whites spoiled easily, depending on the length of time and how they were stored. So they might as well use the whites up first.

"You know," she said, carrying the bottles of wine back into the kitchen, "every Sunday for the past three years, no matter the weather, I've opened a bottle of wine."

"Really?" he asked, turning away from mashing the potatoes to glance at her.

"Corkscrew?" she asked.

He pointed to a drawer and she dug it out.

"Why only on Sundays?"

"It sort of marked the end of another week. And it was the only time I allowed myself to drink."

"Really, why?" He looked at her concerned.

"Don't worry," she said, "I don't think I have any problem with alcohol. I figured that the last thing I needed was to start drinking, and then have some really bad days and feel sorry for myself and drink even more. With an unlimited amount of wine and booze, it sure would be very simple to go down into that hole, make some stupid mistake while drunk, and end up dying alone."

He nodded as he filled a platter full of golden-brown chicken. She could tell he had had the same thoughts.

"After I buried my mom and dad up in Bend, I headed to a local bar I liked when I was home on vacations from college and proceeded to try to drink the entire bar's storeroom dry."

"Oh, man," she said, trying to imagine Matt drunk. "How long did that last?"

"I'm not exactly sure," Matt said. "I woke up under one of the bar stools, with a nasty hangover and hungry enough to eat a house. I haven't really had much more than a glass of wine since. As you said, too dangerous, especially when you're living alone."

She was very glad to hear that story. Both of them had learned to deal with living in the remains of the world in so many logical ways. It was good to hear that he had had trouble at the start just like she had had, and that now he didn't drink much. Both items made her like him even more than she already was, if that were possible.

The dinner turned out to be far too much food, even for two hungry people and a cat who seemed to eat anything. During dinner, she had told him about her friend getting beaten up by the bikers, and why just the sight of them had scared her so much. He agreed that made sense, but they both agreed that they still wanted to go together to meet the visitors.

"Okay, so how do we approach these people?" she asked as the last dish was put in the dishwasher and the counter wiped down. "I really don't feel right going up to them unarmed like you did to me."

Matt smiled and shook his head as he put a couple of wrapped up pieces of chicken in the fridge. "I don't either. I'm just glad you didn't shoot me."

"I'm glad I didn't shoot you as well," Carey said, smiling at him.

"I think we should just have our guns on our shoulders, and just walk up there not showing any threatening actions in any way."

Her stomach twisted. "It seems like we're taking a pretty big chance. What happens if they don't like strangers?"

"Then let's just hope they turn us away without shooting first," Matt said. "I'm betting that people who have seen as much death as we have, and they have, are not really interested in seeing more."

She nodded. "Okay, seems like a better idea than trying to sneak up on them."

"Yeah, I agree there," he said. "And with that many of them, I doubt we could."

"So, we're off to visit the new neighbors. I've only been in the city one night and I already feel like they're intruding. I can't imagine how you feel about them. Or me, for that matter."

"Glad you're here," he said. "Mixed feelings about them. I'm just happy there are people besides me still left alive."

"With that, you get no argument."

They headed out to the foyer area. Before picking up any guns, Matt opened a drawer in a small desk sitting beside the closet and pulled out a metal object. "This is a spare key to the elevator. In case we get separated for any reason, come back here."

He handed her the key as if it were something he did every day, then turned to his gun rack.

She stared at the small, round key in her hand. He was really trusting her, completely, giving her access to his home and all his security. As far as he was concerned, they were together, at least for the moment. And she liked that.

"Thank you," she said, putting the key into her front pocket and then tapping the outside of her jeans to make sure it was securely there.

He slung a thirty-thirty rifle over his shoulder and turned to smile at her. "You're more than welcome. Thank you for walking into my life. Let's just be careful now, shall we?"

"Sounds like a good idea to me," she said, putting her rifle over her shoulder. "How good a shot are you with that thing?"

"Expert with the sniper rifle," he said. "I can break a bottle on the river bank from the top of the roof here. How about you?"

"Good enough."

"That's perfect. Ready?"

"Almost," she said. "All right if I take a bottle of water with me? It's going to still be hot out there."

"Good idea," he said, "grab one for me."

When she got back into the foyer, he was standing there, holding the elevator door open for her.

"You know, in the old days, these things would start dinging in an annoying fashion when you did that," she said, getting on and handing him the bottle of water.

"I know," he said. "I hated that, so I shut off those alarms."

"You're very handy to have around," she said.

"Thanks," he said. "I hope to stay around."

She liked the sound of that a lot.

Thirty seconds later the elevator was again locked, they were across the lobby, and out into the heat of the early evening.

CHAPTER TWENTY-TWO

MATT REALIZED as they started up the hill on the hot sidewalk toward the Hilton Hotel that they had only guessed that was the area the bikers had gone to. Actually, considering how little of the city his cameras covered, they could be anywhere in a very large area.

"You know, this might take us some time to find them," Matt said.

"I don't think so." She reached out and stopped him, her hand on his bare arm, her touch soft wonderful against his skin. "Listen."

She was right. The sound of an engine running was clear, echoing down the street from above them. Then another one started.

"Sounds to me like they are right were we thought they might go," she said, taking her hand off of his arm and starting up the sidewalk again.

"It does, doesn't it," Matt said. He could still feel her touch against his skin, and for the moment that was all he could think about.

"How far do your cameras and alarms stretch in this direction?"

"Four blocks on the motion alarms," he said, "but my cameras can see five or six more blocks than that up each street."

"And the Hilton is at least fifteen blocks. Good thing there's a lot of shade this time of the day."

"You going to be all right?" Matt asked, worried about her. It had occurred to him when they were up on the roof that she couldn't be used to the heat, not after spending the last three years on the coast, where a hot summer's day reached seventy.

"If I keep drinking the water, and we go slowly, I'll be fine," she said.

They moved along in silence for the next few blocks as the hill got steeper. Carey seemed to be having some troubles with walking up the hill on what had been a busy street and sidewalk three years ago. She was getting red in the face, and breathing harder than the slight hill should cause. After she spent an extra few moments staring at one body of a woman in what looked like it might have been a blue dress, he lightly touched her arm and pulled her into a shady alcove.

"Are you all right?" he asked.

"Not really," she said, trying to smile, but failing. She leaned back against the brick wall, staring upward at the sky.

"Memories?" he asked.

She nodded. "The three or four days after everyone died, I was still here in the city."

"Oh," he said, trying to imagine how bad that had to have been. "I left fairly quickly, headed for Bend. This place must have been awful."

"Worse than I want to think about," she said, clearly trying to catch her breath. "Front Street down to the Embassy Suites didn't have this kind of traffic on it, so it didn't bother me as much this morning."

"You want to go back?" he asked.

She shook her head. "No. I've been dealing with death for three years, walking around bodies in stores and on streets. This just brought back those first few days of memories is all. The sidewalks in the area around the lab where I worked were this crowded that day."

"Makes sense this would bother you," he said.

He took the bottle of water she had in her hand, opened it, and handed it back. "Drink."

After a long, gulping drink, she seemed to be doing a little better.

When he had approached Carey, she had come across as a tough, no-nonsense woman. As he learned more about her, he was coming to understand that she was just as afraid of this new world as he was, and had just as many issues dealing with it as he did. It didn't make her weak. The fact that she had survived showed just how strong and powerful she was. But having some trouble made him feel even closer to her, and they were getting close enough as it was.

"I wonder where all those folks on bikes spent that first year?" he said, trying to take her attention from the past to the present.

"I'd like to find that out," she said.

She held his gaze for a moment, then smiled, this time a real smile. "Thanks. I'll be all right."

"Of that I have no doubt," he said.

She took one more drink, put the cap back on the bottle. She pushed herself away from the wall. "Ready to go figure out who these new people are?"

"Ready," he said. "And I'm very glad you're with me on this."

She again stared into his eyes. After a moment she reached out and touched his bare skin on his arm, sending a wonderful sensation through his body. "So am I. We seem to make a good team."

"That we do," he said, taking her hand and squeezing it lightly.

With that, they turned and kept going up the hill, walking side-by-side where they could. He liked having her beside him.

He felt stronger when she was there.

CHAPTER TWENTY-THREE

Somehow, for the rest of the walk up the hill, she managed to keep the memories of walking around the days after everyone died in the background.

Such a brave little girl.

Someday, she was going to have to really get her mom's voice out of her head. She almost laughed out loud at that thought. Fat chance of that ever happening.

She focused on Matt, on the people they were going to meet, on staying alive and working toward some type of future. She wasn't sure what that future might be just yet, but right now a future felt a lot more possible than it did yesterday morning.

That thought almost made her laugh as well. Yesterday morning, her future was exploring a dead world and dying alone. Now she was in lust, maybe in love, with a man she had just met, and was about to walk into a crowd of bikers. Life after the end of the world certainly had taken a turn toward the interesting.

And hopeful.

Matt was giving her hope, showing her things she hadn't thought of before, and making her focus forward instead of backward at that day three years ago. She liked that about him.

She liked everything about him so far. He even had a nice ass. Could a man get any more perfect?

As they climbed the hill, she tried to ignore the heat as much as she could. The heat never used to bother her so much, and she knew the only way to get used to it again was to make sure she drank enough fluids. Beyond that, the only thing she could do was just not think about it.

The sound of a motorcycle starting up echoed through the buildings as they reached the lower east side of the Hilton building. The noise sent shivers down her spine.

Her mother's voice came flooding back once more. *Such a brave little girl.*

Shut up, Mother!

"Sounds like it's coming from just a block ahead," Matt said.

She nodded in agreement, but said nothing. She really wanted to take her rifle off her shoulder and hold it, but they had decided it would be better to just approach with the guns where they were. She wasn't sure if that was a smart idea, or one that might get them both killed.

He reached out and put his hand on her shoulder. "It's going to be all right. These really aren't bikers, like the old gangs. They're just ordinary people traveling in the most efficient manner possible, considering the conditions of all the roads."

She wanted to say, "We hope." But instead she just nodded and stayed beside him.

They reached the front corner of the Hilton and turned north.

She wasn't sure what she expected to see when they found the group, but whatever her expectations had been, what greeted them was not it.

Not even close.

Instead of a street with skeletons and wrecked cars, the street had been completely cleared.

Completely.

A row of motorcycles were now parked down the middle of the pavement in a perfect row that seemed to stretch for two blocks. A couple of men on their backs were working under one that was idling.

The street, except without parked cars, looked like it had before everyone died. Someone had cleaned all the bodies off for as far as Carey could see. And moved all the cars. She had no idea why they would do that, but they had.

"Well, this is interesting," Matt said, voicing a massive understatement.

There were a couple dozen regular people walking back and forth from the front of the Hilton to the buildings across the street, not paying any attention to her or Matt. It almost looked like a normal day in the old city, as if she and Matt had suddenly gone back in time, and the city was alive again, instead of being a vast graveyard.

About fifteen people in all were in sight, doing various things. All of them had ditched their leather coats and were in tee-shirts and jeans, or light dresses. And unlike her, they all seemed comfortable in the heat.

She had to admit one thing. Without the leathers, they looked perfectly normal.

"No one is carrying a gun," Matt said softly as they kept walking toward the front of the Hilton.

Instead of a street with skeletons and wrecked cars, the street had been completely cleared.

He was right. Not even a pistol. In fact, most of the motorcycles still had the rifles sticking up from slings or saddlebags.

A young woman in a light-blue print dress was the first to see them. She stopped, smiled and came toward them, no fear at all on her face.

None.

Carey felt like she might melt into a puddle of fear, but this woman looked as cool and calm as a receptionist greeting someone at an office door.

Carey figured the woman was about her own age, with a nice body that wasn't hidden at all by the summer dress and sandals. The woman had brown hair, cut short, and a dark suntan. She also had a large wedding ring on her finger, and diamond studs in her ears.

Carey was stunned at that. It hadn't occurred to her to put on either makeup or jewelry since the world ended.

As the woman got closer she said, "Hi, I'm Betty Ferguson. Are you two from here?"

"We are," Matt said, shaking the woman's extended hand. "I'm Matt Landel, this is Carey Noack."

Carey shook the woman's strong hand, but said nothing. Carey instantly liked this woman, and her forward nature, even though it wasn't the reaction she expected to have. She had come up here not wanting to like any of these people.

Matt couldn't seem to stop staring at Betty, acting like he had seen her before, or was stunned at her attitude, or something. Carey didn't know what to think of that reaction either. Was she going to lose the first man she had met in three years after just a day?

"Nice meeting you both," Betty said, giving them a smile that could stop any thoughts of problems. "We were wondering if we were going to meet some of the people already living in this area. You have time to talk?"

Matt glanced at Carey, then he laughed. "That's what we were hoping to do."

"Great," Betty said. "Come on. I think it's a little cooler inside. Dan and some of the others are going to want to meet you."

"Dan?" Carey asked as they headed toward the big front doors of the Hilton Hotel.

"Lieutenant Colonel Dan Houghton," Betty said. "He's sort of our reluctant leader at the moment, reluctant being the main word."

Betty held the door for them as they went inside.

Again Carey was surprised at how this group had, in a very short time, cleaned up the lobby. There wasn't a body to be seen, the floors had been swept, and the furniture dusted. If the large overhead lights had been on, the lobby would have looked like a normal day. Instead it was being lit by a series of lanterns set around the big space.

There were two men behind the front desk working on something under the counter. Both wore tee shirts, and one had a baseball cap on backwards to keep the bill out of his way.

"Hey, Steve, have you seen Dan?" Betty asked them as she got closer.

Both men looked up and stared for a moment at Matt and Carey. Then they both smiled.

"Local residents?" the man with the cap asked, then smiled again at Carey.

Carey caught her breath as the man's gaze held her. He was handsome in a rugged way, with a smile that showed perfect teeth, and green eyes that glowed, even in the lantern light. She was betting his name was Steve.

"Someone looking for me," a voice said from off to the left.

Carey and Matt turned to see a man in his fifties, with striking gray hair, walking toward them. He had the look of military, even though he was dressed in jeans and a casual shirt with the sleeves rolled up.

"Some of the local population has come calling," Betty said.

Carey wanted to say the only local population, but she didn't.

Matt stepped forward and introduced himself, then Carey. Carey shook the man's hand. She had hoped to meet new people coming into town, just not so many on the first day. After three years of being alone and talking only to her cats, this was getting overwhelming very quickly.

The man Betty called Dan seemed more like a father figure, or English professor, than a leader. He had a quick laugh, a smile that disarmed, and a deep voice. The most striking thing about him was his chiseled jaw, almost stronger than Kirk Douglas's jaw line.

Dan showed them back toward one of the ballrooms, where the smell of cooking dinner filled the air. They had cleaned out this big room as well, and the tables were in rows, with chairs in position. Clearly this was where they intended to have the group meals.

There was something about these people doing so much work to clean up this area that bothered Carey. If they were just traveling through, none of this would have needed to be done, or at least not to this extent. This group, as far as she could tell, was acting like they were planning on staying for a while.

She wasn't sure how she felt about that.

Dan took a chair across from Carey and Matt. Betty joined them, along with the two men from behind the front desk, and two others. Dan introduced them all, but Carey missed their names completely. She had never been that good with names back in college, and now she wasn't even going to try.

Matt seemed a little surprised by all this as well. He made sure he sat close to her, his leg touching hers under the table.

"Well, sir," Matt said, starting off the conversation as everyone was getting settled. "You folks sure gave us a start coming into town like that today."

Dan laughed. "I bet we did. We scared a group so bad in Boise that they almost opened fire on us before we could convince them we were friendly."

"It's the motorcycles," Betty said. "It would scare me seeing a group like us coming."

Carey thought she might like Betty, now she was certain.

"So two big questions," Matt said, clearly wanting to direct the conversation at the moment. "Where are you coming from, and where are you heading?"

Dan glanced around. "Well, I'd say a large part of this group is from the Area 51 underground testing complex in Nevada, but Steve here, and a couple others, are from Colorado."

Then Dan faced Matt directly. "As for where we are headed, we're there."

Carey took a moment to realize what Dan had said. "Your destination is Portland? Why?" The idea of all these people staying here not only scared her to death, but excited her at the same time.

Dan sort of leaned back. "Let me tell you a story, if you don't mind, that might answer a bunch of these questions before I confuse the issue any more."

"Fire away, sir," Matt said.

"No sir, please?" he asked. "Just Dan."

Matt nodded. "Tell us a story, Dan. After what you said, I think Carey and I are all ears, so to speak."

Dan laughed, and then with a nod to Carey, started into his story.

CHAPTER TWENTY-FOUR

CAREY SAT and listened intently as Dan spoke, making herself breathe slowly and drink regularly. The last thing she needed to do was pass out from the heat or dehydration in the middle of his story. That would be rude, to say the least.

"Three years ago today many of us here," Dan said, "and about three hundred others still back in Nevada, were working the regular day shift in the underground testing areas in the base the press liked to call Area 51. Slowly, as the day went on, we came to realize something had gone very wrong on the surface. The few people that were up there had died, suddenly and without visible reason."

"How long did it take you to realize it was all caused by an electromagnetic pulse from space?" Carey asked, deciding to give the man something to think about right at the start of his story. She figured if that didn't knock him for a loop, nothing would.

Dan and the others stared at her like they were suddenly talking to an alien.

You could have heard a pin drop across the large ballroom.

Then Dan laughed and broke the tension. "Actually, about a week, and it was the people in Colorado who figured out what exactly had happened. And remind me later to ask you how you knew."

Carey smiled at Dan and nodded. She had figured it was a good idea to let him know that she and Matt might be of use, just in case he had other ideas for them. Even though there was no sign of any problems from these people, the lack of trust was still there on her side, and so far she had seen nothing that major to change that feeling.

Matt touched her arm, a sort of signal that she had done just fine with her question. He let his touch linger for a moment, then pulled away. She wished he had left his hand there.

Dan went on with his story. "The base went into a heightened state of alert, thinking that the deaths were some sort of attack from some enemy. It wasn't until days later that we actually discovered it wasn't an attack on the United States, as the scope of the entire disaster was coming in from underground bases around the world."

"And from subs and big battleships and aircraft carriers," Steve added. "On the big carriers, everyone who was above the second deck or near an open port died. But the metal of the ships protected everyone down below. Those survivors had a real mess on their hands, because in one instance, everyone who knew how to navigate had died."

"That would mean that thousands and thousands have survived around the world," Matt said, his voice full of shock at the idea.

Carey was just as stunned. She had figured there might have been a lot, but after three years of seeing almost no one, that thought had faded to a distant dream.

"That's right," Dan said. "The electromagnetic pulse of the cloud that passed over the planet was just strong enough to short circuit the brains of everyone exposed, but not strong enough to penetrate too far underground, or through a certain thickness of metal. There are some guesses that up to a million people around the world survived. Maybe more, considering how many people could be in subway cars or subway stations at the same time around the world."

"A million?" Carey asked, her voice a whisper.

"Amazing, isn't it?" Steve asked, stating the obvious.

"The problem is," Dan said, "the million are scattered everywhere over the globe, sometimes only one or two people in a large area."

Carey could vouch for that, but neither she nor Matt said anything.

"Everyone lost family, husbands, wives, parents," Dan said. "The shock was almost too much to allow any kind of order in any group to be maintained. For some people the loss just drove them completely crazy."

"I hear a large 'but' coming next," Carey said. "It's the *buts* that will get you in any story."

Dan laughed, the sound echoing in the big banquet room. "You're right. *But* after a while, people wanted to be with other people, and the groups started coming back together around the world, especially those in the military. Some of us had maintained a sort of order on the bases, not knowing what else to do.

Slowly, survivors started coming back. We also had one big advantage. We had kept the power running which allowed the communication systems to function around the world."

"Makes sense," Carey said. After three years she had gone in search of other people as well, which had brought her to today, a day she would have never dared dream might happen.

"A lot of very good minds around the world survived the disaster," Dan said. "And those minds started working together to figure out how to best keep humanity alive without dropping back completely into the dark ages."

"At a million," Carey said, "the human race will survive. No doubt there, but you're saying you wanted to help civilization do the same thing."

"Exactly," Dan said.

So far she was following everything Dan was saying, and was liking what she was hearing.

So far.

Dan went on. "This group of scientists and planners figured that the best way to keep humanity alive and growing, and to hold somewhere close to the current level of technology, was to have as many people as possible gather in central places around the world, form towns and cities, salvage what could be salvaged, and focus on the future and education."

Matt laughed. "So let me guess, these people planning this went back to the basics on picking these central places, just as the pioneers did. The places had to have good natural resources like water and building materials, good growing seasons, mild climates, and so on. Everything Portland has."

"Exactly," Dan said, smiling at him. "Five spots in this country were picked.

One area outside of Washington, D.C., for all the people who survived in the eastern corridor, one in northern Florida, another on the Mississippi River in the center of the country, a small town north of San Diego in California, and Portland."

"How many places around the world?" Carey asked, stunned at the scope of the plan she was hearing.

"Fifty-one at present count."

"Fifty-one," she said, softly, shaking her head. She couldn't even imagine that.

"And each place will be in contact with the others?" Matt asked.

"They will," Dan said, smiling at them. "Gathering places for mankind to rebuild, save what we can, and move on into the future."

Carey could feel the weight of being alone the last three years lifting off her shoulders. The death of Paine, her parents, everyone, had forced her into a way of thinking that had no hope, nothing but sameness, survival, and finally death alone. She had come into the city today hoping that wasn't the case, but knowing deep inside that it had to be.

Now this man was sitting her, telling her there was hope, there was a possible future, and that she could be a part of it. The relief was almost too much.

She took a deep, shuddering breath, and stared at her hands, trying to gain some sort of control.

Get it together, Carey.

Such a brave little girl.

Shut up, Mother.

Betty, who had sat down beside her, leaned over and put a hand on Carey's shoulder, patting it for a moment before letting go.

"Let me tell you what's going to happen next here in Portland," Dan said, ignoring the fact that she was having a moment of trouble. "Two more groups are coming in on bikes tomorrow. Those of us here already are going to spend the next day getting an area of the city ready for them, bringing in supplies, cleaning rooms, working on the water systems, setting up generators. We hope to have this two square block area livable in very short order."

"Then what?" Matt asked.

"We clear a two-way road from here to the airport," Dan said, "while continuing to clean up larger and larger areas of the city. Luckily, the bridges are still all in good shape, so no problem there. We just have to move all the wrecks."

"What are you doing with all the bodies you have to move?" Carey asked, looking up at Dan. She could just imagine these people taking a bulldozer and scraping the bodies into piles and burning them.

"We're giving every body the respect it deserves," Dan said, holding her gaze. "We're bagging each one and storing the bodies at the moment, including all the ones we took from this building, the street and sidewalks, and the buildings across the way. When we find the right area, and have the time, we will build a graveyard. We're leaving all the identification with each body, and where each body was found, so each grave can be marked as much as possible."

"That's a massive undertaking," Matt said. "I'm impressed."

"It was agreed by everyone in charge around the world that respect for the dead

She took a shuddering breath and stared at her hands, trying to gain some sort of control.

would be part of the system. The people that died deserve all the respect we can give them."

"I agree," Matt said, "but why go to that much work?"

Dan shrugged. "About all I can say is that it's the right thing to do, and a hundred years from now, our descendants will be glad we did what we are doing. There is already a central database set up in Colorado that will track where each person is buried when that starts happening."

"Everything looking to the future," Carey said, completely amazed that something like that would even be thought of, considering the magnitude of the task.

"Everything," Dan said. "At this point, the future is all we have."

"What happens at the airport?" Matt asked.

"Once we get it secure and working again," Steve said, taking over a moment from Dan, since it was clearly his area, "the rest of the people who choose Portland will start being flown in from Nevada, Colorado, and other areas. After that the airport will be used for what airports are used for now; transportation, shipping, and communications."

Carey nodded. Having contact among the major areas of settlement around the country and the world would be critical over the years.

"How many do you think will pick this city to start with?" Matt asked.

Dan shrugged. "We should have a population here, by the end of the year, of almost twenty thousand."

147

"Twenty thousand?" both Carey and Matt said at the same time.

The number sort of echoed around the room.

Carey couldn't even imagine that many people. Her mind just sort of stopped as she tried to grasp it and failed.

"And that should grow as more people who are on their own around the continent discover the five areas and move closer."

"Not everyone is going to join this idea, move into a city," Matt said.

"Of course," Dan said, nodding. "We expect there to be smaller groups living all over the country, but the five cities picked will be the hubs of this country in a very short time, since they are where all the manufacturing and food production will be happening. Mankind can only scavenge from the bones of what is left for so long."

"I agree," Carey said.

Beside her Matt was nodding as well.

"So, now tell me," Dan said, staring at Carey and smiling, "if you don't mind, how you knew what happened three years ago today."

Carey laughed. "I don't mind at all."

For the second time that day she told her story of working for Dr. Canfield, who Dan, Steve, and Betty had all heard of. She told about the experiment, about how she survived, and about how a few days later she went back to the lab to find out what had happened, before heading to the coast to get away from all the death. She did not tell them where the lab was, however.

"Well," Dan said after she was finished, "What about you, Matt?"

Matt quickly told them what he had done before, and his background, being far too modest as far as Carey was concerned, but she didn't say anything. He also left out where he had been living.

"I sure hope the two of you will join our cause," Dan said. "We can use both of your skills, that's for sure. It's all volunteer, there is no pay besides food, since at the moment there is no money system in place. The work is hard and thankless at times, as I'm sure everyone here will tell you."

Across from Carey, Steve nodded.

"That's an understatement," Betty said.

Dan went on. "But at least, in my opinion, the long-term cause is right, and worth the effort."

"Thank you for the offer," Carey said, standing and offering Dan her hand. "I just need a little time to think about things first. This morning I was convinced I was one of only a few people left alive on the planet. All of this is going to take a little time to digest, if you know what I mean."

Dan nodded, his firm grip around her hand. "I do understand. This is a large planet and there are very few of us left in comparison to the numbers from three years ago. Many people will decide to go their own way, and that is fine. There is more than enough room for everyone, and certainly no housing shortage. Your choice is valid, no matter which one you make."

"You sure know how to say all the right things to a woman," Carey said, smiling at the man in front of her.

"I was married for twenty-three years," he said, laughing. "I should have learned, don't you think?"

CHAPTER TWENTY-FIVE

THE SUN was a distance below the hills to the west, and only the top of Mt.

Hood was still in the bright light as they rounded the corner of the Hilton Hotel and started back down the street.

The shadows of the buildings were deep, and so far there was no sign of a moon. Matt hadn't thought to bring a flashlight with them. They were going to have to be careful getting back. It was lucky they left when they did. Another fifteen minutes and they'd be walking the entire distance in the pitch darkness.

For the first two blocks down the hill, they walked side-by-side, not talking.

Matt was going over what he had heard, how good it sounded, and yet how impossible it was to believe. From Carey's reaction in the middle of Dan's explanation, she was feeling huge relief that people were doing what they were doing. But she was also having doubts, he could tell.

If everything Dan had said was the truth, Matt felt the same relief that Carey had shown. But he wanted to wait, to make sure before offering to help turn Portland back into a city again. He had to admit this group looked good, and sounded good, but were they really what they claimed to be? A day or two would tell the difference on that. And he had a day or two to spare at this point.

"We need to be careful," Carey said, as they crossed the street two blocks below the Hilton.

"We'll go slow," Matt said. "Our eyes will adjust to the dim light and we'll make it before it gets too dark."

"No, I mean we need to be careful to make sure no one is following us," she said, glancing over her shoulder.

"So you're feeling like I am?" Matt asked, a little surprised at her statement. "We need to find out if this group is really doing what they say they are going to do, and if they are who they say they are, before we even get near them again."

"Exactly," she said. "We need to be careful about everything at the moment. I liked them, but not enough to just trust them with my life."

"I agree," Matt said. "And it just so happens I have something set up that might come in handy tonight. And give them a little test in the process."

He reached out and took her by the hand. He pulled her into the street, turning right at the corner, and leading them up the empty pavement. He loved the feel of her hand in his, and she certainly didn't complain.

"What are you talking about?" she asked.

He pointed up at the hill in front of them. Even in the growing dark, it was possible to see the homes perched up there, expensive in the days when a view really mattered. "I set up a generator and a locked house on the hill up there."

"Okay," she said, her voice low enough to not carry. "Why? I'm not following you."

"A decoy," he said, also keeping his voice low. "Two blocks up this direction there is a large office complex that if we were heading up to the house on the hill on foot, we would naturally cut through. We'll start into that building, double back through a place I know we can't be followed, and then a few minutes later I'll light up the house."

"So if someone is following us, they'll think we went up there."

"Exactly," Matt said. "And we can see the area around it from the top of my building. And I have cameras and alarms rigged there as well."

She squeezed his hand and didn't let go. "Have I told you, in the short time

I have known you, that I like how you think."

He laughed, leading them around a wreck. "You mean devious?"

"And careful," she said.

"That I am," he said.

He led her toward the office complex. A few minutes later they ducked inside the dark building and instead of going on through to the next street, they moved to the right down a narrow hallway that he had kept swept clear of dust to cut down on footprints.

Finally, going slowly in the pitch darkness of the hall, they got to a back door and went quietly out into the night. On a ledge there he picked up a remote control that would start the generator up in the house.

"Okay, now we be very quiet," he whispered, moving through the back alley and down the hill toward the street, keeping her hand in his. He had scouted this out, making sure there was nothing that he could trip on in the dark, and since it was getting very dark right now, he was glad he had.

At the edge of the building he stopped, keeping the two of them against the wall, not willing to go out into the open again just yet.

"How long?" she whispered.

"It always took me about five minutes to climb the distance from this office complex to that house. I figure one more minute."

She squeezed his hand showing she understood.

He waited what he thought was long enough, then flicked the switch. From above the edge of the alley a glow lit the night, casting faint shadows on the buildings across the street.

"Drapes are pulled and everything,"

he whispered to her. "They won't know we're not in there."

He let go of her hand and eased out a little, checking the street in both directions for any movement.

There was no one that he could see.

"Ready?" he asked in a whisper.

She nodded and reached out and again took his hand. "Ready."

It took them a long thirty minutes to make it through the wrecks and back into his building, but by the time they got there, he was sure no one had followed them.

He wasn't sure anyone would have wanted to, but he felt a lot better being certain.

CHAPTER TWENTY-SIX

CAREY LET Matt lead her back into his dark apartment. She could just imagine that in the old days, the city would have lit up everything for as far as she could see from the penthouse, but now there was nothing but the outlines of buildings, deep shadows, and the faint pink of the last of the sunset on the top of Mt. Hood.

The coolness of the apartment felt wonderful against her face and arms after the muggy heat of the evening air outside. Just for the air-conditioning alone she was lucky Matt had found her. Not counting the fact that she doubted she would have worked up the courage to go talk to a bunch of bikers alone. More than likely, she would have seen them coming from a distance and just turned and headed back to the coast.

She had almost done just that. It might have been years before anyone found her, or before she might have tried to come back.

Matt was someone special. She had known that from the moment she had first seen him. And her attraction and respect for him had grown with every passing hour. He had treated her as an equal, while at the same time worrying about her, and giving her the use of his apartment for safety.

And as a team, they had gone to the group that came into town. She liked the feel of being beside him, working as a team. She hoped that would continue for much longer than one day.

She slid her rifle off her shoulder as Matt made sure the elevator was locked. "If you need to go down," he said, "use the key I gave you." He pointed to a spot over the top of the call button. "It fits in right here."

"Thanks," she said. "But I'm not going anywhere, except to the bathroom. I want to wash some of the sweat off my face and arms."

"I don't blame you," he said. "I'll take a turn after you. But we're going to have to keep the lights off for the moment," he said. "Can you find the bathroom down the hall in the dark? After the door is closed you can click on the light."

"I can find it," she said, gently touching his arm as he came up to her.

"I'm going to check to see if anyone followed us here, or up to the decoy house," he said, taking her hand and holding it for a moment.

Then he let go and set off through the shadows of the apartment toward the faint light coming from the electronics room, leaving her alone in the semi-darkness.

She let the feeling of his touch linger for a moment longer, then managed to get down the hall to the bathroom. Less than

five minutes later, she made her way back through the apartment to the security room without kicking any furniture, or banging her toe on any corner.

Buddy sat in the door of the security room, the faint light from the monitor framing him like an Egyptian god.

"You waiting for me, Buddy?" she asked, bending down and extending her hand in an offer to pet him. "Or guarding the room?"

Buddy leaned forward into her palm, letting her scratch his ears, telling her clearly that he had been waiting for her to come and do her duty in worshipping him.

"You really are a cat person, aren't you?" Matt said, turning around in his chair to watch her and his cat.

"I am," she said, "and I miss mine. I'm glad Buddy is giving me a little cat fix."

Matt laughed, clearly in a good mood. What he had seen on the screen had encouraged him, that was for sure.

"No one followed us?" she asked.

"Not a sign of anyone," he said. "I don't think any of those people have moved out of that two-block area since they got into town. A deer set off one of my motion sensors off of I-5 an hour ago, but that's about it. With this system, I could never tell there were so many people in town."

She sat on the floor in the doorway so that she could keep petting Buddy. Then she stared up at the monitor and all the green lights on Matt's security map and tried to make some sense out of all this.

"Okay, if I remember right, there's a grocery store close to the Hilton," she said.

"There is," Matt said.

"So with that, and both hotel kitchens, and the nearby restaurants, there would be enough supplies left in those storage rooms to feed those people for a long time. Am I right?"

"You are," Matt said. "And from the smell that was coming from that kitchen off the ballroom, the group probably brought in their own supplies as well, maybe from game they shot along the way."

She nodded. That group didn't need to go anywhere for food, at least for the night.

"They just ignored us after we left," Matt said. "I don't think I could have done that in their position."

"Then it's clear they weren't real worried about the two of us," Carey said. "Why?"

In the light from the monitor she could see Matt shake his head. "I honestly don't know. I'm slowly starting to believe they are doing what they say they are doing. But even that makes no sense. They are in a new place, yet I didn't see any guards as we approached, or left. Did you?"

"Not a one," she said. "And no one had a gun. They didn't feel it was a priority, even though we carried guns walking into the middle of them."

"Which can only mean they are very secure that there are no dangerous groups of people in this area," Matt said. "How would they know that? My security systems would have seen any advanced scouts they sent into the city, and there just hasn't been any."

Suddenly, it dawned on Carey how those new people would know she and Matt were no danger. After three years, she had already forgotten what century they were living in.

"Satellites," she said, laughing. "I bet they know where every person in this entire area lives. If you had the kind of

resources they claim they do, and were planning on moving twenty thousand people into an area, wouldn't you scout everything out first?"

"Of course," he said, shaking his head and laughing. "And most of the spy and weather satellites would be working just fine after three years." He laughed. "It seems our thinking has gone backwards in three years."

"That it has," she said. "It felt odd today even thinking about electromagnetics again. Three years ago that was just about all I thought about."

He reached over and picked up the radio-controlled remote. "No point in keeping the lights on in the decoy house. I have a garden on the roof here. They know exactly where I live, and more than likely, what vegetables we had for dinner."

Carey laughed. "No wonder they weren't surprised when we showed up. They probably got word we were on the way."

"And they sure didn't need to follow us home on the ground tonight," Matt said.

"I'm starting to think these people are the real thing," Carey said. "Their story sure sounds logical on the surface. And they are being very consistent with the story."

"And three years is about the right amount of time that it would take for everything to fall apart, then groups to get back together and start working on something like this."

"True," she said, giving Buddy a good scratching under his chin. His purring was filling the room. "And as you said, Portland is a logical place to start over because of the resources here."

"So what do we do now?" Matt asked, sitting in his chair watching her pet his cat.

She smiled at him, noticing how handsome he was even in the dim light. "How about that movie you promised me. And the popcorn. We can talk about the rest of this tomorrow."

"Perfect idea," he said. "But you're going to have to help me pick out a movie."

"Something classic and pure escapism," she said, pushing herself to her feet slowly. The long day was starting to catch up with her. She could feel the exhaustion creeping into her mind. It was hard to fathom how much had happened today, yet she didn't want the day to end just yet.

"All right," he said. "Popcorn is in the pantry. I'll get the movie if you get the popcorn started."

"Deal," she said. Again he was treating her like a partner and she liked that. She liked that a lot, actually.

"I'll reset the alarms here on the security system, just in case anything comes into the area," he said. "But I have to warn you, my nighttime alarms are louder than the day ones."

"Oh, joy," she said.

He laughed as she moved back into the darkened living room area. A moment later he flipped on the lights.

"Wow, those are bright," she said, shading her eyes as she smiled at him.

"They will dim for the movie," he said, "I promise." He went past her toward the elevator foyer.

"You're not going outside to get a movie, are you?" Carey asked from the kitchen area as he reached the elevator and unlocked it.

"Nope, just down a floor," he said. "I have two rooms downstairs full of movies."

"On the same floor as your second garden?" she asked, smiling at him.

"Just across the hall," he said, as he got onto the elevator and the door closed.

She went over to where her backpack leaned against the wall and kicked off her shoes. Then she took her socks off and stuck them into a pocket of the backpack. Her feet had been hot all day. She would apologize to Matt if they smelled, but she needed to get out of those shoes.

The tile floor of the kitchen area felt wonderful on her bare feet as she got two packets of microwave popcorn out of the pantry and started one.

Then she stood and looked around. With the lights on inside and the windows and city around them dark, she got a much better feel of the immense size of this place. Yet even with the size, it was still comfortable.

The apartment was clearly Matt's, yet she felt at home here, as if she had lived here at one point. She had never been in another person's apartment where she felt this good, this at home. Even Paine's apartment in Eugene was always just Paine's apartment, and when she stayed there with him she had always been the guest. And Paine had said he felt the same way about her place. When they got married they had planned on finding a new home and furnishing it together, to try to make it their place.

But Matt's apartment was another matter, and she couldn't put her finger on exactly what it was, other than Matt himself. She just felt safe and comfortable with him, and he made her feel completely welcome in his home in his every move.

The first bag of popcorn had just finished when the elevator door opened and Matt came out carrying a movie. He locked up the elevator again as she put in the second bag.

"I love the smell of that stuff," he said, flipping the DVD onto the counter in front of her.

She picked it up and then smiled at him, not believing that he had picked one of her favorite old movies. Audrey Hepburn, Gregory Peck, Eddie Albert, in *Roman Holiday*. A movie about two people meeting and escaping from their real lives to fall in love. She loved this old movie and, almost as much, the modern remake called *Notting Hill* staring Hugh Grant and Julia Roberts.

"That all right?" he asked, grabbing a bottle of pop and opening it, smelling to make sure it hadn't spoiled over the years. "You did say escapism and classic remember?"

She laughed. "It's one of my favorite movies. I could watch it over and over. And have. And would love to do so again tonight."

"It's one of my favorites as well," he said, starting toward the living area with two glasses of pop. "Bring the movie and the popcorn."

She did as she was told, putting the popcorn on the coffee table in front of the couch, right beside where he had put the two glasses. He took the movie and indicated she should get comfortable on the couch.

The sofa was as soft and inviting as it looked, and she sank into it with a sigh.

"It's been an amazing day, hasn't it?" he said as he put the movie into the player and then moved to dim the lights.

"It has," she said, watching him come toward her. "Thank you."

"For what?" he asked, sitting on the couch beside her and picking up the remote.

"For everything," she said, not really knowing what to say or how to say it. "For

trusting me, inviting me into your home, giving me a chance to see there might be a possible future for all of us left."

"After three years alone," he said, turning to look into her eyes, "I'm finding it hard to grasp that I might not have to be alone any more. Aren't you?"

She laughed. "I'm having a hard time grasping I've met you, let alone that there might be hundreds of thousands of people left alive out there."

"Yeah, me too," he said.

He picked up his bag of popcorn, sat back on the couch, and started the machine. "Then let's watch a movie and give all this time to sink in."

"I love the idea," she said, taking her bag of popcorn and settling back beside him.

She was sitting on a couch, watching a movie, with a man she hadn't even known yesterday morning, let alone believed existed. Yet she felt completely comfortable with him, and very attracted to him. Just having him beside her felt right.

By the time a quarter of the movie was over she had put her popcorn aside and was leaning against his strong shoulder.

Sometime before the middle of the film she could no longer keep her eyes open.

The next thing she knew, Matt was moving her, stretching her out on the wonderfully comfortable couch, putting a pillow under her head and a soft blanket over her.

"If you need something," he whispered to her, brushing her hair off her forehead gently, "you let me know."

She was so tired, all she could do was sigh and nod under his soft touch. What she really wanted was for him to fall asleep beside her, holding her.

But she didn't even have enough energy to ask.

CHAPTER TWENTY-SEVEN

MATT WASN'T sure who fell asleep first. All he remembered was that he woke up and the sleep mode on the DVD was floating a logo around his screen like an old pong game. The room was silent, the air almost chilly.

Carey was curled up against him, her breathing regular, her head against his arm. He had been sleeping with his head on hers, leaning toward her, the two of them holding each other up. Her hair was soft and smelled of raspberry shampoo. He pulled away slowly, making sure to not pull any of her long brown hair.

She was as beautiful in sleep as awake. Her face was peaceful, her light skin smooth. He studied the lines around her eyes, her eyebrows, her soft lips, her faint freckles, trying to memorize every detail. Her mouth was slightly open, and the feel of her soft breath was wonderful against his neck and face.

He wanted to take her in his arms and hug her, but he refrained. The last thing he needed to do was scare her. They had only been together a short time, and considering everything they had both been through over the past three years, falling asleep together was a great trust on both their parts.

He eased himself away from her, leaving her sitting for a moment with her head on the back of the couch, breathing softly. Then he clicked off the television and went for a blanket and pillow.

He got the pillow in position on one end of the couch, then gently eased her head down, covered her, and brushed the hair from her face, enjoying the touch of her smooth skin against his fingers. She was so beautiful, all he wanted to do was kiss her and crawl in beside her and hold her. But it wasn't the right time, and he knew it.

She awoke a little, but didn't object to being stretched out on the couch. She was asleep again before he walked away.

He turned off the dimmed lights in the main area, leaving on only the hall light so she could see where she was when she awoke, and could find the bathroom again. He had planned on making up a place for her to sleep in one of the spare rooms, but for the moment, the couch would work just fine. Over the last two years, he had spent many a night on it, and he knew it was comfortable.

He barely made it to his own bedroom, got his clothes off, and crawled in before he was back asleep as well.

The next thing, he knew the sun was lighting up the city outside his large bedroom window, and his security alarm was going off, the loud beeping more annoying than any alarm clock could ever be.

As always, it took him a moment to realize what it was.

"Damn deer," he said to himself. He crawled out of bed, nude and headed for the door. He got a half a step into the hallway before he remembered he had a guest.

Carey!

His world had changed, and changed drastically. And more than likely this alarm wasn't a deer, but more of the group coming into town.

He had not been jolted so awake, so fast, in a long time.

It took him a long few seconds before he could pull on a pair of exercise shorts and a sweatshirt and get out of his room again.

The couch in the living room was empty, the blanket folded under the pillow on the coffee table. A glass of orange drink sat half-full on the counter top.

Carey must have already been up when the alarm sounded. Her backpack and rifle were still against the wall near the elevator, so she hadn't left. That realization made him feel even better. He didn't want her to leave.

He headed for the security room. Carey was in there, shaking her head at the monitor, sitting on the chair they had moved there for her yesterday. Her hair was wet and she had on clean clothes.

"Morning. What's happening?" he asked, dropping into his chair and trying to make sense of the images on the monitor.

"Sorry, I couldn't figure out how to turn off the alarm," Carey said over the noise. She smiled at him, sort of a fond grin. He realized he must look a mess. Most of the time he awoke in the morning with his hair going in all directions and he had no doubt this morning would not be an exception.

"Right here," he said, punching off the alarm and then running a hand through his hair to try to smooth some of it down. He was going to need a shower as well.

The alarm that had been triggered was on the Chambers Street exit off of I-405. A dozen people were working their way along the wrecks blocking that exit and off ramp, and along the area on the freeway below the exit. They were opening the car doors and putting the bodies, clothes, purses, and all, in black garbage bags. They even emptied the glove boxes of the cars into the bags and checked the trunks.

Matt stared in shock. They were doing as they had told them they would do. The bodies were being treated carefully, and the bags, once sealed, were put in certain areas beside the road.

Up at the top of the exit, where they were clearly done with the body removals from the cars, a large bulldozer was shoving the wrecks to one side, clearing the street. Matt remembered that same bulldozer being down on a construction sight about four blocks east of the Hilton. These people had people who knew how to operate heavy equipment, and get it started again after three years. They had come prepared, that was for sure.

Three others were loading the body bags into a pickup truck. Another pickup quickly took over as the first left with its load and disappeared out of the camera range.

"They're starting on the road clearing to the airport," Carey said. "It sure seems that what they were telling us was the truth."

Matt just stared, nodding. "It does seem that way, doesn't it?"

They sat and watched. Matt didn't know what to think, other than he had to use the bathroom and take a shower.

He turned to Carey. "Nothing we can do now but watch and think about our choices. But first I need a shower, then some breakfast. I have more eggs and all that stuff. You up for that omelet I offered a few days back?"

"I'd love one," she said. "You take your shower, I'll get out the supplies for breakfast and get started."

"Good idea," he said. They stood and headed for the kitchen.

"You sleep all right?" he asked, stopping in the hallway and watching as she opened the refrigerator door. "I'm sorry we didn't get a bedroom set up for you."

"The couch was great," she said, pulling out some eggs and placing them on the counter. "If I had one that comfortable in my place, I'd never get off of it."

"I know that feeling," Matt said. "I spent many a night on that thing, too tired to even bother to get up and go to bed."

"Climbing poles putting up cameras will do that to you," she said, laughing. "Now go get that shower before we both starve to death."

He smiled at her, then turned and headed down the hall, the sounds of another person in his kitchen the most wonderful noises he had heard in over three years.

CHAPTER TWENTY-EIGHT

WAKING UP on Matt's couch had been a shock.

The sun was bright in part of the room, flooding the entire main area with more light that she thought possible in a room. It had taken her a moment of squinting to remember exactly where she was.

She had climbed off the couch and looked around, checking out everything, including her backpack, making sure it was still where she had left it. She didn't expect it to be moved, but after living alone for so long, she found it hard to trust anyone. Even Matt, no matter how much she was attracted to him.

The apartment was quiet, the sun already high in the east over Mt. Hood. She stood, staring at the fantastic view for a moment, then turned and headed quietly down the hall. The first bedroom was Matt's and she glanced in at him through the open door, feeling a little like a peeping tom as she did so.

He was breathing evenly, not really snoring as he lay on his side. He had one bare leg thrust out from under the blanket. She stared at his bare skin, wanting to touch it.

There was something about this guy that hit her buttons. More than just about anything, she wanted to be in his arms right at that moment.

Or maybe that was just anyone's arms.

Snap out of it, Carey.

Three years was a long time to go without other human contact. She wasn't sure yet if it was Matt she wanted, or just the companionship. Better she have a very clear answer on that before she moved any farther with him.

Buddy lay on the corner of the bed. The cat looked up at her, its eyes half-closed, then laid its head back down and went back to sleep.

Damn she missed her cats. Both of them slept with her as well every night. She was going to have to get back to the coast soon and see how they were doing.

She stood there in his door, silently staring at him, studying the lines on his face, the messed up hair, how he held his mouth. She really was attracted to him, more than she remembered being attracted to Sam.

Far more.

She wondered what he would do if she took her clothes off and just crawled in beside him. More than likely he would welcome her. But it didn't seem right, no matter how much she wanted to.

Actually, it seemed very right, just not yet.

Finally, she forced herself to move on into the bathroom, picking up a fresh change of clothes from the dryer as she went.

She took a long, hot shower, letting the water drain the tiredness and worry from her muscles. Then she put on clean clothes and headed back for the kitchen, glancing in at Matt as she went past.

He was now laying on his back, his mouth open, snoring softly.

She could sleep with that level of snoring.

She shook her head, surprised at the thought. Everything seemed so normal with him there sleeping like that.

Again, she considered crawling in with him, then forced herself to move away.

Go slowly. You've only known him for two days.

It seemed so much longer.

She went back into the kitchen and made herself a fruit drink. She was sitting at the counter, staring out at the city when the security alarm went off. It sounded like a cross between a really loud buzzer on an alarm clock, and the siren of a cop car. The apartment had been so silent, the sudden noise startled her, making her heart pound as she looked around trying to figure out what it was.

"Security alarm, dummy," she said as she headed across the apartment.

"Damn deer," she heard Matt say from down the hall as she got to the security room where the alarm was coming from.

The moment she got inside the security room, she knew it wasn't deer, that much was for sure.

She dropped into her chair, searching for any obvious buttons or switches that would shut off the loud alarm. She couldn't see anything, and after a moment figured it was just better to not touch anything. Matt was going to want to see this.

He came in a moment later and dropped into his chair. He had on shorts and a baggy sweatshirt that looked like he had done gardening in it. His hair was sticking out in all directions, and he had a sheet mark crease across one cheek. He looked so damn cute, she just wanted to hold him.

She apologized for not being able to shut off the alarm as he silenced the awful racket, then they spent the next ten minutes watching the new people work clearing the road. The fact that the newcomers were actually treating the bodies from the cars and sidewalks well gave her a feeling that Dan and the rest had their priorities in the right place and really were looking to the future. With so many dead, it would have been easy to just push them aside, worry about it later, after the living were taken care of.

But not this bunch.

They seemed to know they were going to succeed, that there was going to be a new world coming up out of the ruins of the old one. And because of that, they were treating every body from every car, from every building, like a fallen war hero, putting the bones and clothes and personal effects in bags and handling the bags with respect.

The future, if this all worked and the human race survived, would be very glad this was done the way they were doing it.

She doubted the new people knew she and Matt were watching. This was just the way they were going to work, as Dan had told them they would last night.

That gave her a vast amount of hope for the future. At least far more hope than she had held at this time yesterday morning. So much, in fact, that she didn't even want to say anything.

Finally, Matt suggested he take a shower and then cook them both breakfast, which she had readily agreed to, since her stomach was rumbling and his offer of omelets that first morning had sounded fantastic.

He went off to shower, leaving her to get things started in the kitchen. By the time he got back, wet hair combed into place, she had chopped up some onions, a green-pepper,

They seemed to know they were going to succeed, that there was going to be a new world coming up out of the ruins of the old one.

and cut some bread left over from dinner for toast.

She had been right about the feel of his kitchen. It fit her, as if she knew where every utensil, every appliance was before she actually found it. It was exactly like something she might have designed for herself. Maybe better.

Within minutes they were sitting at the table eating breakfast like a normal couple after sharing a night and a life.

She and Paine had had a few of these types of mornings. Usually they had been on a Sunday, when they both sat and read the paper, sharing different things that interested them. There hadn't been many of those mornings with their work schedules and school. Not near enough.

Now Matt sat across from her, staring intently at her as she ate.

"What?" she asked, using a napkin to wipe off her mouth. "I have egg on my nose or something?"

He laughed. "No, just sitting here thinking about how beautiful you are, and wondering what you were thinking about."

She could feel her face blush slightly at his compliment. "Thank you," she said. "But actually I was thinking about how nice this felt having breakfast like this, and how Paine and I hadn't gotten the chance very often to do it."

"I'm sorry," Matt said, the smile instantly gone from his face.

Oh, damn it all, she had screwed up. She held up her hand. "No, no, it's all right. I know he's gone and there's nothing I can do about it. I just meant that this feels nice is all."

"It does, doesn't it," Matt said, nodding.

He took another bite of toast covered in raspberry jam, then looked at her with a very serious look. "You know, we can bury Paine and your parents, if that's what you'd like to do. I'll be glad to help."

She smiled at him. His offer was very kind, and from what she had already seen from this man, not unexpected. Clearly Matt had a very big heart.

"Thanks," she said. "That's very kind. Maybe at some point down the road, after we figure out what to do about those people out there, and Dan's offer for us to join them."

Matt nodded. "What are you thinking about the offer?"

"That I need more information," she said. "I'd love to know what being part of what they are attempting would mean for me. And their expectations. And if I can even be of help."

"Exact same questions I was wondering about," he said. "I'm having fewer and fewer doubts about them being what they say they are. Especially after this morning. This city is going to be a very different place when twenty thousand or so people show up."

She looked out at the sea of empty buildings. "It will come alive a little, that's for sure," she said. "If they have the ability to get that bulldozer working, I bet they have the type of people with them that could start up the hydro-plants up on the Columbia, and get the power flowing into the city again."

Matt laughed. "Yeah, and picking Portland was a good choice as far as the water goes. The system that brings in the water from the Bull Run drainage up in the hills is more than likely just fine. With power, it will be very easy to clean and get back up to standard. But it's going to take a lot of people going around and turning off water faucets left on three years ago."

"Maybe that's what they want us to do," Carey said, and laughed. But she was half serious. With her background, she really didn't have anything practical she could offer in building a new society from the rubble of another. Matt, on the other hand, would be a golden find for them considering all his skills.

"Why don't we just go ask them after breakfast?" Matt said. "Before it gets too hot out there."

"You know," she said, taking the last bite of her omelet, "I think that's a splendid idea."

"I'm glad you do," he said. They held each other's gaze for a moment before both began laughing.

Twenty minutes later they had cleaned up the breakfast dishes and were headed down the elevator. Both of them still had rifles slung over their shoulders, but Carey doubted they needed them.

CHAPTER TWENTY-NINE

CAREY WAS very glad that Matt had suggested they go out early, before it got hot. It was still only around nine in the morning, yet the air was starting to turn warm, and she could feel that the wind was from the Columbia Gorge, which meant it was going to get much, much warmer.

It didn't take them long to get back up to the Hilton. And for some reason, the knowledge that all the bodies in the cars, and on the sidewalks, would be taken care of at some point in the future, made it easier for her to move among them. It still brought back the memory of that first day, but the memory didn't eat at her as bad, wasn't as close to the surface, as it had been the night before.

She would never forget that day, and the days that followed. She doubted anyone left alive ever would. But at least she might be able to deal with it better now.

Amazing how focusing on the future instead of the past could change an attitude. She hadn't felt this good, this positive in three long years.

There were very few people around the Hilton, and even fewer inside. Amazing how sixty people could just seem to vanish into the buildings and empty city.

They finally found someone who thought that Dan might be in the communications room. She and Matt were directed to a building across the street, an office building, and then upstairs to what must have been a large, second floor meeting room.

One wall of the room had been filled with communications equipment of different types, filling a dozen different shelves. It was an impressive display that clearly hadn't been there yesterday. Matt stopped and stared for a moment.

The large sliding doors at the end of the room were open. Carey could see a couple of satellite dishes on the balcony outside. And other wires going out another open window and leading up to the roof.

Dan was sitting at one conference table, talking to a man about something to do with an uplink, while two other men worked on equipment. Carey could tell by the way Matt moved slowly from one shelf to another that he was impressed at the set-up.

"Wow, you folks really know what you're doing," Matt finally said.

"Not really," one man said. He was on his back, under a large piece of equipment, and he sounded disgusted. "More like we're making it up as we go."

Matt laughed. "Boy do I know that feeling."

Dan looked up from his conversation and smiled at them, standing and moving toward them. Carey could tell the smile was real. He was actually very happy they were there.

"I was hoping you two would come back," Dan said. "More questions about what we're doing, I assume."

Carey was shocked at how much she liked the older man, and felt comfortable around him. When she had worked with Dr. Canfield, she had had to deal with a few military types. They were always nice, but they had made her uncomfortable. But Dan put her at ease just with a smile.

"More questions," Carey said, agreeing.

Dan motioned them over to a few chairs near a fairly empty table. Then, after they were all seated, he said, "Ask anything. We could use both of your help, so I'll give you as much information as I know. Straightforward, no punches pulled. How's that?"

"Sounds good to us," Matt said, glancing at Carey.

She nodded and let Matt start the questions.

"First off," Matt said, "How do you know you could use our help?"

Dan laughed. "Fair enough. We knew there were a few people living in this area. After you came by last night, I got in touch with our main base back in Nevada." He pointed to one of the machines near the window. Carey had no idea what it was, but from the way Matt nodded, he must have had an idea.

Dan went on. "I gave them your names, and they, in turn, contacted Colorado where there is a vast storage area of information about people around the country."

"And our names were in that database?" Carey asked, clearly amazed.

"They were," Dan said, nodding. "Of course, this data was meant to be for people working on family trees on the Internet. It was a fantastic project that had gathered records from just about every public place around the country and put them all in the same database, then cross-referenced it all."

"Wow, that was some work."

"It was," Dan said. "For example, I know what degrees both of you have from university records, what was on your last driver's licenses from an Oregon database, and your last known addresses."

"And you've tapped into this data just to find out about people?" Carey asked.

"Actually, no," Dan said, smiling at her. "But it does come in handy for meeting new survivors like you two. The database was activated and backed up in three different places because it will help in the body recovery and location of graves for the future reference work. That data will be the starting point when we actually begin putting all these poor souls into final resting places. We'll add into the data the information about how we found the person, and where exactly they are buried."

Matt glanced at Carey. She could tell from the look in his eyes that he was impressed. And she was amazed that after just two days how much they could talk to each other simply with a look.

"If we did come to work for you," Matt said, getting the conversation back on track, "what exactly would that entail?"

"You mean hours and such?" Dan asked.

Matt nodded.

"Actually, as many or as few as you wanted to put in. At this point, everyone is sort of in this together. We're going to be helping each other set up places to live, begin food distribution of salvaged items, and so on. To be honest, what we're discovering is that people want to work on this too much, and we end up having to make people slow down, take time off."

"Are you trying to match skills to jobs needed?" Carey asked.

"As much as the skills allow," Dan said, nodding.

One of the men working on connections under a table covered in electronic equipment laughed. "Yeah, I was a plumber in Vegas. I'll be glad when I can get back to pipes. This wiring stuff is for the birds."

Everyone laughed.

"We've got almost twenty thousand people headed here over the next six months," Dan said, "and with luck, even more after that. We need everything in the way of skills, and all the help we can get to give everyone a place to live, clean water, electricity, and enough food."

Carey could feel herself getting excited. Society might not be completely dead after all, if this worked. And even if it didn't, it was worth the fight. She certainly had nothing else to do.

"You know my degrees," she said to Dan.

"I certainly do, Dr. Noack," Dan said.

Carey sat back. She had been a post-doc. Granted, she had a Ph.D., but no one had ever called her doctor before. It took her a few seconds to take that inside.

Matt smiled fondly at her, clearly trying not to laugh at how Dan had surprised her.

"I'm not so sure I like the doctor stuff," she said, ignoring Matt for the moment, "but since you know I have that degree, what could I do to help? I doubt you're going to be doing much work in electromagnetics at any time in the near future."

Dan actually laughed. "You're young, you're smart, and you know computers and how to do research. We're going to be reinventing a lot of wheels over the next ten years, if you know what I mean. We're going to need scientists, people who know how to keep thinking ahead, as well as take information from the past and apply it now."

Then, before she could say anything more, he turned to Matt. "And you, Mr.

Landel, are also a real find for us. Not counting your education in electrical engineering, your ability with electronics would help us a great deal. I assume the cameras on the poles near the freeways are part of your security system?"

Now it was Carey's turn to try not to laugh at Matt's shocked look.

"They are," Matt said.

"And keeping a building the size of the Baxter building in water, electricity, and a working elevator, all by yourself, isn't an easy task. Yet you managed that as well. In case you haven't noticed, I'm almost begging you to come and help us."

"In case you haven't noticed, I'm almost begging you to come and help us."

"Dan," the plumber guy said from under the panel, "I'll join you on my knees if it helps get him on board, so I can go back to my pipes."

Everyone in the room laughed again.

Carey could tell that Matt was shocked they knew so much about him, and how he had been living. It surprised her as well, until she remembered the power of those satellites orbiting overhead. As Matt had said, they probably knew what vegetables he picked for dinner out of his garden.

Dan went on with his pitch. "I'm not saying this isn't going to be a lot of work. It will be. Some of it will be just basic work, like helping deal with the bodies. And for nothing more than you could do for yourself over the first few years, since it will be some time before we have a money system again."

"There is planning for one?" Carey asked, shocked.

Dan nodded. "There is. Everything we do is aiming at a longer term goal of getting back to farming, manufacturing, and all the other infrastructure it takes to supply the needs of all the survivors."

"Is this military?" Carey asked, realizing there were some pretty basic questions they hadn't gotten to yet. "Did the United States Government survive?"

"It did, sort of," Dan said. "No one in congress or the executive branch survived that we know of."

Carey was not surprised at that news. No one on the planet thought the wave of energy coming toward Earth could be dangerous. It had been just another day, with another strange thing happening out in space.

"Right now everything around the country is just being run as you see it here," Dan said, "a sort of volunteer work project, half directed by a military structure because of the nature of the majority of who survived. After each of the five cities are populated again, we'll have local elections, and those governments will take over, with the military side stepping back into a sort of police function. The first national election is slated for five years from two days ago, on the eighth anniversary of the disaster. We'll elect a new President and Congress then, starting over with five states at first."

Matt glanced over at Carey. She knew, without a doubt, she wanted to help Dan and the others. Something like this was so much better than sitting alone on the beach, wondering how she was going to die alone.

But she didn't want to commit unless Matt did. She had decided on her way up the sidewalk that she wanted to be with him more than she wanted to help Dan and the rest.

"Well?" she asked Matt, "what do you think?"

Matt smiled at her, the excitement in his eyes. "I'm in if you are."

Carey turned to face Dan. "I think you just found two more volunteers."

"Wonderful," Dan said, clapping his hands.

From under the electrical equipment came the sound of applause.

"We only have one delay in starting," Matt said, smiling at Carey. "It's going to take us a few days to get Carey and her cats moved over here from the coast."

"Oh, that's right," Carey said, annoyed at herself for forgetting that she actually didn't live here, and that her cats were expecting her to come back soon.

"You've been living on the coast?" Dan asked. "What area?"

"North of Depoe Bay," she said.

"Can you fish?" he asked.

"Well," Carey said, glancing at Matt, then back at Dan. "I've managed to catch my share of crab and dig my share of clams. And I used a Native American net system near the mouth of a small stream for other fish. But beyond that, I wouldn't have a clue."

"Well, I was hoping," Dan said, smiling. "One plan we have is to set up a supply line for fish from the coast sometime over the next six months."

"I don't think I'd be much help in that area," Carey said, remembering her cold mornings trying to get anything out of the ocean to eat that was fresh. More often than not she had come away empty handed.

"Well, take as much time as you need," Dan said. "Just hurry back, we need you."

"I'll get moved as quickly as I can," she said.

"If you need help, just find me," Dan said.

"Actually," Matt said, "if you could lend us two motorcycles, that would be a large help."

Carey managed to not shout *No!* She would have to climb over her fear of the things and learn how to ride. Until most roads were cleared, it was going to be the main way to travel any real distance.

"Not a problem," Dan said. "I'll have two waiting for you on the sidewalk in front of the Hilton."

"Great, thanks," Matt said. "And no problem with me continuing to live right where I'm at?"

"None that I can think of," Dan said, shrugging. "I don't think we're going to be dealing with a housing shortage anytime soon. Our plans are to spread out in this area, and into the Northwest section, where there is a lot of single-family housing."

"One more thing," Matt said, glancing at Carey. "If I start working for you, I could use a little help with another project I have going."

Dan looked puzzled, but Carey smiled, knowing what Matt was about to say.

"I've been raising some chickens," Matt said.

That stopped all activity in the room almost instantly.

"Fried chicken," one man said.

"Eggs," another said. "I can't remember the last time I ate eggs."

"Well," Matt said, "with a little help on feeding and harvesting the eggs, and some good management, I don't think that's going to be a problem for the future. I have about five hundred or so birds trapped in the Rose Garden. I think that place can hold a lot more than that if I have help with feeding."

Carey could have cut the thick silence that filled the room.

Finally, one man said, "Sorry, Dan, I'm going to work for him. He's got fresh chickens."

Everyone laughed, and Dan smiled even larger. "I have no doubt we can find more than enough people to help with the chicken project. I'm *very* glad you two are joining us."

"I'm glad you're here and doing all this," Matt said.

"So am I," Carey said. "It's amazing what having a hope for a future can do for the spirit."

"That, and a piece of fried chicken," the man under the desk said.

CHAPTER THIRTY

DAN WALKED them to the doorway, shook both their hands, and told them to hurry back. Carey felt as if he actually meant it. Nice to be wanted again.

Then she and Matt were back in the mid-morning heat, headed down the hill. They were a block into the walk before either one of them spoke, but Carey didn't care. She was thinking about what Dan had said, about the promise of a new government, towns with social aspects, people gathering and having families and surviving. Even if only a part of it happened, it was fantastic.

Now all she had to do to get to work helping this cause was to learn how to ride a motorcycle, get her cats, and then find a place to live.

Or maybe in a different order, now that she thought about it. Having a place to go to when she got back here to the city might be a good idea first.

Finally, as they crossed the second street headed down the hill toward the Baxter building, Matt broke the silence.

"Looks like we have jobs again."

"Retirement just isn't the life of luxury it's made out to be," Carey said. "I just have to figure out where to live."

"I'm assuming you don't want to go back to your old apartment," Matt said.

"No," she said, surprised at how firmly that came out. "Although I wouldn't mind getting some things from there at some point. And from my parent's home as well."

The idea of actually having some of her old possessions again pleased her, and got her a little excited. Everything she had on the coast, besides the cats, could just stay there, to maybe be used later. It could be her coast retreat when she needed to get away. She wanted to start fresh here, with new things combined with old stuff from her past.

"I can help you with finding a place," Matt said, smiling at her. "I have an idea on where you might want to live."

"Where?" she asked, glancing at him. He had this impish look in his eyes she hadn't seen before.

Was he going to suggest that they live together? Or that she take one of his spare bedrooms? It would temp her, she knew that. But it also might be too close, too soon, even with the way she felt about him.

But if he asked, right at this moment, she didn't honestly know what she would say. That's how much she had come to like, maybe even love, this man.

"Let me show it to you first," he said. "I think you might like it. And it has some advantages."

His smile told her that no amount of coaxing was going to get his idea out of him, so she didn't even try.

They made it the last few blocks back to the Baxter building in silence, and when they got on the elevator, her stomach was fluttering. She didn't know what she would say if he asked her to live with him. The idea felt right, and really wrong at the same time.

"Matt," she said, her voice shaking a little, "I don't know if—."

Instead of punching the button for his apartment on the twenty-second floor, he punched the button for the twentieth floor.

"Yes?" he asked, smiling, more than likely knowing exactly what she was going to try to stammer out.

"Nothing," she said, now even more confused.

The elevator opened on a foyer area with two large, double doors on each end. Matt moved toward the doors labeled "A", pushed them open, and walked inside.

"Someone was living in "B" when I moved in," Matt said, walking ahead of her. "I took care of their bodies when I cleared the building. But this place was empty. I could never figure out what to do with it, since I'm using all the space on the two floors above. I think this is almost better than my apartment."

Carey stood in the door and just stared. She had found her home, she knew it without even stepping inside. The apartment had a big kitchen area, floating in the center of a large tiled space like Matt's kitchen. The windows were floor-to-ceiling and over ten feet tall, giving the large living and dining area almost a cavern feel, since it was empty.

The carpet was a light brown, and everything was trimmed in beautiful oak. An oak desk surrounded by massive bookcases covered one interior wall.

Matt walked to the kitchen counter and ran his finger through the layer of dust. "It will take us some time to clean it and wash the carpets, but otherwise it's in good shape."

She moved over and stood beside him, staring at the fantastic space, the view of Mt. Hood in the sunlight, the river spread out below the apartment, the city basking in the first day of its new future.

"I can get the power hooked up here easily," he said. "The plumbing might take a little more, but I think that if I can't make it work, then that guy fighting the wiring back in the communications room might help."

He turned and took her hand, looking her squarely in the eyes. "I'm being selfish here," he said. "I'm hoping you'll stay close, so we can really get a chance to know each other."

"I want the same thing," she said, squeezing his hand gently, but not letting go. She liked the feel of his skin against hers, and the powerful feel of his hand in hers. "And I'll make you a deal."

He smiled, taking her other hand in his so that they now faced each other. "Always interested in deals."

The closeness of him made her want to get even closer, to pull him against her fully and kiss him. But somehow she managed not to. Instead she kept talking.

"If I move in here, you'll have to let me help you with both of your gardens and the chickens, in exchange for vegetables and meat, of course."

"Another thing I was hoping you would say. We both are going to be working. Keeping up gardens the size I have is going to get to be more work than I want to do alone."

"And I'll do some extra cleaning around the building in exchange for you keeping the water and power flowing. That fair?"

"I think I'm getting the better part of that deal," he said, smiling at her.

"So we have a deal?"

"We have a deal," he said. "I'm just glad you like this place. I have, from the moment I first walked in here. I've been in every room in the building and my place and this place are the two best by a long ways."

She laughed. "It seems from the moment we met you've been helping me find a place to stay."

"It's been my pleasure," he said, staring into her eyes as he squeezed both of her hands lightly.

"Thank you," she said. "Without your help I might have missed this chance at a new future."

With that, she pulled him toward her, keeping his hands in hers.

She kissed him, letting her body press against his.

She held the kiss longer than she had intended.

Actually a lot longer.

She just didn't want to let go of the wonderful sensations that were surging through her, the feeling of his lips against hers, the way his body fit against her.

He didn't push, he didn't object, he didn't pull away. Instead, they seemed to become one in that kiss.

After a moment, or maybe hours for all she knew, she ended the kiss and eased back from him, feeling the loss of his lips on hers.

She felt hot, and she had no doubt that her face was flushed. The empty apartment around them suddenly felt very, very warm.

That had been some kiss. Best she had ever had.

Ever.

Matt's face was also flushed, and the surprise in his eyes was wonderful.

They stood there, close, hands grasped, staring into each other's eyes for a long moment, then she decided that she either needed to break this up or she would end up kissing him again.

And again.

She stepped completely back and let go of his hands.

"You know," she said, proud that her voice only broke once as she tired to speak, "we're going to have to do something about the air-conditioning in here as well."

All Matt could do was stand there and nod as she turned to explore the bedrooms and bathrooms of her new home.

CHAPTER THIRTY-ONE

MATT WATCHED Carey as she worked on building them two salads for lunch. He had added in a couple pieces of cold chicken from last night's dinner and poured them both diet Coke to drink. He was now sitting at the table, waiting and watching her. He couldn't imagine ever getting tired of watching her.

That kiss, thanking him for his help, had left him stunned and almost gasping, just like his first kiss back in junior high had done.

Everything about Carey stunned him. Never in his life, not with any past love or infatuation, had he ever felt so strongly for a person. Not only did he want to take her in his arms and make love to her, but he wanted to talk to her over meals, walk with her through the city, work beside her.

He just wanted to be with her.

And that scared him a lot.

This wasn't like him, falling so hard after only knowing a woman for a couple of days. He needed to take a deep breath and try to separate out how many of his feelings were from being alone for three years, and how much was truly feelings for Carey, the person, the woman. That separation was going to take a lot longer than two days.

And now, by asking her to move into the apartment on the twentieth floor, he had just risked his entire world here in this building. If she turned out to be some nut case, he was going to have to move out. But he just couldn't imagine, no matter how hard he tried, Carey being anything but what he was seeing.

But that got him right back to not trusting his own emotions, mostly because the emotions that he had used to deal with other people had been shut off for so long.

One thing that encouraged him, more than he wanted to admit, actually, was her worry about getting too close to him too fast. It seemed odd, but he considered her worry a very good sign that she was sane.

She slid his salad in front of him. It looked wonderful. Fresh tomatoes, lettuce, sprouts, and some sliced cucumbers, all topped with an oil dressing, and garnished with sliced hardboiled eggs.

And it had been prepared by someone else. The salad was better looking than anything he would have gotten in most restaurants, back when there were restaurants.

Maybe someday there would be restaurants again. He just hoped when that day came, he would be sitting across the booth from Carey.

"This looks fantastic," he said, grabbing his fork and digging in.

"Thanks," she said. There was a moment of silence and then she went on. "I've got a confession to make."

Her voice was full of worry.

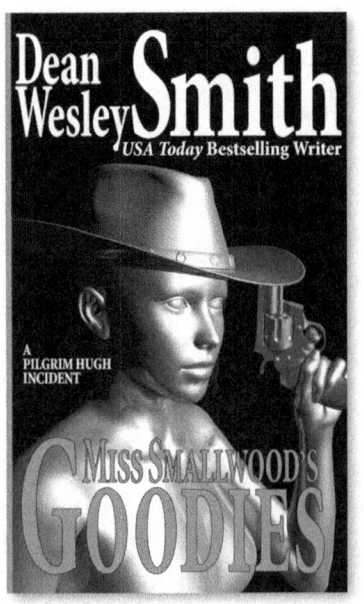

He glanced up. She was playing with her salad, sort of moving lettuce around but not seeming to care if she ate anything.

"Oh, oh," he said, trying to make light of the sinking feeling he had in his stomach. Every time a woman had said that "she had a confession to make" to him in the past, it had meant trouble, and things changing. He was liking the way things were heading at the moment between them. He didn't need any confessions, but it looked as if he was going to get one.

"Go ahead."

She looked up at him, a forkful of salad in her hand. Then as if blurting out the worst crime imaginable, she said, "I don't know how to ride a motorcycle. In fact, I'm afraid of them."

He stared at her for a moment, shocked that that was all she was worried about. Then, even though he knew he shouldn't, he laughed.

"It's not funny," she said, still not putting the forkful of salad in her mouth. "Motorcycles are the only way we're going to get to the coast and back with any speed. The roads are a mess all the way. And I've been thinking about it. We need to take two bikes so that we can get both of my cats back here."

He could see how upset this had her. It was no wonder she had picked coming with him yesterday over being on her own with people on motorcycles coming into town. Beyond her friend getting hurt from the bikers, she had a real phobia about motorcycles that she had clearly never dealt with.

So, what could he do to help her?

"Maybe I should just walk back," Carey said, still clearly upset. "You go to work to help Dan and I'll figure out a way to get the two cats back here to Portland. I could rig up some sort of child's wagon and just pull it with them in it."

"Does that mean you would rather I not help you?" he asked, afraid of the answer.

"Oh, no," she said. "I want you to help me. I just have this problem with motorcycles, and that's the only logical

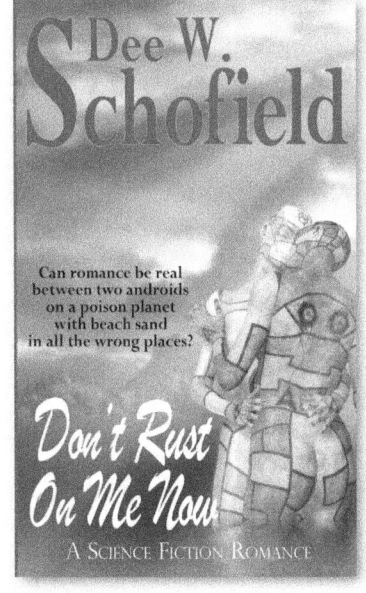

way we both can go, besides both of us walking. I just don't see how I can learn to drive one of them. At least not quick enough to do us any good on these roads."

"Actually," he said, "we only need one bike. All you have to do is ride behind me."

He reached across the table and put his hand on her arm. He wanted to stroke that soft, light skin, but instead he used his touch to try to calm her.

She shook her head. "We can't get two cat carriers on one motorcycle with both of us on it as well." Then she looked at him with a questioning look. "Can we?"

"Sure we can," he said. "Do you have much else at your place on the coast that you want to bring back, besides the cats?"

"Nothing really," she said, shaking her head. She paused for a long moment, then said, "Maybe a few small things that would fit in my backpack. The rest can be left for some future use. I'll furnish the apartment here with new stuff, and things from my old apartment and parent's home."

"Then it's not a worry," he said. "Problem solved. One of those big bikes is enough. Keeping the cats from totally freaking out on a motorcycle is another matter altogether."

"They will just have to deal with it," Carey said. "If I have to, they have to." She tried to smile at him, but the smile didn't reach her eyes as it normally did.

He took his hand away from her arm and made a show of going back to eating, trying to make her believe that it wasn't a problem. Actually, it wasn't. And he had no doubt that once they had been headed to the coast for a few hours, she would be comfortable on the bike as well, and past her fear. But he now knew he was going to have to take it very easy at the start,

and work with her fear to get them going. He could do that.

"Okay," she said, her voice hesitant. "You've ridden motorcycles before?"

"A bunch of times," he said, taking a bite of a chicken leg. "That's why I just assumed you had as well."

"Okay," she said again.

He could tell she didn't like the idea of getting on a motorcycle. And right now he needed to give her an out. "Look, if the motorcycle doesn't work for you, we'll find other ways of getting there and back. You walked here, didn't you? I want to go with you, if you want me along, and walking is no problem as far as I'm concerned. Dan will just have to wait for us. We really aren't in any great rush."

She thought for a moment, then nodded. "I suppose you're right. We're not in that much of a hurry, are we? Dan will put us to work no matter when we show up."

"Of that I have no doubt," Matt said. "Let's just play it by ear and see how the trip goes. If the motorcycle works, fine. If it doesn't, that's fine as well. The focus is getting your cats, and getting all of us back here safely. Right?"

"Right," she said, smiling at him.

"But I would suggest," Matt said, "that we get your new place set up, and at least partially furnished before we leave. That way you and your cats have a place that is comfortable to come back to."

"Good idea," she said. "And the first thing is cleaning."

Matt laughed. "That, and power, and water, and air-conditioning."

"Oh, yeah, those too," she said, shaking her head and smiling. This time the smile reached her eyes.

"There may not be a housing shortage for all the new people coming in, but I bet there's a cleaning and maintenance shortage."

"Now we know why Dan wants us as soon as we're ready," he said. "Cleaning help."

"More than likely," Carey said, taking the last piece of cold chicken off the plate. "And you know, I won't mind in the slightest."

Matt realized he wouldn't either. Cleaning homes and getting a city ready to be reborn seemed a lot more valuable a job than putting in security cameras in bank vaults. Of course, doing that had given him the chance to survive.

And to meet Carey.

CHAPTER THIRTY-TWO

CAREY HAD just finished wiping down the three bedrooms and the walk-in closet, and was just about to start on the hallway when the lights came on.

The cleaning had been doing great. She had had to carry three buckets of water from Matt's apartment so far, and she had no doubt she was going to be carrying more before she was finished.

Actually, the fact that the apartment had been completely empty helped a lot. No furniture or old drapes or bedding to have to take care of. Just walls, counters, and windows. She would vacuum last.

She and Matt had replaced light bulbs in all the ceiling fixtures, then he had gone off to see if he could hook this apartment into his electrical system. She had worried that it would overload it, but he had brushed the comment away.

"Trust me," he had said, "those three generators on the roof could handle this entire building if they were forced to."

She would have to trust him, as if she hadn't trusted him enough already.

She wiped the sweat off her face and stood looking at the room that would be her bedroom. She loved her new place, more now that she was working in it. It just felt good, even empty. And the light from the tall windows in the main room was amazing, almost as if she was outside. She loved places that were filled with light, and now she had found one. Even the master bedroom had huge windows.

She would have never been able to afford an apartment like this one when everyone was alive, let alone furnish this much space. It was only because she had survived, and everything was free that she could do this.

But she had survived, and since there was no one left to protest, she felt she deserved this beautiful place. It would just sit here and go to waste if she didn't use it.

"It seems we have light," Matt said, coming through the double front door. "And come over here and feel this."

He motioned her to follow him. He led her to a vent in the wall beside the pantry door. He showed her where to put her hand.

The cool air coming from the vent sent chills through her hot, sweating body. "Oh, a miracle worker."

"Don't say that until I get the water running," he said, laughing. "Electrical is easy for me. Plumbing, on the other hand, is a nightmare. Luckily I did most of the heavy lifting getting water to the two floors above you. With luck, this floor will be easy to open up as well."

"Just don't flood my new apartment," she said, smiling at him as she sat down on the floor in front of the cool air, letting it blow over her. She hadn't realized just how hot she had gotten washing down the walls and windows.

"No worry there," he said. "But I take no bets on the basement. Thermostat for temperature is room-by-room. You might want to check them."

"Thanks," she said. "I will. Would you toss me that water bottle? I think I just want to sit here and get chilled."

"You have a thing about heat, don't you?" he said, laughing as he grabbed the water bottle from the kitchen counter and handed it to her.

"I didn't used to," she said. "But three years living on the Oregon coast will do that to you. Trust me, you'll be freezing when we get over there, after this kind of heat here."

"It's not going to be that much difference," he said.

"Now it's your turn to trust me," she said, smiling at him as she finished taking a long drink. "If it's this hot here, more than likely the coast is socked in with a fog, and the temperature is a cold fifty-five to sixty. Of course, that's also the temperature of a winter day when it's below freezing here, but that's beside the point."

"Amazing what a hundred miles can mean to climate," he said, shaking his head.

"A hundred miles and an ocean," she said. "But give me enough time and I'll get used to this climate again."

"I think we have all the time in the world," he said. "Now I'm going to go see if I can figure out a way to turn on your water."

"Thanks," she said. "And good luck."

She watched him walk out the door. He had the build of an athlete, was clearly in very good physical shape, and carried himself well. She remembered the wonderful feel of that body against hers when she had kissed him. She hoped that at some point soon, she would be against him again.

And kissing him again.

She took another long drink of water, letting the cold draft of air brush over her arms and neck and face. Then she stood, feeling the sweat that had dried on her skin crack. She hoped he got her shower running soon, or she was going to have to borrow his again.

She had finished wiping down the walls and was starting on vacuuming the carpets with his vacuum cleaner when Matt came back through the door. He arms were covered in grease, some of which had made it to black streaks across his face.

She flicked off the machine and smiled at him, wiping sweat from her face. "Any luck?"

"Time to test this and find out," he said, heading toward the kitchen sink. He took one of her dirty towels and used it to protect the sink handle from the grease on his hands. He twisted the cold open and then waited, leaning down to listen.

No water came out at first, but by the time she had moved over beside him, the water was flowing through the tap.

At first it was red and dirty in color, but then it quickly changed to a clean look.

Matt nodded. "Get all the taps running, about half open, including the shower and the bathtub and the utility sink, and leave them running. I'm going to go check to see if I have any leaks where I brought the pipes to this floor into my system."

She did as she was told, and by the time she was finished, the apartment sounded like it had a bubbling stream running down the hall. And all the water looked clean, from every tap, almost instantly.

Matt came back in a few minutes later, smiling. "No leaks."

"Water looks great here," she said.

"Good. Let's turn them off."

Together they turned off every faucet, with Matt checking each one to make sure it worked, and that there were no leaks in the drains under the counters.

Then, as they headed back for the kitchen, he said, "I'm going down to a store about six blocks from here, off of Front Street, to get a new water heater."

"The old one won't work?" she asked. She had no idea at all about plumbing.

"I doubt it would after having water sitting in it for three years without movement."

"Oh," she said. "Do you need help?"

"I have my little tractor with the bucket on the front," Matt said, smiling. "And I have a good path cleared through the car wrecks to that store. I'll just load a water heater into the bucket and bring it up the freight elevator. I might need some help getting the thing from the elevator in here."

"Just shout when you get back," she said.

"I will." Then he moved over closer to one of the big windows and pointed across the river. "The next wave of settlers is arriving."

She joined him, staring at the dots that were bikes moving along the freeway toward the bridge. The crews working to clear the road had made it past that point, so the bunch of bikers were moving at a pretty reasonable speed.

Again the sight of them twisted her stomach, even though she knew who they were, and why they were here. She was going to have to get over this fear of motorcycles at some point. It was silly

and she knew it. More than likely, on the trip to the coast, she would get past it. At least, she hoped that would be the case.

"Looks like we're at the end of a new Oregon Trail," Matt said. "They're not quite in covered wagons, but close."

"Same reason, though," she said. "They are coming here searching for a new home to start over."

"That's true," Matt said. "More than likely, a hundred years from now they'll be writing history books about Dan and those folks out there, and their trek to Oregon."

"I hope so," she said. "I sure hope so."

CHAPTER THIRTY-THREE

IT WAS AMAZING how much plumbing a guy could learn out of books. Matt was actually starting to gain some confidence with it. And considering the only thing he had done with plumbing before three years ago was pour Drano down a sink, he was doing all right. Better than all right if he said so himself. It sometimes took him a few tries before he got a joint to not leak, but this time he'd gotten it right the first time.

Amazing. Simply amazing.

Adding her apartment onto his closed water system turned out to be easier than he had expected. He just opened a few values he had closed off before, and ran a pipe from his clean water system to the main line to her apartment. He installed a shut-off valve as well just in case something happened in the future.

No leaks anywhere. He checked it three times because he couldn't believe it.

Carey helped him move the new water heater into her place and drain the old one. It still weighed a lot and it took both of them to get it into the bucket of his tractor out into the dumpster area behind the building. Doing that, he discovered that Carey was a lot stronger than she appeared. That was a good thing to know, considering the world they were living in.

Then he hooked up the new water heater without a problem, watching for any leaks as the water moved into it.

"You're going to have to give it some time to heat up the water," he said, sounding like he knew what he was doing. He hoped he did. He had read the installation instructions at the hardware store twice.

"Then I'm going to need to borrow your shower again," she said, "if you don't mind. Even with the air-conditioning on, cleaning this place was hot work."

"But it looks great," he said, slowly scanning the apartment. And it did look good. She had even managed to wash the inside of the windows while he was off getting the water heater. The apartment smelled of lemon cleaning solution and was as bright and shiny as if it had just been painted.

"It does, doesn't it?" she said, smiling. "This is a simply wonderful place."

"I thought you'd like it," he said. "I sure do."

"I do more than like it," she said. "I love it. Thanks, for everything."

"You're welcome," he said, smiling at her. She seemed radiant as she studied her new place, the fear she had shown at lunch now gone. "But it needs furniture, don't you think?"

"Not today," she said. "It has to be over ninety degrees out there. If you don't mind, I'd like to take a shower, help cook a nice dinner for the both of us, and maybe watch another movie. We

can get some basic furniture and supplies tomorrow morning when it's cool."

"You know," he said, "that sounds like a perfect evening to end a perfect day."

"A perfect day is doing plumbing?" she asked, smiling at him with that twinkle in her eye that he was starting to love.

"No, a perfect day is being with you all day and not having any leaks in the plumbing."

She laughed. "You sure know how to charm a girl. So what do you have up in that wonderful kitchen of yours that I might help cook for dinner?"

"I always have more chicken," he said. "And I make a mean spaghetti sauce from scratch."

He watched her as she thought about the choices, then said, "I seem to remember I used to do a pretty good lemon and herb chicken. How does that, with some asparagus out of your garden done in a light cream sauce, all served with a salad, sound to you?"

He laughed. "No leaks and asparagus in a cream sauce. Now I know I'm having a perfect day."

"Well then," she said, "I'll get the chicken defrosting and then take a shower."

"I'll do one more quick check of the water system and be right behind you."

He didn't offer to wash her back, but he wanted to.

CHAPTER THIRTY-FOUR

EATING DINNER with someone besides her cats felt great, and after just a few meals, it was starting to feel almost normal. She would have never thought that possible three days ago. Dreamed about it, maybe, but never thought it would happen.

Her lemon chicken tasted better than she remembered it tasting, and the asparagus and sauce came out perfectly. She almost felt human again after the shower, and while the chicken cooked and Matt took a shower, she had gone back down to her apartment to just walk slowly through it. She had no doubt, she would be very comfortable here. Actually, more than comfortable. This was a dream apartment for her. She could see herself living here the rest of her life.

When she got back to Matt's, she checked on dinner, then wandered into the security room. A large group, maybe the biggest yet, were coming into town, the motorcycles seeming to stretch into the distance. The sight of them jarred her again, but not as much as the first time she saw the bikes. And this time there was no fear making her want to run away. Knowing who they were helped. And seeing that there were young children and a few babies in this group made them seem very non-threatening.

Humanity rebuilding itself, getting up off the mat from the knockout blow and fighting on.

Matt joined her a minute later, his hair wet and combed back. He looked so damn good, she just wanted to kiss him right there.

Instead, she pointed at his monitors. "More company."

"Wow, that's a lot of people," he said. "Am I glad we went and talked to Dan. Sitting here and seeing this without knowing what was happening would be really scary."

"True," she said. "Now it looks hopeful."

"That it does," Matt said.

At that moment a timer dinged from the kitchen, calling them to dinner.

About halfway through the wonderful dinner, they switched the conversation over to when they should leave for the coast.

"You know," she said, realizing what she had been feeling when she was downstairs while dinner cooked, "the furniture in my place isn't really that important to have in place before we get back. I'd rather take my time and get some stuff I really liked. Cat boxes is all that needs to be ready, if you don't mind me crashing on your couch the day we get back."

Matt smiled. "Not at all. Consider my place as yours until we get you set up."

"Thank you," she said, keeping her gaze locked with his for a moment. "For everything."

"Trust me," he said, smiling that smile that she was growing quickly to love. "It's been my pleasure." He paused for a moment, then said, "Missing your cats, huh?"

"Very much," she said. "And getting worried about them." More worried than she wanted to admit. It felt like she had been gone a lifetime in just the last two days.

"So, we roll out real early tomorrow morning. Buddy's got a spare cat box he hasn't used that I'm sure he wouldn't mind loaning the new neighbors."

She laughed. "What we do for our cats."

Later, she once again fell asleep on his shoulder while watching a movie. But this time, when he tried to cover her with a blanket, she woke up enough to pull him down to her and kiss him again.

Long and hard.

It was a perfect kiss, far, far better than she had ever imagined or dreamed since this nightmare of a world had started.

After a few minutes, he picked her up and carried her into his bedroom, kissing her all the way.

Slowly, very slowly, they undressed each other and all she could do was marvel at how wonderful he was, how perfectly built, how great his skin felt against hers.

And how wonderfully he kissed.

Two hours later, she fell asleep once again, this time nude in his arms.

Somehow the nightmare of the last three years had turned into a wonderful dream.

And for the first time in years, she had no desire to wake up.

CHAPTER THIRTY-FIVE

THE FANTASTIC smell of toast and sizzling eggs woke her. The sun wasn't over the mountains to the east yet, and Matt was gone.

She stretched and lay there smiling, remembering how wonderful everything had been with Matt last night. The fear that she was moving too fast now completely gone. That made no sense considering that she had only known him for a few days, but somehow she knew him in far deeper ways than just being together.

They had both survived the last three years and there was a new world lying in front of them to help build. And build together.

She climbed out of bed and wrapped the bathrobe Matt had draped across the bottom of the bed around her, then walked barefoot down the hall into the kitchen.

Matt saw her coming and smiled that wonderful smile that she knew she was never going to tire of seeing.

"I was hoping to serve you breakfast in bed."

"After last night, I'm not sure I could have handled that as well."

He laughed and came over and kissed her, then quickly went back to the eggs, indicating she should take a seat at the table. He had already showered and was dressed.

"Isn't this awfully early?" she asked, noticing that the lights were still on because the sun was a distance from being up.

"I figured we'd get an early start for the coast before it got too hot," he said.

The image of him naked beside her was pushed aside by the sudden realization that very shortly she was going to have to climb on a motorcycle.

He smiled, not really laughing, but clearly almost reading her thoughts. "Don't worry, I'm doing the driving and we'll get your cats back here soon, I promise."

"Thanks," she said as he slid a plate of scrambled eggs and toast in front of her. The smell was wonderful and the plate had barely stopped moving before she had the first bite to her mouth.

The idea of riding a motorcycle just scared her to death, but that seemed just silly now considering what she had already come through. And for the first time she had someone in her life she could trust.

Granted, she really didn't know him yet, not completely, but she felt she did, and she felt she could trust him. And right now that was enough.

More than enough.

Outside, she could see movement on the interstate bridge. Clearly humanity was up and working early as well, getting the highway cleared and working to build a new future.

And she needed to do that as well.

She needed to move into a future because suddenly she had one again. With Matt and with all the people pouring into town.

She took a deep breath. She had survived three years alone in all the death and destruction. She had come up with the courage to come back to Portland, to meet Matt, and to join the rebuilding.

She could ride a motorcycle and face whatever else needed to be done in the coming years.

Just as she had done coming into town just a few days earlier, she slotted her fears away and felt a calmness come over her.

She finished the last bite of her eggs and pushed the plate aside.

She stood and kissed Matt hard, not allowing him to come up for air for a good thirty seconds.

"Thank you for breakfast."

All he could do was nod and smile.

Then she started toward the bathroom to take a shower. About halfway down the hallway she stopped and looked back at Matt. "I can be showered and dressed and ready to go in about fifteen minutes."

Then she slipped the robe off, holding it in one hand as she stood there naked, smiling at the shocked look on Matt's face. "But I don't think we need to leave for thirty minutes if you'd like to scrub my back."

She turned to the bathroom grinning as behind her Matt scrambled to his feet and followed.

One hour later, she was in the passenger seat of a motorcycle, holding onto the man of her dreams as they headed off into their future.

A future she never dreamed she might have.

~

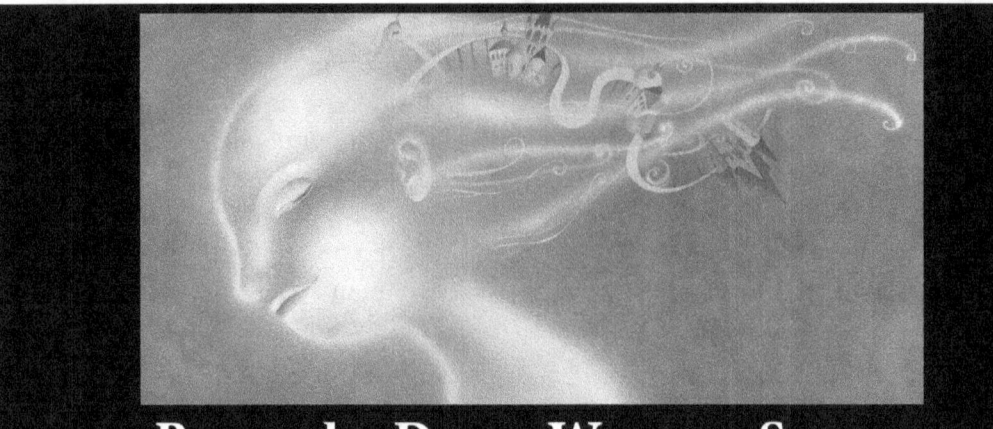

Poems by DEAN WESLEY SMITH

The Last Croak

After the man spread the myth,
the damn frog sat there, waiting on his lily pad,
just a few feet from the pond's shore, aloof, yet willing.
Croak. Croak. Croak. The sound echoed through the night.

The man hired a publicist,
the press releases went out,
the media played up the idea of the greening of a prince.
Nothing happened. The damn frog just sat there. Croak. Croak.

The man tried a want-ad which read,
"Prince trapped in frog body. Need woman with big lips,
strong stomach. Reward." No one showed.
The damn frog still sat there. Croak.

The man bought a rifle, with a scope, night vision,
two boxes of shells. The man only needed one shell.
From ten feet away the man shot. The frog exploded.
Finally, the man would get a decent night's sleep.